INCINERATED

COAST GUARD RECON BOOK 2

LORI MATTHEWS

ABOUT THE BOOK

From the bestselling author of the Callahan Security Series.

Meet Axel Cantor of the US Coast Guard's TEAM RECON. As in reconstructed. As in broken and needs fixing.

When a cargo ship gets stuck in the Suez Canal and an American journalist on board ends up dead, Axel is sent in to investigate. He didn't count on running into Sloan Bishop, another reporter, and the love of his life. Or maybe the hate of his life. Ever since he ended up in one of her articles.

Sloan is a driven reporter who fights to get the story at any cost, even if it means jeopardizing her personal safety. She's on board the *Sea Jewel,* to document the first-ever female pilot to navigate the canal. But it all goes sideways, literally, when the ship becomes mired in the narrowest part of the canal. As worldwide shipping backed up, the female pilot is blamed. But Sloan knows there's more to the story. When one of the other journalists covering the historic story is murdered, Sloan casts aside her misgivings to find out why.

As the body count rises on the stuck cargo ship both Axel

and Sloan must lower their defenses to work together to undercover the real motive. There is something much bigger at play here, so big that Axel has to call in reinforcements – his RECON teammates.

Incinerated

For my readers.
You have made my dreams come true.

ACKNOWLEDGMENTS

Once again, a big thanks to Parvez Mansuri for sharing his knowledge of the shipping industry. This book would not be possible without the support of Joseph D'Elia (Lieutenant, USCG) who has the patience of a saint and answered all my questions and frantic texts about the Coast Guard. I couldn't have created Team RECON without his help. Any mistakes are my own.

My deepest gratitude also goes out to my editors, Corinne DeMaagd and Heidi Senesac for making me appear much more coherent than I actually am; my cover artist, Llewellen Designs for making my story come alive: my virtual assistant who is a social media guru and all round dynamo, Susan Poirier. My personal cheer squad which I could not survive without: Janna MacGregor, Suzanne Burke, Stacey Wilk, Kimberley Ash and Tiara Inserto. My mother and my sisters who told me to dream big. My husband and my children who make my hair turn gray but also make me laugh.

And to you, the reader. Your emails and posts mean the world to me. The fact that you read my stories is the greatest gift ever. Thank you.

PROLOGUE

Omar Balik leaned back in his desk chair and stretched his long legs out in front of him, crossing them at the ankles. He looked out the window beside him at the Bosphorus strait in the distance. Istanbul was not only his home city but also his favorite. Usually, he found the sight of it refreshing. Today it did nothing for him.

He ran his hand through his short black hair and closed his chocolate brown eyes. He was exhausted. His father had been riding his ass for months, years even. There was always something else to do. Some other crisis brewing. Omar had been working on the deal with the Germans for months. It was supposed to be all signed and sorted by next week. *I'll take a few days off then.* Surely, his father would agree that he'd earned the time off.

Hakan Balik had built the company from scratch, and they were one of the biggest textile suppliers in all of Turkey. The deal they were making with the Germans was massive. It would escalate them to the next level. It would put Omar's name on the map. He had put the deal together. He'd approached the Germans and gotten them to agree. This would establish him as a serious player in the textile game, and he would finally be out from under his father's shadow. His father would *have* to see him as worthy of inheriting the company *when* the deal came through.

It had been the longest fucking five years of Omar's life. His father had insisted Omar go to work for him immediately following his graduation from university. He'd taken no breaks other than a few long weekends, and he'd worked long hours, but it was never quite good enough for his father.

Well, this deal was good enough. It was better than that. It was the best deal to come to the company in a long time and he, Omar, had made it happen.

"I am the head of one of the biggest textile companies in the world," Hakan would say when Omar complained. "And you need to toughen up. Stop whining. If you want to take over the company someday, then you need to earn it."

Earn it. He'd been earning it since the day he'd been born. Always trying to live up to his father's dreams. It had been brutal.

Omar's gaze roamed over his office. He'd decorated it in the latest modern fashion. All white. White furniture, white walls, and white floors only broken up by splashes of color from the view over Istanbul and the Bosphorus and the artwork he'd purchased. It was perfect. "Divine" was what the designer had called it, and Omar agreed. One day he would be the god running the company. Best to look the part.

His cell phone vibrated, and Omar glanced at the screen. *Aysun.* He didn't feel like talking to her now. She was… boring. He only dated her because it made his father happy. He liked women who were more willing to party. That's what he needed right now. Some drinks and a good fuck. He was too tense about the deal with the Germans. He needed some stress relief.

There was a quiet knock on the door before it opened.

His assistant, Fatma, walked in. She was carrying some papers. "You need to take a look at these." She walked over and placed them on the desk in front of Omar.

He nodded his thanks and then watched her walk out. She had her long black hair up in a bun. Her white blouse and navy skirt emphasized her generous curves. Fatma was someone he'd like to party with. She had a great ass and those big dark eyes. He'd love to hear her scream his name as she came. But she was off limits.

"You never fuck at the office," his father reminded him time and again. "It's bad for business."

When this deal came through, that was going to change. A lot of things were going to change around here. He sorted through the papers Fatma had dropped off. At the bottom of the stack was a magazine. As soon as Omar saw the picture on the cover, he froze. A familiar face smiled up at him. The face from his nightmares. The face of the man that his father had held up as the one to beat. And he never could.

Omar grabbed the magazine as he ground his teeth. It was one of those "top thirty under thirty" lists. *Tristan St. Claire, The Man to Watch*, the headline screamed. He was the best of the best because he not only tripled the size of his family's textile business, but he was also helping the environment and trying to help the less fortunate in Australia where he was from.

"Fuck!" Omar spat.

St. Claire had been his nemesis at Lassard Alpine Academy, the boarding school they'd both attended. They'd hated each other on sight. That had never changed. At least not from Omar's end. St. Claire was everything he was not, tall, blond, athletically gifted, and smart. Very smart. He'd come first in everything. Now here he was first again. He flipped to the article and started scanning. St. Claire was nothing short of a god, according to the magazine. And Omar? Where was he on the list? He flipped the pages until he found himself. Number twenty-three. Twenty-three. Not good enough. Not even close. That's what his father would tell him.

Heat crawled up Omar's neck to his cheeks. He swallowed hard. Even St. Claire's picture was mocking him. Where Omar's picture was taken at his favorite restaurant, St. Claire's was taken while he was working in a field. In a fucking field, for fuck's sake!

Omar crushed the magazine in his hands. Then he froze. His father would see this. He would call Omar into his office and ask in a deceptively quiet voice if he'd seen the article and what was Omar going to do about it? How was he going to stop coming in second to this man?

Last time Hakan had brought up St. Claire, it was at Omar's college graduation. He and St. Claire had, of course, ended up at Oxford together. St. Claire had taken extra classes and finished early with a double major. Omar had taken the standard amount of time and only studied one thing: business.

"This man is wiping the floor with you," Hakan had said. "You, you're known for your parties. What's he known for? Saving the fucking world! Developing some machine that will clean the oceans. Now he wants to revolutionize the textile industry so the materials are organic and produce less waste. What are you going to do? How will you beat him?" His father had been livid.

Omar had partied at university, and he'd thrown the best ones. No one wanted to miss any of Omar's parties. He'd been proud of that, but it wasn't good enough for Hakan. Why wasn't Omar out saving the world like St. Claire?

Omar released the magazine from his fists. He would have to face his father but, this time, *this time* he had an answer. The deal with the Germans. It would catapult them to number one. Their revenue would be the largest. His father would be the top man in the number one textile company in the world, and Omar had been the one to make it happen. His father would *have* to be proud of him then. He was ready this time. Ready for when his father called.

The phone on his desk beeped. He hit the intercom button. "Yes?"

Fatma's silky voice came through the phone. "Your father wants to see you."

Omar smiled as he stood. He straightened his tie and put on his light grey suit jacket. Things were definitely going to change, and it was all due to him.

CHAPTER ONE

S loan Bishop wiped sweat off her forehead with the back of her arm as she lay on the single bed. It had to be a hundred degrees in the small cabin she'd been assigned. As the only woman reporter on board the *Sea Jewel*, she got her own room, but it was the size of a broom closet with just enough space for a bed and a small table with a lamp. There was a tiny mirror over the table. Probably for the best since she was sure she looked like shit.

The size of the room didn't bother her. Neither did the beige walls with their peeling paint or the ultra-thin mattress with its thread-bare blankets that she was now lying on. Even the smell, a mix of metal, salt water, and years of wear and tear didn't really get to her. This was actually a step up from some of the other places she'd stayed, and wasn't that a sad statement? What kind of life was she leading that a cell-like room was a step up?

No, the thing that bothered her the most was the fact that the air conditioning was non-existent. Oh, there was a vent, but the limp flow of air coming from it was more like a hot breath than a cool breeze. Being in a metal box in the middle of the Suez Canal in spring was not her idea of fun. Normally, it would be in the eighties, but they'd been having abnormally hot days with temperatures in the high nineties, and it wasn't getting much cooler at night. She imagined this was what being slow roasted in an oven would feel like. At least, it wasn't summer. She'd be well cooked by now.

She checked her watch. Just after two a.m. local time. Her navy T-shirt was sticking to her, and her khaki cargo pants were making her legs sweat like crazy, but she didn't feel comfortable sleeping in anything less. If something happened, she wanted to be fully dressed and ready to go. Plus, the lock on her door was flimsy. She wasn't taking any chances.

Sloan rolled off the bed and slid her feet into her sneakers. It was too damn hot to sleep. Maybe if she went up on deck, she could at least get a breeze. The Suez Canal is an engineering miracle. The man-made shipping channel connects the Red Sea and the Mediterranean but it's also a pathway through the desert. She hadn't paid enough attention to *that* fact in her research. She would have packed more deodorant. The desert was supposed to be colder at night and it was, just not enough to cool down her room before the sun rose again.

She piled her shoulder-length dark brown curly hair on top of her head and pinned it there. A few tendrils escaped but Sloan didn't bother redoing it. It was the middle of the night and too damn hot to care what she looked like. Having it off her neck made her slightly cooler. She glanced in the mirror and wished she hadn't. Her big blue eyes had large dark circles around them. The lack of sleep was definitely getting to her.

This had seemed like a dream assignment when she was picked to be on board when the first Egyptian female canal pilot took her first ship on its voyage through the Suez

Canal. Canal pilots work for the port authority. Sloan composed the introduction to the article in her head: the pilot's job is to guide and advise the ships on how to proceed through the canal. It's a big deal for a woman to succeed in this traditionally male-dominated field.

Perhaps dream job was a bit strong, but it was a hell of a lot better than running around, trying to scrape together scraps of other people's interviews to write a story. Charlie Philips, a good friend of her father's before he passed away, had pulled strings to get her the assignment, and she was truly grateful.

Being a newspaper reporter was damn hard in this day and age. She wasn't a full-time employee, and she had to shop around everything she wrote. She'd been lucky enough to break the story about the Tarchuarani, and *The New York Times* had run that and all of the follow-ups she'd written, but she needed to come up with something good if she was going to keep getting picked up by the Times. Sloan liked to win, and she was ambitious, but even she had to admit that a lot of being a reporter was luck, and hers seemed to have turned sour lately.

Sloan opened her door and slid quietly into the hallway. She moved as silently as possible through the freighter. Being one of the few women on a ship filled with men meant keeping her head down and staying out of the way.

Most of the crew was nice enough, but there were a few of them that looked more like mercenaries than crew and they made the hair on the back of her neck stand up. She had no intention of running into one of them at this hour. Extra security for the ship and cargo, the captain had explained when she'd asked him about the abnormally large number of security guys on the ship. Security for something to be sure but what remained to be seen.

After breaking the story for *The New York Times* about

the Tarchuarani, she'd thought she might get an actual job offer from them, graduate to being a salaried employee, but after a couple of weeks, that bubble had burst and she was back trying to dig up something of interest. When the Egyptian government had announced they had their first female Suez Canal pilot, she'd jumped at the chance to interview the woman. Zahra Nabil would be the name on people's lips for at least a news cycle or two. She would be held up as an example of how things were changing in North Africa and the Middle East, albeit much more slowly than women would like.

Or she would have been if catastrophe hadn't struck, and the ship hadn't gotten wedged sideways in a narrow part of the canal. The bow was stuck in the left bank and the stern was beached on the right bank. There was even some talk that the stern might be stuck on the bottom of the canal as well. The ships that had been ahead of it made it through but now the *Sea Jewel* was blocking all the canal traffic from both directions, and Zahra Nabil was famous for all the wrong reasons.

Some people, the hardline religious groups were pointing to her and saying she was why women shouldn't have jobs that were traditionally male. They'd given a woman a chance, and she'd screwed up. Now everyone could see why women shouldn't have certain jobs.

Stupid.

And Sloan was pretty damn sure Zahra hadn't screwed up. Sloan had been on the navigation bridge when Zahra was advising Captain Svensson on entering the canal. She heard the argument between the two about the wind and how it might not be the best time to take the ship through. They'd started in English, but then Zahra had switched to Arabic and got the interpreter to translate to Norwegian. Sloan thought she switched languages because the captain wasn't listening, and Zahra was probably worried she wasn't communicating well enough for him to understand. Or, at least, that was Sloan's theory. Who the hell knew what really happened? She spoke neither Arabic nor Norwegian.

Then the second in command, Rohan Patel, had pushed her and all the other reporters out of the bridge onto the bridge wing, saying it was dangerous to have them in there. They were distracting the captain. With a strong wind pelting sand at them, the rest of the reporters left except for her and Eddie. He'd stayed right along with her like she knew he would. Eddie had a nose for a story just like she did.

Sloan was about to leave when she felt something, a shuddering of sorts. Zahra and several other people on the bridge looked around in alarm. Then the whole ship rocked slightly. Patel saw her standing outside and signaled to one of the other officers. The officer chased her and Eddie out of the area. That had been two days ago and it was the last time she'd been able to speak with the canal pilot about anything.

Sloan quietly moved through the doorway out onto the walkway on the left side of the ship. *Port.* She needed to use the proper terms so she didn't forget them. She'd had to look them up continuously when she'd written the first story about the ship getting stuck.

There was a slight breeze, and it felt like heaven. The air was dry, and she knew from experience that she would end up with sand in her hair and her mouth—the fine flecks that were carried on the breeze stuck to everything—but the cool air of the desert night was worth getting sandblasted.

She walked along the rail toward the bow. The outside lights were dim, but a bright waxing moon provided enough light to cast shadows. She made her way to a set of steps up to the main deck. There, she picked a container to lean on. She was about a third of the way down the ship toward the bow. The spot gave her a nice view of the canal as well as a cool breeze. It also meant she could see anyone coming from either direction. Of course, they could also see her, but she didn't imagine too many people would be around at this hour.

She sat down, stretching her legs out in front of her and crossing them at the ankles. What could she write about? Being on a massive container ship was interesting for her, but she wasn't sure it would be something people wanted to read. It was daunting being a small speck next to all the containers. The sheer volume of them was intense. She'd filed her story about the ship being stuck as soon as the incident happened and filed several more updates, but there was nothing new to report. Well, nothing she was allowed to report.

She'd tried to ask Zahra about the shudder that she'd felt, but the captain had cut her off. He said Ms. Nabil couldn't talk about it because the incident was under investigation. Sloan had tried to approach the woman twice more, once during lunch and once when she bumped into her in a hallway, but each time Zahra had refused to speak to her. Her entourage, two of the "security" men, was determined to keep anyone from having any meaningful exchange with her anyway.

Sloan might have let it go if the woman's eyes weren't so filled with terror. There was more to this story, but how to dig it out was the question. How could she get access to Zahra without those goons around?

She closed her eyes and let the breeze roll over her skin. They weren't allowed to leave the ship yet. As far as the world knew, everyone was staying on board because they would be free any minute now and the historic journey would continue, but the reality was different.

She'd asked to get off but was told by the captain it wasn't possible at the moment. He hadn't given her a reason, and when she'd pointed out the interpreter got to leave immediately, the captain just told her to leave his office. Her reporter instincts were screaming at her but so was her well-developed sense of self-preservation. There was something major going on. She just had to figure it out before anyone else did, or at the very least, at the same time so she could get credit for breaking the story.

Off in the distance, a door clanged loudly, metal hitting metal. She heard footsteps and then the murmur of voices. The voices were getting louder so they must be coming closer. It sounded to her like people were arguing in English. She could catch the occasional odd word.

She peeked around the edge of the equipment and looked up at the flying bridge. Two men stood arguing in the middle of the deck, but at this distance, she couldn't tell who they were. There were too many shadows.

Then one took a step back, and the light hit his hat. Eddie. Who else would wear a fedora? He was the only guy she knew who could get away with the hat and the swagger. He was a damn good reporter, and it didn't hurt that he was charming as hell. He claimed his dimpled smile and his charm were his secret weapons. Sloan didn't doubt it.

Eddie was definitely arguing with the other man. He had his hands up in front of him like he was trying to calm the other guy down, but the other guy wasn't having it. He took a step closer to Eddie. He was taller than Eddie, and the moon shone off his hair, but she couldn't tell the color. They were too far away. A good chunk of the men on board, including the scary security guys, were taller than Eddie. The man moved closer still, and Eddie backed up another step.

Should she go help him out? There was a sound off to the right, and a man came into view. Sloan watched as he headed in her direction. He was one of the normal crew, but she still did not want to be discovered. She had mentally divided the crew into the "normal" category, those who were usually thin and strong with deep tans and calloused hands and the "secu-rity" group, those who were bigger, very muscular, less tan, and meaner.

They scared the crap out of her.

Her heart pounded, and her palms broke out in a fine sweat. Why was she panicking? She wasn't doing anything wrong, but this whole situation had her spooked. Being stuck on the ship and knowing no one was telling the truth made her nerves raw. The crew member stopped about twenty feet away, checked something on his hand-held device, and then turned and left again.

She tried to calm down. She took a deep breath and then another. Her heart rate was returning to normal. She was turning to look at the two men once more when she heard a sickening thud. Her stomach rolled. She instinctively knew the sound. Her hands started shaking. She slowly leaned out a bit and looked back up at the flying bridge. Eddie's body was lying on the deck about fifty feet away. He wasn't moving. She wanted to move, to go to him, but her limbs refused to move. Her mouth was open in a silent scream.

The sound of boots on the deck cut through her paraly-sis. The light that had illuminated Eddie went out and then a man appeared from the shadows. She got up and scooted around the corner of a shipping container so they couldn't see her. She leaned out just so she could see Eddie with one eye and then quickly held up her phone. She snapped several pictures of Eddie before a man with a flashlight came to a halt next to him.

It was too dark to make out the man's features, but it was probably the man who had been arguing with Eddie moments earlier. She couldn't tell anything about him except he was tall. Two more men joined him on the deck. They all looked down at the body while they were talking. They were still too far away for her to hear exactly what they were saying. She wasn't even sure they were speaking English. A lot of the crew didn't and the security guys appeared to be from all over the world so they spoke in various languages at different times depending on who they were speaking to. Sloan snapped another few pictures, but she knew it was too dark to make any of them out. She wanted to turn on the flash, but then they would know she was there, and who knew what they would do to her. When her stomach rolled, she tried not to retch.

The three men all bent down and picked up Eddie's body. Sloan whirled around and leaned back against the container. She swallowed hard, fighting to keep the lamb kofta she'd eaten for dinner down in her belly. Eddie's head had lolled at an odd angle and his eyes had stared sightlessly at her. He was dead, no question.

She closed her eyes and then opened them again. She needed to get up to the flying bridge to see how the incident had happened. Her friend was dead, and she needed answers. But her limbs wouldn't move. She got up and tried to take a step, but her knees wouldn't cooperate. They wouldn't move. Nausea rolled through her. Maybe just another couple of minutes. Eddie was dead. There was no rush now.

She sat on the cool steel decking and tried to gather herself. Her hands shook so she balled them into fists. Eddie's voice rang out in her head. *Get it together, doll. You've seen dead bodies before*. Which was true, but it had never been someone she knew and never under those kinds of circumstances.

She heard voices again and another sound like water being sprayed. *Come on, doll, you have to go after the story. Snapping the pictures was quick thinking. Don't stop now. Follow it wherever it takes you. Get to the truth*. She could see his goofy grin in her mind's eye.

"I will Eddie. I promise," she murmured as she wiped

away a few tears that had escaped and rolled down her cheeks.

A few minutes later, after more tears than she would ever admit to, the sound of multiple voices reached her ears. The smattering of multiple languages seemed more excited somehow. They were also much closer. She got to her feet and walked out from behind the container. The captain and several crew members, both regular and security, were standing on the deck closer to the cabin area. They were looking over the side.

Sloan bit her lip. She didn't want anyone to know she'd been on deck when Eddie fell. *Or was pushed.* At least not yet. She needed to find out what people were saying before she said anything herself. Moving quickly, she stepped out from her spot and crossed to where the others were standing. With any luck at all, they would think she came from somewhere in the midst of the containers tied down on deck, *if* anyone noticed her at all. They were all engrossed in something that was happening over the side of the ship. Maybe they were finally getting freed from the deep sands of the canal.

Sloan hesitated as she passed the spot on the deck where Eddie had fallen. There was nothing but a wet spot now. No blood. Nothing to mark where he fell. Certainly nothing the police could use as evidence of a crime. That was the sound she'd heard. A hose spraying down the metal decking. All signs of Eddie's demise had disappeared.

Her heart rate increased again. How dare they? How dare they erase him like that? He deserved better. Sloan marched over to where the captain and crew had gathered at the rail. "Captain Svensson, I need to speak with you," she demanded.

He glanced over his shoulder at her. "It will have to wait, Ms. Bishop." He gestured over toward the railing. "I am dealing with a serious situation at the moment." His accent was thick, so it was hard to understand him.

"I'm afraid I must insist," Sloan said. The other men glanced at her but returned their gazes over the railing. She put her hands on her hips. Was he seriously going to ignore her?

The captain turned to her. "Ms. Bishop, we lost a person overboard. They are pulling him out now. You'll have to wait." He turned back to look over the side again.

Sloan frowned. Someone overboard? She moved closer to the railing and the gathered crew made room. With all the lights shining on the water from the side of the freighter, it was bright as day out there. The water looked black but calm. There were people out on the decks of all the other boats that were waiting to enter the canal, watching what was going on.

Sloan leaned over the railing slightly and gasped. On the deck of a smaller boat was Eddie's body.

CHAPTER TWO

C hief Petty Officer Axel Cantor leaned on the railing of
the U.S. Coast Guard Cutter, *William Fitzgerald*, and
raised his binoculars to check out the massive container ship.
His blond hair was slightly longer than it should have been,
and the breeze pushed it across his forehead. He squinted
against the sun.

"The *Sea Jewel* is stuck alright. Her bow is well into the
sandbank." He shifted his gaze slightly. "Her stern looks
wedged as well. Hard to tell from this angle. I can't see the far
corner of the ship." He then looked around the waterway.
"There are a lot of ships waiting, and Suez has only been
blocked for forty-eight hours. I would imagine it's the same
on the Mediterranean side as it is here in the Gulf of Suez. If
they don't move her soon, there will be hundreds of ships
waiting." He dropped his arms. "Take a look, sir," he said to
the Coast Guard Executive Officer next to him.

XO Bill Schwartz raised his own binoculars with the letters
XO stenciled on the side. His salt and pepper hair, clipped to
regulation length made him look older than his years. He kept

himself in excellent shape despite filling out a bit recently. His lips tightened. "This is a shit show. The Suez Canal being blocked for even an hour or two backs everything up. The fact that it's already been blocked for two days is going to cause mass panic around the world." He lowered his arms. "And we're going to be in the middle of it. The higher ups have already been on the captain's ass to keep them "well informed." They want to be kept in the loop about any activity we see. Specifically, you have been requested to find out all you can. It appears the higher ups know of your…network of contacts."

"Er, yes sir. I will keep my ear to the ground."

Schwartz growled, "I can't believe we're stuck here, waiting on gossip to find out what the hell is going on. If we'd just made it to the Mediterranean before the ship got stuck, it would be someone else's problem." He shook his head. "Sometimes I wish we would just stick to the U.S. All this traipsing around the world only gets us involved in more shit than necessary." He turned to face Axe, his grey eyes hardening. "If you repeat that, I'll deny it and have your ass hauled off to Alaska."

"No sir. Didn't hear a thing." Axe grinned. "And off the record, I sometimes agree with you." Being stationed in places like Bahrain weren't his favorite. He was glad the *Fitz* was on her way home. Not that there was anything wrong with Bahrain. He actually really loved the food, and the people he'd met had been fantastic, but he was tired of being immersed in another culture. He missed a good ol' fashioned barbeque and knocking back a beer with friends.

He missed Tag and the rest of the misfits that he'd been on a team with when he was recovering from burns he'd received while in the line of duty. They called themselves Team RECON, as in "reconstructed." They were good guys. Friends. And friends were something he needed these days.

Not too long ago, he'd lost a few and it was a hard pill to swallow.

He took a deep breath causing his shirt to pull across his muscular chest. The smell of the salt water was a nice change. He'd been working mostly below deck for the last couple of days. It was nice to be up in the fresh air and sunshine. Too bad it was so damn hot. He adjusted the sleeves of his blue uniform shirt, so they covered his wrists. It would be significantly cooler if he wore the short-sleeved version but there was no way in hell he wanted the world to see the grotesque scars on his forearms.

Schwartz raised the binoculars again. "Do you know who they're calling in to deal with this?"

Axe shrugged. "Not sure. Help has been offered from all over the world, but I don't think they've accepted any as yet. I know the locals have organized heavy equipment to dig it out."

Schwartz snorted. "That's not going to work. You can tell by looking at her she's dug in deep, and not just in the bank. I'll wager she's wedged on the bottom. The canal is not that deep, and *Sea Jewel* is one of the largest class of ships that go through here. The middle would be the only safe place for her."

"Sir," a young ensign said as he approached, "message for you.

Schwartz dropped his binoculars and let them dangle from around his neck and accepted the offered piece of paper. "Here we go again," Schwartz muttered as he read the paper and then started moving along the deck. "Cantor, keep an eye on the *Sea Jewel*. Let me know if anything changes. I'm needed on a call."

"Yes, sir." It wasn't normal for the XO to be so candid with a Chief Petty Officer, but Schwartz had served as a new recruit under Axe's grandfather, Captain James Axel Cantor.

He claimed that Jimmy Cantor had saved his life on more than one occasion. He had nothing but respect for the old man and he'd promised his former captain that he would take care of Axe the way Jimmy had taken care of Schwartz.

Axe went back to leaning on the rail. Schwartz wasn't wrong. This was not going to be an easy fix. He was damn glad it wasn't his responsibility to sort out the container ship. Blocking the Suez Canal was going to have global repercussions. Heads were going to roll for sure.

He raised the binoculars and ran them over the ship. There were people on deck now, peering over the side, which was ridiculous because there was no way they could really see the part of the ship that was stuck. Maybe they were watching the heavy equipment that was arriving on the bank.

Axe started to move the glasses away from the people but halted and refocused on the crowd. He squinted into the lenses. It couldn't be. *No fucking way*. His heart thudded against his ribs. He zeroed in on the woman who was climbing up on the rail and leaning over. Her dark curly hair was tied up on top of her head. She was wearing a long sleeve white top and jeans. A man, one of the ship's officers by the look of his clothing, stepped up next to her and pulled her back from leaning over the edge. He started gesturing and pointing. The woman straightened and nodded.

"Turn your head," Axe mumbled, but the woman kept her face aimed away from his view. The conversation between the woman and the man on deck continued. The woman nodded again. The man gestured some more. The woman finally looked in Axe's direction. His heart which had pounded so hard before stuttered to a stop for a beat or two.

"Shit."

It was her.

Sloan Bishop.

The woman who had smashed his heart to bits and the

most fun he'd ever had. What the fuck was she doing here? Why was she on the ship? Stupid question. As a reporter, where else would she be? This was a huge story. But how the hell had she gotten on the *Sea Jewel*?

The man gestured to Sloan again, and she stepped down from the rail. He walked with her until they disappeared from view.

Axe ground his teeth. They were broken up, he reminded himself. She'd hung him out to dry. She could walk and talk with whomever she pleased, but he didn't have to watch.

He lowered the binoculars and moved away from the edge. Striding down the deck, he knew he needed to avoid seeing Sloan again. He'd been crushed when things didn't work out. As much as he'd wanted to rekindle things after Panama, he just couldn't forget or forgive. Axe had made sure whatever had remained of their relationship after Panama had blown up in a spectacular fashion.

He'd used her job as an excuse. Sloan wanted to chase every story, even those that involved him, and she wasn't above sacrificing him and their relationship to get it. It didn't matter that he wasn't allowed to discuss things. She would snoop and dig until she discovered the truth. Saying she had an unnamed source didn't help. Everyone knew they were dating. It didn't even matter that he had never told her a thing. When her story about a Coast Guard screw up broke, everyone had assumed it was him, and his old commanding officer had made it part of the daily routine to punish Axe for it.

No, Sloan had cost him too much. He needed to stay as far away from her as possible.

Axe pulled on the cuffs of his uniform. He was having a hard time living with his scars. That was part of the problem with Sloan. She just didn't understand that the scars were a reminder of his mistakes. It was bad enough that everyone knew he was scarred; there was no need for them to see the proof of his failure.

He entered the ship and headed toward the bridge. It was cooler inside, and he felt less conspicuous with his long sleeves.

That had been another bone of contention between him and Sloan. She just didn't understand about…the incident. Andy had died, and Axe had to live with the fact that he hadn't been able to save one of his best friends. Sloan kept telling him it wasn't his fault, but it was. He should have been able to save them both. Andy and Kyle. Instead, Andy died, and Kyle wishes every day that he had died right along with Andy and he blamed Axe for saving his life.

All that pain and anger was tough for Axe to deal with. Sloan thought he should work on letting it all go but he couldn't. These were his brothers, and he'd let them down. He was responsible for the misery and death of his friends, and he had to live with that. It was a part of his life now. Sloan wasn't. At least not anymore. Whatever Sloan was doing on the *Sea Jewel*, it was no business of his. He would just forget he ever saw her.

CHAPTER THREE

"Sloan, you can't see anything by leaning over the side. I promise," Rohan Patel said as he pulled on Sloan's arm. He was a tall, lean man somewhere in his thirties with thick black hair and deep brown eyes. He had a warm smile. His brown uniform seemed slightly large on him as if he'd just lost weight.

Sloan sighed. "I know. I guess I just…" Just what? Needed a distraction. Eddie's death had thrown her. Not just his death but the cover-up. She desperately wanted to speak to someone about it but didn't know who to trust. She studied Rohan. As the ship's Chief Mate, or First Officer as she thought of him, he should be made aware of the situation, but he seemed awfully deferential to the "security" men. MacGregor, the head guy, was scary as hell, and Sloan had no intention of letting him know she knew the truth.

Rohan nodded. "I understand. You need to write another story, but it's not worth risking your life over. We've already had one…accident. We don't want another."

Sloan quickly searched Rohan's face. Had that been a threat? But no, there was just genuine worry and maybe even a touch of sadness. She nodded. "I guess I was looking for a distraction. It's hard being stuck here but not really getting the full story. I actually feel like if I was on the canal banks, I might know more of what's going on. Svensson won't give me an interview or even give me a hint as to what they're doing to get the ship unstuck, apart from the obvious." She gestured at the heavy equipment on the bank.

Rohan frowned. "Captain Svensson is in a difficult position. He isn't allowed to speak about what happened. Surely you can understand that?"

Sloan nodded. "But can you tell me what's going on?"

Rohan sighed. "I can't speak about it either."

"Are you going to try anything else besides the heavy equipment? What's the backup plan?"

He shrugged. "Sloan, I cannot speak about that. Truly."

Sloan tried another angle. "Hypothetically, if a ship got stuck in the canal and heavy equipment couldn't dig it out, what might be the next option?"

Rohan cracked a smile. "You are very persistent."

She grinned. "So?"

"Hypothetically, I would suggest that tugboats, and many of them, would be helpful. But you didn't hear that from me." He smiled and gave her a wink.

"Do you really think tugboats will work?"

Rohan tilted his head. "Off the record?"

She nodded.

"Maybe. But…" He hesitated. "I think she's also run aground underneath. I don't believe it is just the banks. It will be very hard to get her out if that's the case."

"Rohan, do you think there was something strange about the whole thing? I was there and saw Zahra Nabil and Captain Svensson arguing. Why did Svensson go into the canal when she advised him not to?"

The Chief Mate turned and faced the water. His shoulders slumped. "I don't know." He turned back to face Sloan. "You cannot quote me on that." His eyes pierced her as if holding her in place.

"I promise it's all off the record, Rohan."

He gave her a brief smile. "Now I have to get back to my duties. Please remember not to hang off the side. And…just be careful, okay?" He gave her arm a quick squeeze and then took off down the walkway toward the stern.

Sloan stayed on the deck, enjoying the shade. The white blouse she had on was light and even though it had long sleeves, it let what little breeze there was through to her skin. It also protected her from the sun. Her jeans were a different story but she didn't have much choice clothing-wise. She'd only packed a small bag for the trip.

She fanned herself with her hand. It was still hot in her cabin, and at least there was something to look at out here. She glanced back at the mouth of the canal. The number of ships seemed to be increasing at an alarming rate.

Her phone beeped, and she pulled it out of her pocket. Glancing at the screen, she frowned. Yet another article blaming Zahra Nabil for the blockage. It was from one of the radical right-wing online sites. Well, of course, they'd blame her. As the first female Suez Canal pilot, she had a target on her back no matter what. Sloan bit her lip.

Most of the mainstream press weren't declaring it anything more than an accident, but the conspiracy theory nuts were alive and well, pumping out story after story. Her heart went out to the Egyptian woman. At least the Egyptian government was doing a full investigation. They'd already spoken to everyone on board but said they may have more questions so everyone needed to hold tight and stay on the *Sea Jewel*.

Sloan really needed to speak with the canal pilot. She'd tried to approach her, but Captain Svensson had cut her off.

He said Zahra Nabil wasn't allowed to discuss what had happened until the investigation by the Egyptian government was complete by order of Pacific Overseas Express, the company that owned the *Sea Jewel*. Then he said Ms. Nabil had received death threats so he was assigning security to be with her twenty-four-seven. When Sloan had asked if the captain thought Zahra Nabil was in danger while on board the ship, he just refused to answer and kicked her off the bridge.

One of the security goons pushed past her on the walkway. He was wearing a blue shirt and a baseball cap that covered his dark blond crew cut. He was very muscular, but there was something in the way he carried himself that said military rather than cargo ship security officer. She'd heard him called "Christo," but who knew if that was a first or a last name. He had an accent that she suspected was Afrikaans but she wasn't about to ask him. The less interaction she had with these guys the better.

Sloan shook her head. She was totally pissed at Eddie. How could he go and get killed like that? There were a couple of other reporters on board, but they were from the local papers and steered clear of her. Eddie had been her only friend on the ship, and now she was alone. He had kept telling her she needed to push to get the whole story, but maybe he pushed too much. A shiver traipsed across her skin.

She heard a man speaking somewhere farther down the walkway. If she leaned back from the rail, she could see down the side of the ship to identify him, but she already recognized the voice. Hamish MacGregor, head of security on the *Sea Jewel*.

MacGregor wasn't a tall man but what he lacked in height, he made up for in girth. He had a big barrel chest and strawberry-blond hair. His pale blue eyes were like ice chips, and his Scottish accent was thick. He often spoke in a quiet voice, but just the sound of it put the fear of God in Sloan. He was the one that scared her the most. He was a cold, calculating man, and she just knew in her marrow he would have no qualms about killing anyone who got in his way.

Sloan would have thought it was MacGregor up there with Eddie, but he was actually the wrong shape to have been the man on the upper walkway. Christo was a better fit. Maybe MacGregor had ordered Christo to kill Eddie. But why?

Sloan *knew* there was way more to this story. Whatever was happening on board this ship had to be big. Big enough to risk killing Eddie. The heat prickled across her skin. Eddie was a sharp guy. They'd run into each other many times over the last few years. Sometimes she got somewhere first, like the story on the Tarchuarani, and other times he did, but they had a good working relationship and he'd watched out for her a few times.

And now he was gone.

"What did you know, Eddie?" she murmured. And more importantly, why was it worth killing over?

CHAPTER FOUR

A xe let out a curse as he hopped out of the shower and started to dry himself off. He had about thirty seconds to be dressed and on deck ready to go before Schwartz would be yelling. He'd overslept, which wouldn't normally be the end of the world, but Schwartz had summoned him for some reason, so now Axe was keeping his XO waiting.

He cursed again as he pulled on his operation dress uniform. The dark blue shirt stuck to his broad shoulders as he tried to do up the buttons. He was going to have to get a larger size if he kept up all this time at the gym. He fixed the cuffs on his long sleeves and cursed colorfully. The heat was going to kill him again today. It wasn't just the shirt, the matching dark blue cargo pants were also brutally hot in the Egyptian weather, but he didn't have a choice there. Shorts weren't an option. At least the uniform brought out the blue of his eyes, or so Sloan had told him.

Sloan. Thoughts of her had kept him up until the wee hours last night, and he'd only fallen asleep just as he was supposed to be getting up. Now he was exhausted, starving, and generally pissed off. Toddy, the Chief Cook had better have coffee ready, or Axe was likely to snap someone's neck today and he would put the blame squarely at Sloan's feet. She always wreaked havoc on his life, damn her, even when she wasn't actually in it.

Axe finished tying his boots and left his quarters. He moved swiftly down the hallways toward the Chief's Mess. He quickly stepped through the mess into the galley where Toddy had a cup of coffee sitting on the counter. "Thank you, Toddy. I owe you big time." He took a big gulp of the bitter brew.

Toddy was a giant of a man with big dark eyes and skin to match. His belly laugh was one of the best sounds Axe had ever heard. Deep and rolling, it came from the depths of his soul. "My man, you owe me nothing. I have a bet going with Simons over here. He said you wouldn't stop because you're too late and Schwartz is going to have your ass. I told him you'd stop no matter what. You can't go on no caffeine. So now I am twenty bucks richer. Coffee is on me."

Axe grinned. "Glad I could be of assistance." He took another large gulp and then put down the cup. He left the galley at a jog and made his way onto deck to join his commanding officer.

"You're late," the older man said as he looked through binoculars focused on the cargo vessel mired in the middle of the canal.

"Yes, sir. I'm sorry, sir."

"They're still stuck."

"It would appear so, sir."

Schwartz lowered the binoculars and glanced at Axe. "The captain got pulled into a meeting so I'm giving you an assignment. We have a problem, Cantor, and the powers that be seem to think you should be the one to solve it. Or at least keep things secure until another team can get here and solve it."

"Er, what kind of problem, sir?" Axe groaned silently. He'd been hoping for a quiet day, one where he could just phone it in until the end of shift and then he could crash for a good twelve hours.

"The dead kind."

Axe swallowed. "I'm sorry. I'm not following you. Can you be more specific, sir?"

Schwartz sighed. "The body of an American citizen was discovered off the side of the *Sea Jewel* at oh-two-twenty this morning. It is presumed to be an accident, but because the world is watching, the higher ups want a full investigation. They need to be seen as taking the loss of an American life very seriously.

"The Egyptian government is not thrilled with the idea, but they can hardly refuse at the moment with all eyes on the Suez. My boss's boss requested you by name. Rear Admiral Bertrand seems to like you for some reason." Schwartz looked Axe up and down as if the reason he was liked would somehow become apparent. "Anyway, he found out you were here and requested that you transfer over to the *Sea Jewel* immediately and oversee the investigation as the closest American law enforcement officer."

Icy fingers gripped Axe's heart. A dead American from the *Sea Jewel. Sloan.* He tried to speak, but his mouth had gone dry. It couldn't be Sloan. She wouldn't be that sloppy. He saw her in his mind's eye, standing on the railing yesterday. Yes, she would have if it meant a better story. Axe cleared his throat. "Ah, do you have any more details on the dead person, sir?" His voice cracked on the last word, and the captain turned to look at him sharply.

"Are you alright, sailor? You aren't sick or anything?"

"No, sir." Axe shook his head.

"The body is that of a male. They faxed over a copy of his driver's license. One Eddie O'Mara. In his early thirties from

New York City. Looks like the fall killed him. That's all the details I have."

A male. Axe's shoulders sagged for a second. It wasn't Sloan. Then aware that his boss was still watching him, he straightened up. "So, I guess I should head over to the *Sea Jewel.*"

"Yes," the XO agreed. "That would be a good idea. Hard to manage the investigation from here."

"Right."

Schwartz eyed him. "Are you sure you're okay? You seem…off this morning."

"Sorry, sir. I'm fine. Just didn't sleep well last night and not enough caffeine yet today."

Schwartz shook his head. "Well, get yourself together. They have an FBI team flying in to take over the investigation. Admiral Bertrand wants you to oversee things 'til they get here in the next eighteen hours or so."

Axe nodded. "I'll do my best, sir."

"See that you do. Dismissed."

Axe turned and walked down the deck and back into the ship. He stopped at the galley.

"Back already?" Toddy asked as he glanced up while chopping potatoes.

"Coffee, please," Axe managed to choke out. He was still having issues speaking. The image of Sloan dead in the water was haunting him. Even though Schwartz had said it was a man, he wasn't going to be able to relax until he saw her with his own eyes. Or saw the dead guy. That was probably better. Safer for Axe.

Toddy came over and offered Axe a mug. "You aren't looking so good. As a matter of fact, you look a bit gray. You okay?"

"I… Yeah."

Toddy shook his head. "You look like you just lost your

best friend. Why don't you come sit a minute?" He stood in front of Axe, studying him.

Axe shook his head. Toddy had been in the Coast Guard longer than most people roamed the earth. He'd also come up under Jimmy Cantor. Besides Axe's grandfather, Toddy was the best sailor, best man really, that Axe knew. He and Axe had served together on a couple of different ships over the years, and the old man had always looked out for him. Probably another tribute to Axe's grandfather. "Thanks, Toddy. I appreciate it, but I'll be okay. Just…had a bit of a… shock, I'd guess you'd call it." He took a sip of the strong, hot brew. "Duty calls. Can you put this in a to-go cup for me?" Axe offered a smile.

Toddy nodded as he took the mug. He pulled down a cup made for hot drinks and a lid. He poured the coffee into the new cup and put the lid on. Axe reached out for it, but Toddy held on to the cup. "Listen, you take a minute to get yourself right. Don't go out there off-kilter. Not sure what's going on, but no doubt you're gonna need all your wits about you."

It was Axe's turn to nod. "You're right, and I promise to get my shit together." He gave the other man a brief smile. "Thanks for the reminder, Toddy. I really do owe you one this time."

"You owe me thousands, young man, but that one was free." Toddy turned and went back to his vegetables.

Axe made his way to the Chief's quarters and gathered his things from his bunk. He was going to have to stay on board the other ship until the FBI arrived. He grabbed his go bag and his coffee and started out the door but stopped. He put everything down and took a moment to breathe. Toddy was right. He was a mess.

He glanced down at his hands. They were shaking. Ever since he'd gone back to regular duty, anytime there was an incident, his body went into overdrive. It was stupid and, if he was being truthful, dangerous. Being on the ship again, he'd lost his edge. Running through the Panamanian jungle was fine, but just hearing about some stranger dying on a cargo ship had him falling apart.

This was ridiculous. *He* was being ridiculous. He didn't even know the guy, although he felt bad for any family he might have had. The main thing was Sloan was fine. She wasn't even his girlfriend anymore, so he needed to get his shit together and stop with the shaking bullshit. He took a deep breath.

The image of Kyle flashed in his mind, and he ground his teeth. Losing Andy had been hard enough, but Kyle cutting Axe out of his life because he blamed Axe for making him *survive* the fire, well, it was slowly killing him. He didn't want to lose anyone else. Even if he and Sloan weren't together anymore, he needed to know she still walked the earth.

Axe adjusted the cuff of his sleeves once more. Then he squared his shoulders and grabbed his stuff. It was his job to look after the dead American until the FBI could arrive, and he would do it to the best of his ability. Sloan was just another person on that ship. He needed to put her into perspective if he was going to get through this. She was no longer his, and that was just fine. She'd broken his heart and his trust. He needed to move on. He had bigger problems to deal with.

Axe walked out onto the deck and went to the launch that was waiting to take him to the *Sea Jewel*. After dropping his bag and climbing aboard the launch, he settled onto the bench and took a large sip of coffee. The transfer wouldn't take long, and he was determined to use his time to rein himself in.

The boat wound its way through the traffic at the beginning of the canal. The number of ships building up while the canal was blocked was increasing daily, and the problems the blockage was causing couldn't be understated. He knew there were at least two-hundred ships waiting now. That was a big number when it came to delays. It would take a few weeks at this rate to get them all through the canal.

As they cruised around one of the other container ships, Axe noted the livestock. Those animals needed to be fed. He knew that the shipper had only packed enough to get the animals to their destination with little extra. Several more days on board and those animals would run out of food, and then what? That problem was multiplied by every ship there. They all were on a schedule, and they only had supplies enough to last for maybe a few more days.

Also, people were waiting all over the world for what was on those ships. The longer they were blocked, the longer people were without items they needed. The whole world's economy was being held up by one ship. Right now, it wasn't too bad, but if this lasted a week or more, there would be serious consequences.

They finally came alongside the *Sea Jewel,* and Axe gathered his gear. He waited for the boat to come alongside the pilot stairs before he threw his gear onto the platform, and then a few beats later, he made the jump. He gathered his gear and took the stairs two at a time. It was a long way up from the water, at least one hundred feet. By the time he reached the top, he was breathing heavy. It didn't help that the wind had picked up and had been blowing against him.

There were three men standing there when he arrived on the deck. The first one stepped forward. "I'm Captain Svensson." The man was tall with light blond hair and lots of freckles. He spoke with a slight accent, Norwegian if Axe had to guess. Svensson's face was lined, and his handshake was firm. This man had spent a lifetime at sea.

"I'm Chief Petty Officer Axel Cantor of the US Coast

Guard Cutter *William Fitzgerald*. Permission to come aboard, sir."

The captain nodded. "Granted. This is Chief Mate Rohan Patel." He pointed to the tall, slender man on his right. "And this is Mr. Hamish MacGregor, the head of security," he said as he gestured to the great barrel of a reddish-blond man on his left. "The body is downstairs in the refrigerated unit. Mr. MacGregor will show you your berth and then take you down to see the deceased. Let one of these men know if you need anything else."

Axe nodded. "I also would like to speak with any witnesses and see for myself where exactly the gentleman was said to have gone overboard."

The captain's lips thinned. "Fine. Chief Mate Patel will assist you by rounding up the crew you need to speak to. I have been told the FBI should be here in the morning, but there's a dust storm coming, and they are having some difficulties with their flights."

Axe nodded. He'd checked the weather before he'd left the *Fitz*. It wasn't unheard of out here to have dust storms. They stopped everything. Nothing can fly with all that sand in the air. Damn hard to drive, too. People usually just stayed inside and waited out the storm.

"I'll leave you to it," the captain said and then turned on his heel and left.

MacGregor crossed his arms over his brawny chest and glared silently, his gaze roving from Patel to Axe and back.

Axe said nothing but was slightly surprised by the head of security and the captain's brusque attitudes. He could excuse the captain, after all, the man was under a lot of pressure. His ship was holding up the world. No telling what had crawled up MacGregor's ass. But Axe imagined having a man go overboard on his watch would have made Axe a grump as well.

Then again, Axe was used to being the person who comes

to everyone's aid. People were usually overjoyed to see the Coast Guard unless they were smugglers. Was the captain a smuggler? Nah. Was MacGregor hiding something? Who could tell? Axe mentally shrugged. He was just letting his imagination get away with him, but he made a decision to pay close attention to the happenings on the ship.

"If you'll follow me, sir." The Chief Mate turned and walked along the deck toward the bridge. Axe had recognized him as the man Sloan had been speaking to on deck yesterday. He slammed the brakes on those thoughts. *No sense borrowing trouble in the form of the sexy brunette.*

Patel was a lean man with serious eyes. He moved efficiently but looked like he could be blown away in a strong wind compared to the other beast of a man walking with them.

Axe made a point to make sure MacGregor was in his line of sight the whole time. There was something about the guy that inspired an instant dislike. He seemed like a stone-cold killer. But what he was doing on a cargo ship was a mystery. Maybe the captain really was smuggling something.

"How are things going with getting unstuck?" Axe directed the question to the second in command.

Patel shot a glance at MacGregor before he said, "Slowly."

"Are you calling in special teams to help?" Axe was actually shocked there wasn't a US Navy team on site already. The US reached out immediately. The Suez was very important in worldwide shipping and the US, as one of the dominant powers in the world, wouldn't want this blockage to happen any longer than was strictly necessary. It could affect military movements in a delicate region. *Politics.* Had to be. He gave himself a mental shake. All above his pay grade.

Patel looked at Axe and then gave a quick glance at MacGregor before looking back at Axe. "I'm sure the captain has it under control." He opened the door and led the way down a hallway.

Axe's gut tensed. The Chief Mate did not want to discuss anything in front of the head of security. Not good. MacGregor seemed more mountain than man. He was at least twice the size of Axe across his chest and arms, and Axe was no slouch. MacGregor was a human wall of solid muscle and bone. The fact that the first officer thought of MacGregor as the enemy, or at least not a friend, made Axe's gut churn all the more. The coffee he'd slugged down now burned in his stomach. The situation was turning bad, and he hadn't even bumped into Sloan yet.

They walked through the rabbit warren of hallways that always made up the inner workings of a ship this size. It would take Axe a couple of days to get the whole layout down pat, but he understood the gist of where everything was. Hopefully, he wouldn't be on board that long.

They came to a stop in front of a nondescript door. Patel turned and addressed Axe. "This is where the body is kept. It's refrigerated, so be prepared."

Axe nodded, and after Patel opened the door, Axe stepped into the room. It was refreshing after the heat of the day but Axe knew he'd be cold in a few minutes. The room was on the small side. It had metal shelves on all four walls that stacked from floor to ceiling. There were boxes on most of the shelves, but they didn't appear to be labeled. At least not on the sides that Axe could see. Given his thoughts about smuggling, Axe was tempted to ask about them but, in all likelihood, Patel wouldn't answer his questions.

MacGregor stood leaning against the wall out in the hallway. The hair on the back of Axe's neck stood up. MacGregor was effectively blocking Axe's exit and could lock him in the cold storage room in the blink of an eye. It put Axe on edge, but there wasn't much he could do about it at the moment.

He sure as hell wasn't going to say anything because that would be admitting MacGregor had the upper hand. MacGregor knew what he was doing, and he was doing it on purpose. He wanted Axe to know who was boss. Was he just being a territorial asshole, or was there more to it? Axe was betting on the latter.

Directly across from where he stood in the doorway was a black body bag laid out on a shelf about waist high. Axe went over and unzipped it. The only reason he wanted to see the body was, in fact, to confirm that the guy was dead and so he could compare it to the ID picture to verify he was American.

He pushed the body bag out of the way and looked down at the dead man. He was the man from the driver's license. Edward O'Mara. He couldn't tell much because the right half of the guy's face was crushed, but Axe knew he was in his early thirties.

He looked over the body. O'Mara was still clothed. He'd been wearing a khaki shirt and a pair of jeans which were now frozen, probably due to being wet when the body was put into cold storage. There wasn't a huge amount of blood.

Axe then looked at O'Mara's arms and hands. There were no obvious defensive wounds, so it didn't look like he'd been in a fight. The fact that he'd also been in the water meant some of the blood could have been washed away. The guy had probably died instantly, possibly from massive internal hemorrhaging or head trauma, from the look of things. Hitting the water from a height as tall as the ship would be like hitting concrete. He would love to examine the body more closely, but it wasn't his place.

"You guys think he fell over the side?" Axe asked as casually as possible.

"Yeah," MacGregor said from the hallway. No more details were offered.

Axe nodded and zipped up the bag. As a law enforcement officer for the Coast Guard, it was his job to see that this man was taken care of properly until the FBI arrived and did their own investigation. That was it. Even if he knew for sure this guy died differently than MacGregor was saying, it wasn't up to him to challenge the notion or launch an investigation. But he knew in his gut something weird was going on. He just didn't know if it had to do with the dead guy or not.

"Can you take me to my quarters now and then organize the witnesses so I can verify the facts? The FBI will go over everything in detail. I'm just here to sketch a broad outline for them."

MacGregor pushed off the wall. "Patel, go get the witnesses set up, and I'll take him up to his stateroom." It wasn't a recommendation. It was an order, and the first officer took off to follow it without question.

Something was definitely off here. Axe needed to speak to Patel without MacGregor being around. He also wanted to poke around the ship a bit. "Can you show me where he went overboard?"

MacGregor slowly nodded his head. Axe just stood there and waited for MacGregor to either say something or start moving. Finally, MacGregor turned and started down the hallway. Axe's shoulders relaxed just a fraction. He left the room and closed the door. MacGregor was waiting at the end of the corridor. Axe quickly caught up and followed the huge man back through the twists and turns of the hallways.

A few minutes later, MacGregor stopped in front of a stateroom door. "This is yours."

Before Axe could respond, the door next to his opened, and Sloan stepped out into the hallway. Axe stiffened, and his heart slammed against his ribs. *Damn if she didn't look fine.* Her curly dark hair was pulled into a messy bun at the top of her head. Her white blouse clung to her curves in the heat. A tingle went from his stomach to his groin. She always had that effect on him. No matter what was going on when he saw her, she could stir his blood in an instant.

But when she looked at him, his heart stalled. Her blue eyes were huge, and they had dark circles under them. Her skin was pale despite her tan. She was stressed and more than a little upset. Her eyes flashed with something akin to relief. His first instinct was to grab her and hold her close. She looked scared, and that was like a punch to the gut.

"Axe!" she said. "What are you doing here?"

"You two know each other?" MacGregor demanded, his Scottish accent sounding thicker than before.

Axe cursed silently. He needed to rein in his instincts. He had to keep his distance from Sloan if he was going to do his job properly. "Yes, I have run into Ms. Bishop before. She's done some…reporting," he said with a sneer, "about the Coast Guard in the past." He put as much derision in his voice as he could. Instinctively, he knew it was better if MacGregor didn't think they were friendly. He deliberately turned his back to Sloan. He knew he was insulting her, but he had no choice. "Where should I meet Patel and the witnesses?"

"The crew mess. They'll be there shortly. Don't waste their time."

"Understood," Axe said and then went into his cabin and shut the door. He leaned on the back of the door and rubbed his chest.

Seeing Sloan look lost and scared physically hurt him. He needed to find a way to deal with her. This was quickly turning into the assignment from hell.

CHAPTER FIVE

Sloan stood there and stared at the spot where Axe had been. Had she imagined him? Conjured him up because of her deep-seated fear of the men on board? Men like MacGregor? She glanced up at the head of security and mumbled. "Er, he's not my biggest fan. Broke a story about a Coast Guard screwup."

MacGregor just looked at her with his blank stare. She'd heard about men who had nothing behind their eyes but had never met one until she boarded this ship, and now it seemed they were everywhere. She knew instinctively this man wouldn't hesitate to kill her just like one of the others had killed Eddie. Despite the day's warmth, she shivered.

Sloan turned and went back into her room. She closed the door softly and locked it. Not that the flimsy lock would keep out a man like MacGregor, but it might slow him down a minute. But what good would that do? She needed a weapon. Today when she went to eat, she would steal a knife. It wouldn't be much, but having even that meager protection in her possession would make her feel infinitely better.

She flopped down on her bed. *Axe*. Axe was here in the room next door. Her shoulders sagged and she almost gave into the urge to cry. He'd said some awful things to her the last time they were together. He blamed her because his last CO gave him a hard time. He argued that the guys all believed he was her source so they'd all given him the cold shoulder. The ironic thing was that her source was his commanding officer, but she couldn't tell Axe that. It was an awful situation and she felt badly about breaking the story, but it was a good story and she was a reporter, writing good stories was her job.

She tucked a loose tendril behind her ear. On the positive side, she wasn't alone anymore. She didn't have to deal with everything on her own. Axe would help. He could make sure Eddie got the justice he deserved. Axe might hate her guts, which was most likely the case if the reception she'd just received was anything to go by, but he wouldn't let her be killed nor would he let these people get away with murder. That would go against his moral code, and Axe didn't break his moral code for anything or anyone. She knew that first-hand. As far as he was concerned, she'd screwed up, and he cut her off. She just knew he wouldn't let her in ever again, and that hurt. A lot.

She leaned back against the wall. She wanted to talk to Axe, but he obviously didn't feel the same. She wanted to do a lot more than talk. She missed him. His laugh, his smile, the amazing sex they'd always had together. Life without Axe was…boring. No one else had ever made her feel so alive, so ready for adventure.

She ran her hands over her face and thought about how to tell Axe what she knew. Would he believe her? She sat up again. If she didn't move now, there was no telling when she would get another chance to talk to him by herself.

Sloan opened her door quietly. Then she went out into the hall and locked it behind her. She walked the few steps necessary to put her squarely in front of Axe's door. She took a deep breath and raised her hand to knock.

The door opened before her fist made contact, and Axe stood there looking down at her. "Can I help you?"

She blinked. "Ah, yeah Axe. It's good to see you," she stammered. He looked good. Really good. She let her glance do a quick run over his whole body. He was as she remembered him, all hard angles and rippling muscles, not that she could see through his shirt, but his body was burned into her memory. His chest was bigger. He must be working out more. As he stood in the doorway, his shoulders almost touched both sides of the frame. She longed to touch him. She cleared her throat. His hair had been lightened by the sun, and his face had a healthy tan. He was wearing a long sleeve uniform shirt to cover his arms, so he must be still sensitive about his burns. His blue eyes were cold, though, and she had to steel herself from taking a step back. He was still pissed off. Well, he'd have to get over it because Eddie needed his help.

"I have to go. What do you want?"

"Eddie."

Axe frowned. "The guy who died."

She nodded. "He was a friend and a fellow reporter. He didn't deserve to die."

"Most people don't." Axe wasn't budging. He seemed to be determined to be an asshole.

"Axe," She glanced in each direction before lowering her voice. "He didn't die like they said he did. I was there. I—" She broke off when she heard footsteps in the hallway off to her left. When she turned, MacGregor was heading toward them.

"You." He pointed at Axe. "I told you not to be late. I don't like it when my people are held up. They're waiting for you upstairs. Move now."

Axe leaned casually against the doorframe and crossed his arms over his chest. "I was on my way when Ms. Bishop here decided she wanted to interview me about why I'm on board. I told her I'm just keeping an eye on the deceased until the FBI show up. She can ask them whatever it is she wants to know."

When MacGregor turned his glare on Sloan, her stomach lurched. "People all over the world want to know what's going on." She offered him a smile. "You can't blame a girl for trying." She jammed her hands into her pockets so he wouldn't see them shaking.

"You"—he turned back to Axe—"upstairs to the crew mess now."

Axe remained leaning on the doorjamb. "Waiting on an email from my superior. I'll be up as soon as I can. You know what the higher ups are like—you can't rush them. He'll get back to me shortly, and then I'll head up. I'm sure the captain won't mind the guys waiting a few more minutes."

When MacGregor clamped his jaw down hard, Sloan was pretty sure she heard his teeth grind, but he didn't say another word. He turned on his heel and strode down the hallway. His bulky frame made his arms stick out from his body so he had to turn slightly sideways when he came to the end of the hallway to get through the opening. Then he turned the corner and disappeared.

She let out a pent-up breath. "He scares me," she said as she looked in the direction he disappeared.

Axe made some non-committal noise. "I've gotta go. He won't wait long before he's back."

"I thought you were waiting on an email."

"No. I just don't like being ordered around like some snot-nosed kid." He straightened up and took a step toward Sloan. "You need to keep your nose out of things. MacGregor won't think twice about hurting you." His low voice sent shivers across her skin. She licked her lips. He scowled. "The FBI will be here tomorrow. They'll want to talk to you, and then they'll get you off the ship. Until then, don't talk to anyone and don't do anything stupid." Axe was glaring at her now.

"I—"

He took another step toward her. In the same low tone as before he said, "I'm serious, Sloan. We're not on U.S. soil. There's only so much I can do to protect you, so don't push everyone. It won't end well."

She knew he was being serious, and she should be paying attention, but he was close enough that his scent reached her, and memories of their time together flooded her brain. She couldn't focus.

Axe reached into his room and grabbed his backpack off the desk and then he stepped out into the hallway again and closed his door. He strode down the corridor before she could clear her brain long enough to formulate another protest.

Did he really think she was going to stay out of it? He knew her better than that surely. She had to know what happened to Eddie. She wasn't going to let her friend's killer get away, nor was she going to miss out on the story. Eddie would be really disappointed in her if she walked away now. No, she was going to stick it out 'til the end on this one. She owed it to Eddie and to herself.

Sloan opened her door again and grabbed her phone. If she was going to poke around, she needed to be able to record what she saw and heard. Hopefully, she would run into the female pilot. She closed her door and locked it again. Then she proceeded down the hallway.

She had so many questions for Zahra Nabil starting with what the hell happened? Sloan didn't speak Arabic, but she didn't have to to know there had been a major problem on the bridge. Zahra had been arguing about something with the captain. Sloan had the distinct impression that the pilot didn't want to go into the canal, but the captain hadn't listened to her. He blatantly ignored her, or that's what it seemed like to Sloan, but she could be wrong.

The interpreter would know. He had been translating from Arabic to Norwegian. He'd even seemed agitated, but he'd left the ship almost immediately after it got stuck. Zahra tried to leave as well but they wouldn't let her. The captain had said something about paperwork and being interviewed as part of the investigation.

And then there was that shudder, the feeling like the ship was slipping sideways. It had been odd. Eddie said he had noticed it, too. The pilot certainly had noticed it. Sloan had seen her through the window. She'd looked at the instruments and then asked questions in rapid-fire Arabic. The captain ignored the translator, and then a few minutes later, it was all over. They were drifting sideways with no way to stop the ship from getting wedged across the canal.

Now the world was angry and looking for someone to blame. As the first female Suez Canal pilot, Zahra Nabil was being held responsible, at least in the Middle East. She really needed to speak with Ms. Nabil. There was so much more to all this. and now with Eddie's death, Sloan wasn't sure what was going on, but she sure as hell wasn't sitting on the sidelines.

When she arrived at the crew mess, she was relieved to see it was fairly busy. It was almost lunch time, so people were filing in.

Sloan grabbed a tray and made a few selections and then looked for a table. She wanted to be close enough to hear what was being said during Axe's interviews, but when she located him, she realized he'd chosen a table in the back corner, and there was no way for her to get close enough without being obvious.

She headed to the table where the other reporters on board were sitting. Two of the three sitting there wrote for local Egyptian papers and the other wrote for a newspaper in Saudi Arabia. None of them were overly friendly with Sloan. She really missed Eddie at that moment. Glancing around the room, she saw the pilot sitting by herself. That hadn't happened before, and Sloan immediately looked around for the two men that always seemed to be near her. One was being interviewed by Axe and the other was nowhere in sight. Sloan hustled over to the table and sat down next to the pilot.

"Is this seat taken?" she asked brightly.

Ms. Nabil opened her mouth and then just shook her head.

"Great. I'm famished. What about you?" How much English did the woman speak? She had seemed proficient when she was on the navigation bridge, but it was hard to know for sure.

The pilot just gave her a small smile.

Sloan tried again. "I'm Sloan Bishop. We didn't get to formally meet up on the bridge." She offered her hand.

"Zahra Nabil," the woman said as she hesitated and then accepted Sloan's handshake.

"Zahra, may I call you Zahra?" Sloan asked. At the other woman's nod, Sloan continued. "I want to tell you how impressed I am that you're a canal pilot. That's totally amazing."

Zahra smiled a bit bigger this time and nodded her head. "Thank you. I am very pleased, too."

Glancing around, Sloan tried to keep the conversation going. "Have you piloted a lot of ships?" Sloan knew the answer already but it was important to break the ice.

"No. This was one of my first." The woman looked down at the food on her plate. "I may not have a career after this. I know they blame me."

"It wasn't your fault. I was there. The captain didn't listen to you." She had no idea what really had been said because the rest of the conversation was in Arabic and Norwegian, but Sloan was willing to take the gamble.

"Yes. Yes. He refused to listen." She shook her head. "But it will not matter. The news blames me. They say it is my fault. I did nothing wrong, but I fear I alone will bear the punishment."

"It doesn't have to be. Tell me what really happened. I am a reporter. I will tell the world what happened"

Zahra frowned. "But you are a woman as well. They will not listen to you."

"My last big story broke in *The New York Times*. They'll listen." Sloan said it with a firmness she didn't feel. Who knew if the *Times* would publish the story? But she would give it her all.

"They have forbidden me from speaking to…anyone."

Sloan frowned. "Who? Who told you not to talk?"

Zahra's eyes filled with tears. "They won't even let me have my phone. I want to speak to my family, my mother, but they refuse. They said I can't speak to anyone until the investigation is over, but they won't tell me how long it will take."

Sloan's heart broke for the woman. Clearly, she was distressed, and not being allowed to speak to her family was just ridiculous. "Is it the captain? Is he the one saying you can't speak to anyone?"

She shook her head. "No. It is that man, the head of

security. MacGregor. He took my phone. He has men guard me all the time. He says it's for my protection, but it is not. It is so I do not talk."

"Zahra, this is your chance. Tell me what really happened on the bridge, and I will do everything in my power to get your story out. At least you will have had your say. Then they'll have to let you speak to your family because the story will already be out. As it is now, no one will know your side."

Zahra bit her lip and looked around the room. Axe was still questioning one of her normal escorts. The other man was not in the mess hall. She leaned in and whispered, "Okay. I will tell you."

Sloan took out her phone and turned on the app she used to record interviews. Then she put her napkin over the phone. She didn't want to make it obvious what was happening.

"Tell me what happened from the moment you got on board the ship."

Zahra swallowed. "Myself and my interpreter both came on board the ship. We were taken directly to the navigation bridge. The captain introduced himself. We spoke briefly about the ship, the size, the cargo, that type of information. I filled out the forms I had with me, and then the captain started to move the ship. I asked him to stop."

"Why? Wasn't it your job to guide the ship through to the Mediterranean?"

"Yes, but it was very windy, and many other ships had decided it was not a good time to traverse the canal. I asked him at first if he would consider waiting a day. The weather for the next day was better. The winds would diminish. He said he was on a schedule and needed to keep moving."

She licked her lips. "I was nervous. I did not want to insult the captain or make him angry, but it was a poor decision. I told him with the wind, it would be hard to control the ship and keep it where it needed to be to guarantee a safe passage. This ship is so large, there is not as much room for it to maneuver. He told me it was my job to tell him where to be in the canal to ensure the ship made it safely through."

Zahra put her hand on Sloan's arm. "It was my job, yes, but as I told him, the conditions were not good for going. It was also my job to tell him not to go, but he refused to listen. He proceeded on his course. I called my boss, but it was too late. We were already past the entrance."

"What did you do then?"

"My job. I told him because of the size of the ship, he needed to keep it straight and stick to the middle of the canal. Instead, he went in a…" She frowned and then moved her hand back and forth.

"A zigzag?"

She nodded. "Yes, that is it. A zigzag pattern. He was too close to one side and then too close to the other. I kept trying to get him back in the middle, but he ignored everything I said. Even Khalid, my interpreter, tried to explain that the captain needed to listen to me, but the captain refused. He zigzagged on purpose." The frown on her forehead deepened. "Why would he do that? It was obvious he was having a hard time controlling the ship with the wind, and then all the zigzagging made it worse."

"Then what happened?" Sloan glanced around the room again. The security guy talking to Axe was starting to rise from his chair.

"There was a…a weird movement of some kind, and we got stuck."

"Do you know what the shudder was from?" Sloan asked quickly.

"No. It felt as if the ship was… I thought…" She squeezed Sloan's arm again. "I thought the ship was being pushed sideways, as if there was a tugboat maneuvering it."

A small jolt of electricity shot through Sloan. She had thought the same thing, but now Zahra was confirming it. "You think something pushed the ship sideways and wedged it across the Suez on purpose?"

The pilot nodded her head. "The captain, his actions and the shudder, there could be no other explanation. He blocked the canal on purpose."

"What are you doing?" a harsh male voice demanded.

Sloan whipped around. The security guy leaned on the table, shoving his face close to hers. She smiled. "I was chatting with Zahra about Egypt. She was telling me what I should see and do while I'm here." Sloan glanced over at the other woman, and Zahra nodded vigorously. Sloan turned back to face the angry man. "It's just nice to have another woman to chat with on board. Do you know when they're going to let us off the ship?"

The man's eyes narrowed. "I have no idea." He looked at Zahra. "Lunch is over." She immediately stood up and moved out from behind the table.

"It was nice chatting with you," Sloan called, but Zahra was moving out of the room almost at a run.

Sloan waited a beat and then collected everything onto her tray. She grabbed the napkin with the cell phone underneath and placed it on the corner of the tray. Then she took the tray to the garbage cans, where she set it on top and started sorting the garbage into the correct containers. She had her back to the room, blocking anyone's view, so she took the opportunity to grab her cell phone and shove it in the front pocket of her jeans. She also grabbed her knife and wrapped it in a napkin. She stuck it in her other pocket. Then she threw away the last bit of her lunch. She turned and started out of the room.

The second security guy was now leaning on the wall by the door. He watched her approach. She held her breath.

Was he going to grab her? When she moved by him, he did nothing more than give her a hard stare. As soon as she was in the hallway, she fought the urge to run. Nevertheless, she walked quickly all the way back to her room. She didn't let out the breath she'd been holding until she was inside with the door locked.

CHAPTER SIX

"What the fuck is going on? Why is there a dead American on board? It's all over the fucking news!" Omar Balik yelled into the phone. He was desperate for his deal to go through. To beat Tristan St. Claire at his own game. He'd hired help to make his dream happen. Now it was becoming a nightmare.

"Mr. Balik, we ran into some slight difficulties, and the situation was dealt with appropriately. You need to trust us to do the job you hired us to do. We did discuss that there could be a possibility of complications, and if I remember correctly, you said to do whatever it took to solve the problem."

"Yes, but I never thought that meant killing someone." Omar wiped the sweat off his forehead. He needed to calm down.

"Didn't you?" asked the calm voice on the other end. "I think you did. You want us to handle things, and we are. Getting cold feet now won't help you. What's done is done. The glitch has been dealt with, and we are back on track. The question is are you on track?"

"Wha…what? Yes. Everything is fine on my end." Omar swallowed. That wasn't quite true, and he was afraid the man on the other end of the phone knew it. He seemed to know everything.

Omar bit the inside of his cheek. He deeply regretted calling the Silverstone Group and asking for help. This man scared the hell out of Omar. He knew too much about Omar and his family and he'd made clear that once Omar engaged their services there was no going back. Then with his soft voice and accent, he was even more menacing. The man had promised him they could solve his problem—whoever "they" were.

His best friend Ivan had given Omar the number of the Silverstone Group. Ivan said they were miracle workers. He'd told Omar that they could put St. Claire in his place without breaking a sweat.

For the amount Omar was paying them they had better come through. He'd have to find a way to hide that expense in the company somehow. Ivan had guaranteed it would be worth it. Now, Omar wasn't so sure.

"Is anyone suspicious? Is it going to be another problem?" He sincerely hoped not. If there were more problems and his father found out what he'd done, well it didn't bear thinking about.

The truth was Omar was afraid of his father. But who was he more terrified of dealing with? His father, who might skin him alive for fucking up the German deal, or this man, who might kill him for getting cold feet?

"As I said, Mr. Balik, it's been handled. Now I must get back. Good luck with your deal. I understand you're going to need it." The line went dead.

Omar stared at the burner phone then dropped it onto the table. He was so paranoid that his father was going to find out about the deal going south that he'd taken to making phone calls at random bars and restaurants all over Cologne. He needed to stay away from prying eyes and ears.

His father. The man had become a constant thorn in Omar's side. He never gave Omar any credit. He would scream and rage at Omar if he found out that the Germans had decided to go with St. Claire, at the last minute. Omar would never be allowed to live it down. He needed his father gone.

Omar froze. An idea blossomed in his head. Was it possible? If the Silverstone man was successful which it appeared he was, and if Omar could get the Germans back on board, a big ask to be sure. But if those two things happened then maybe, just maybe Omar would be in a position to take his father out of the equation.

His regular cell phone pinged, and he glanced at the screen. Another email from the Germans. He'd had to sweeten the pot more than he'd anticipated to get them back to the table. He skimmed the email. Yes! The deal was back on. They'd finally agreed to the new terms.

Breathing came easier, as if a great weight was lifted from his chest. Things would work out after all. The deal wasn't quite as good as before, but it was still a strong deal. His father still would make hundreds of millions of dollars and, quite possibly, Omar could get rid of his father permanently.

He stood up and dropped some bills on the table to cover the cost of his drink. He needed to get his people working on finalizing the revised deal right away. He needed it signed, sealed, and delivered before the *Sea Jewel* was free. He wanted everything to be locked in place by the time the world righted itself. Then, and only then, would he be able to start putting his new plan in place.

CHAPTER SEVEN

Axe sighed to himself as he looked across the table at the last crew member he had to interview. Billy Seaver. The kid looked like he was still in high school but spent all his time in the gym. The baby face with the blond hair and eyes that were just slightly too close together made it hard to take him seriously or see him as any kind of a threat, no matter how hard Axe tried.

Oh, Seaver did his best to look tough with his arms folded across his chest and what Axe could only assume was supposed to be some sort of intimidating expression on his face. But it just made the kid look constipated.

Talking to Seaver was a colossal waste of time. Actually, the whole interview setup had been a joke. Apparently, MacGregor thought Axe was an idiot. He'd done his best to keep his temper in check, but he had hit his limit.

"So, in your *own* words, tell me again exactly what happened."

Seaver shifted in his chair. "I was out on deck, checking some of the tie-down lines and locks on the containers when

I heard MacGregor yell. I went to see what was going on and the guy was over the side in the water. He was dead."

"How about some details?" Axe wanted to smash the kid in the nose. It was the same story, word for word, he'd heard from the five other guys he'd spoken to before Seaver. He was usually a good-natured guy, but this asshole was making him see red.

"What'd ya want me to tell ya? That's what happened."

"Where were you on deck?"

"Checkin' the locks. I already told ya."

Axe ground his teeth. "Where were you checking the locks on the deck? Bow or stern? Port or starboard?

Seaver blinked, and his mouth fell open a bit. "Um, I was…checking the locks," he repeated, but the confidence had gone out of his voice. He shifted in the chair and looked at the floor.

Now we're getting somewhere. Axe calmed down and altered his tone so it was less adversarial. He threw the kid an easy question. "Why do you check the locks? Once the containers are loaded and locked into place, do the locks usually come undone?"

"Nah, but ya gotta check. The first layer is locked to the deck and all the layers after that are locked to the container below it. Sometimes, if the weather gets bad, we lose some over the side, but that's why we check the locks. Make sure nothing gets loose."

"So, were you checking locks towards the front of the ship? Maybe on the starboard side, meaning the right side? Does that sound correct?"

Seaver blinked again. "Um, yeah, that's right. I remember now. I was toward the front right, checking the locks."

Axe nodded. "Okay, so what time were you there? Could it have been a little bit after two-thirty?"

Seaver's response was faster this time. "Yeah, about then."

"And you heard MacGregor yell about a man over the side, so you came to help?"

"Yeah. He yelled, and I came to see what the problem was. I didn't know it was a guy over the side 'til everyone else was looking over the side, so I looked, too."

Those were probably the only true words Seaver had uttered. Axe stared at Seaver for a minute. Was it worth confronting him? MacGregor had been at the back of the ship on the left side, the port side. If Seaver had been where he said he was, then there was no way in hell he could've heard MacGregor yell.

"Okay, Seaver. You're good. Thanks for answering my questions. The FBI will pick it up when they arrive."

Seaver stared at him with his mouth open again. He cursed as he shot out of the chair and then marched away. Axe surreptitiously shut off the recording on his phone. He had no doubts MacGregor would try and coach the kid more before the FBI had him answer any questions. Axe wanted to make sure the Feds knew the real score.

MacGregor had staged all the witnesses. There wasn't a doubt in Axe's mind.

They all said the same thing. But the big question was why? Why have all these men lie to him about what happened? There was so much more to this, and he wanted to follow the trail, but it wasn't his job.

Axe gathered his notes, such as they were, and left the room. He wondered if Sloan was back in her stateroom. He'd almost stood up for her when the security guy had gotten into her face here in the mess hall, but he'd thought better of it. Sloan knew what she was doing. She could handle herself. She didn't need him jumping in, and it wasn't going to help him any, so it was best not to interfere.

He made his way to his cabin and, once inside, sat down on the bed and created a report on his laptop. One version for his boss and another for the FBI. His boss just wanted to make sure he was doing what he should be. The FBI would want to know if he'd found anything interesting.

But what was interesting was what he hadn't found. Proof that Eddie took a header off the side of the ship.

He needed to find Patel again and see where exactly O'Mara was supposed to have gone over the side. Axe stood up and left his cabin once more. After a couple of wrong turns, he found his way topside. He stood in a patch of shade and watched as the crew moved around the deck, performing their duties.

It soon became apparent there were two different groups when it came to the crew. One group that seemed to be doing all the work. They looked like sailors, tanned, weathered faces and bulging muscles from working hard.

The second group were men that were all standing around in various locations, looking relaxed and like they belonged there but weren't actually doing any work. They were just making a show of it. What they were really doing was watching. They were keeping an eye on everyone else. They also stood out because they looked less like the other crew members and more like, well…him. This group was some sort of trained security, possibly ex-soldiers or mercenaries. As Axe watched them, they watched him.

He was turning to go just as MacGregor stepped out onto the deck and walked toward him. Axe glanced at his watch. Less than five minutes had passed since he'd been on deck. *Not bad.* MacGregor's guys were a well-oiled machine by the look of things. They must have alerted MacGregor the moment Axe emerged from below. Good to know. Axe was going to have to get creative if he was going to do any poking around without MacGregor knowing. He smiled. He loved to be creative.

"What are you doing?" MacGregor demanded.

Axe just kept smiling. "Just looking around. Haven't spent much time on a container ship." Not exactly true. He was used to boarding ships like this to carry out searches for contraband. It could take hours, or even days, sometimes.

"This isn't some sort of tourist trip. Go back inside." MacGregor broke into a ghost of a smile. "We wouldn't want you to get hurt."

"I appreciate the concern"—Axe nodded—"but I do need to see where O'Mara went off the side."

MacGregor's eyes narrowed slightly, but he nodded grudgingly. "Ackerman," MacGregor barked. A tall dark-haired man came toward them. He was about Axe's height and weight. He had on mirrored sunglasses and a khaki T-shirt. His cargo pants were light brown like the desert. He practically screamed military.

MacGregor nodded toward Axe. "Take our guest to see where the journalist fell overboard."

Ackerman gave a stiff nod then turned and headed off across the deck. Axe followed in his wake. They crossed the ship to the port side and around toward the stern slightly. Ackerman came to a spot maybe twenty feet or so from the main door to the inside of the ship and stopped.

"Here," was all he said.

Axe approached the spot and looked around. There was nothing to differentiate this spot from any other. "Can you tell me how you came to determine this was the spot he went over?"

Ackerman just shrugged. "Where he was in the water. He must have gone off here."

Axe looked around. "Any security cameras?"

Ackerman shook his head, his mouth compressed into a hard line.

"So, you're guessing. There's nothing that really indicates this is where he went overboard."

"Like I said, he ended up in the water right there," Ackerman pointed at the water below. "So, he had to go off here."

Axe looked around, but with no security cameras, there was nothing to say whether Ackerman was telling the truth. If he'd gone off the other side, there were fifty ships that might have seen him, but being on this side, there was nothing but empty canal and desert. Wasn't that convenient? Axe's intuition was screaming at him. This was a setup. O'Mara was a reporter. Maybe he found out something he shouldn't have.

The sound of the heavy equipment on the bank of the canal reached Axe. They'd been bringing in more diggers and dump trucks over the course of the morning. He couldn't see the site from where he was standing but it sounded like they were in full swing.

Axe took one more look around. He looked over the side once again and then nodded at Ackerman. Ackerman started back across the deck, but Axe didn't follow. Instead, he ducked inside the forecastle and made his way up to the bridge. He had to find a way to speak with Rohan Patel without MacGregor's guys being there.

It took him a few minutes, but he finally found his way to the bridge. He asked after Patel and was told he was in his office. Another couple of wrong turns later, he was standing in Patel's doorway.

"Chief Mate Patel," he said affably, "do you have a minute or two to chat? I have a couple of questions."

Patel looked up from his desk. An expression flitted quickly across the other man's features. It looked suspiciously like fear. "I, um…that is, yes, I can spare a few minutes." He got up from behind his desk. "Why don't we chat while I take you on a tour? I am sure you are anxious to see the container holds." Patel stepped past Axe and hurried down the hallway.

Axe followed the Chief Mate through the maze of hallways and down several flights of stairs until they finally arrived in the container holds. Like other cargo ships, this section resembled a big warehouse with several levels of containers stacked in rows. The mesh walkway was suspended from the ceiling and bounced as Axe moved. It had several levels so every container could be accessed. Sound echoed around and the area was loud. A rank odor of like stale water, diesel fuel dominated, along with other scents Axe couldn't place.

Patel turned to him. "Sorry about that. MacGregor and his men are everywhere. They don't like it down here as much, so we might be able to chat uninterrupted."

Axe nodded. "What is going on with MacGregor? He seems to have an abnormal amount of authority for a guy in charge of security."

Patel leaned against the side of a container and ran a hand over his face. "I am not sure what happened. Svensson is usually an excellent captain, but just before we left Mumbai, MacGregor and his men boarded. Svensson told me new security protocols were being put in place and that the ship was under a threat of some kind. We were taking extra men with us this trip as a precaution. I was to tell the crew that these new men were part of a new training program. It didn't make sense, but when I asked questions, Svensson became very angry and threatened my job. I had no choice but to go along."

"So, they boarded in Mumbai and have been with you ever since?"

Patel nodded. "They don't really do anything but stand around and stare at the real crew. At first, I thought that maybe there was a secret cargo on board and these men were security for it, but I've watched them, and they pay no real attention to the cargo at all. Then when we got stuck, things changed."

"How do you mean?" Unease filled Axe's gut. His instincts were bang on. There was trouble on board.

Patel crossed his arms in front of his chest. "First, we never should have gotten stuck. The poor pilot argued with Svensson in both English and through the interpreter, but Svensson wouldn't listen. It was too windy to take the ship through the canal. We should have waited a day." He sighed. "It just defies logic. Svensson would never have made a mistake like this. And to blame that poor woman, just grossly unfair. And so unlike him."

"So, the wind knocked the ship off course?"

Patel shook his head. "That's the most frustrating part. Svensson grounded her on purpose. I'm sure of it. And he had help from some of MacGregor's men."

Axe frowned. He heard a sound off to his left and saw a man approaching. Patel nodded to the man. The newcomer tipped his head and disappeared down a row of containers.

"Explain what you mean by he had help. How did he wedge the ship on purpose?" Now it was Axe's turn to cross his arms. This whole situation was making him uneasy. A captain blocking the Suez Canal on purpose amounted to a terrorist act. The ship groaned. Axe cocked an eyebrow.

Patel frowned. "They're trying to dig her out while Svensson uses the thrusters to help. It's bound to cause a bit of noise but to answer your question, Svensson kind of veered the ship back and forth a bit. He said it was the wind, but that was only partially true. It was rather windy, which was an issue, but he was helping the wind along by steering into it and then out of it again. Obviously, it was done slowly. Nothing quick on a ship this size but once he started those motions it made the ship slowly turn across the canal. And then…" Patel paused and ran a hand over his face. "And then I—I would swear someone pushed the ship sideways."

Axe blinked. "You lost me. What do you mean *pushed the ship*? Like with a tugboat?"

The Chief Mate shrugged. "Yes and no. Obviously there was no tugboat, but yes it was like that. This ship wouldn't have needed much of a push at that point. With Svensson's erratic steering and the wind, just the slightest push and the ship would turn sideways, which is what happened."

Axe studied the man. There was no doubt in his mind that the man was telling him what he thought was the truth. Now he understood the look of fear on Patel's face. If what he was saying were true, this was an incident of massive proportions.

"So, if it wasn't a tug or any other kind of boat, then what is it you think pushed it sideways?"

Patel pulled out his phone and touched the screen a few times. Then he gave it to Axe. "I noticed a smaller vessel leave the Mumbai port the same time as we did. There was nothing unusual about it. I'm not sure why I noticed it. Anyway, it stayed in the vicinity, again not unusual. I assumed it was trying to get to the Mediterranean as well.

"Then at about zero-two-hundred hours on the morning before we got stuck, I couldn't sleep so I was out on the deck and noticed a small launch come alongside the ship. I've gotten pretty adept at avoiding MacGregor and his men, so they didn't know I was there. I watched several of them get into the launch and then watched as the launch took them over to the other boat. It made me uncomfortable, so I stayed up and waited. I took that video at around four-hundred hours."

Axe hit play and waited. The screen filled with a boat some distance away. The boat appeared to be lowering something into the water. Axe looked more closely. The object swung out a little bit and caught the moonlight. Axe froze the frame and looked closely. "Are those thrusters of some sort?"

"Yes. I think they are portable versions of the thrusters that are on the bow and stern of ships. They pull water in and push it out to move the ship. People would normally use them when docking. They provide more mobility in tighter spaces. At least that's what they look like to me."

"And someone put them on a platform of some sort. It almost looks like an oversized piece of plywood."

"Yes but plywood wouldn't hold that much weight. I'm not sure what the platform is made of, but they needed something to mount all of the thrusters on. It looks like there were at least five of the devices."

Axe played the rest of the video, and then he played the whole thing again. "Do you mind if I send a copy to myself?" he asked as he furiously typed away on Patel's phone.

"You can't. The file is too big, but I can send you a link to where I have a copy stored." The Chief Mate took his phone back. A second later he said, "There. Sent."

Axe felt his phone buzz in his pocket. "So, you think they applied thrusters to the side of the ship to drive it sideways." Axe couldn't get his brain around it. The audacity of the plan was mind-blowing. "But this is a big-ass ship. Even with those thrusters, I'm not sure there would have been enough power to turn the ship."

"Agreed"—Patel nodded—"but factor in Svensson steering erratically and that he was going thirteen knots, well above the seven-point-six knot speed limit. The ship was already on an angle in the shallow part of the canal, and then it wouldn't have required all that much force. Since Svensson knew what was going on, he was working with the thrusters, not against them. And they got lucky with gale-force winds, which helped their cause."

"But they couldn't have known they would block the whole canal."

"They didn't have to. If their objective was to stop traffic, all they had to have was a ship jammed in the canal. It would hold traffic at least for a day or two. The Egyptians wouldn't let any other ships by until they deemed it safe, and they wouldn't do that until they had at least tried to move it first."

Axe ran a hand through his hair. "So, what you're saying is Svensson worked with MacGregor to block the canal on purpose."

"That's what I'm saying." Axe was trying to absorb what Patel had told him when the man said in a loud voice, "And if you rinse the lentils, I think you'll have better results."

Axe stared at Patel. What the fuck was he talking about? Lentils? Then he heard it, soft footfalls. MacGregor or one of his men. "Thanks for that. I've been trying to figure out a good lentil soup recipe for ages."

Patel gave him a slight nod. "No problem. Do you like to make your own bread? I have a great Naan recipe as well."

"What the fuck are you two doing down here?" snarled Ackerman. He came from the row to the right of Axe.

"Discussing recipes. Mr. Patel is into cooking, and I was getting some pointers." Axe shifted his weight so he was facing both men now.

Ackerman pointed at Patel. "You're needed topside."

Patel nodded and turned to Axe once more. "It was nice chatting with you. Don't hesitate to ask if you run into more problems with your lentils."

"Thanks, I'll do that." Axe smiled as Rohan Patel left the container hold. He turned to Ackerman. "I think I'll head up to my cabin."

Ackerman moved to stand directly in front of him, mere inches from Axe's face. "You do that. And stay there."

Axe didn't blink or move. He wanted to smash the guy in the face, but there was really no point. It wouldn't help the situation. The guy was just a complete asshole, and he wasn't the only one on board. Axe ground his teeth and then moved around Ackerman. He made his way quickly back to his cabin. Several of MacGregor's men were stationed along his route. Watching to make sure he didn't go anywhere else.

He entered his cabin and locked the door behind him. Axe stood in the middle of the room and ran through what Patel had told him. The hair on the back of his neck stood up. This wasn't just about murder anymore. This was terrorism, and it affected the entire world.

Axe started pacing in the small space. He had to find a way to communicate with his CO and others without tipping off MacGregor. Axe brought his laptop out and started to write an email but then thought the better of it. Patel had been so nervous about talking, he'd moved them to the farthest reaches of the ship. The Chief Mate didn't trust his own office.

Axe looked around the room. Chances were good at this point that his room was bugged as well. He stared at the screen. Had they hacked into his laptop?

He ran a hand through his hair. If they could jam a ship in the Suez Canal, they could hack his laptop. So far, there was nothing of any real interest on there. He wrote up a basic report for his boss and the FBI. He didn't go into too much detail so he should be good. But how was he going to communicate with his commanding officer now? How could he get the word out about what was happening without alerting MacGregor?

Axe started a fresh email.

Nick,

How's things in your neck of the woods? Am bored here.
Stuck on the Sea Jewel *in the middle of the Suez. Some*
guy died and I have to babysit until the Feds get here.
Uncle Bertrand was right. This is not the usual posting.
Had a great chat with the Chief Mate. He seems like an
okay guy. The captain is a bit uptight, but I guess if you
got your ship stuck in the Suez, you would be uptight
too. Anyway, don't let Uncle Bertrand gloat too much
about being right. I should have known postings in this
part of the world never go smoothly.
Axe

P.S. There's a Scottish guy here who is in charge of secu-
rity. Could be a good job when I leave the Coast Guard.
Still trying to keep my options open. You never know
your luck.

Axe read over the email. He wasn't sure if he had managed to get his point across, but it was worth a try. Bertrand had sent him to keep an eye on things. The man must have thought something was off and, hopefully, this would confirm it for him. Plus, the email was just crazy enough that Nick Taggert, the head of Team RECON, would check on things anyway. All Axe could do now was sit and wait. Too much investigating and there could be another "accident" on board with another dead American.

He put his laptop away and lay down on his bunk. It wasn't half bad. He'd definitely slept on worse. He thought about Eddie O'Mara. Axe was now convinced it was no accident. He must have found out something, and MacGregor threw him over the side. That's probably how he knew where Eddie went over because he'd done it.

Axe blew out a breath. How was he going to explain that to the Feds when they arrived? It wasn't like he could just come out and tell them if Patel was to be believed, and Axe had no reason to doubt him. Rohan Patel seemed very much like a standup guy doing his best in a bad situation.

He didn't want the FBI to lose the element of surprise because, at this point, it would be brutally hard to prove MacGregor or Svensson did anything wrong. They weren't even here to investigate the ship getting stuck. They were just supposed to look into O'Mara's death, but the two things were related, Axe was sure of it.

Svensson could blame the pilot and the wind. There's no hard evidence. Even Patel's pictures are dark and grainy. It would be difficult to show that to a jury and expect anyone to be able to tell what was going on. He really hoped Nick reached out to Bertrand in the next few hours. Bertrand had been smart enough to send Axe over to the *Sea Jewel*. That hadn't been an accident. Axe just had to hope Bertrand trusted him enough to believe his email and send help.

Axe sighed. Sloan was a problem. She was a distraction he didn't need but really fucking wanted. Her scared and vulnerable look from earlier had almost done him in. O'Mara had possibly died because he'd found something out. Sloan wouldn't stop digging until she found out whatever Eddie knew. That was just her nature, and in this case, it was likely to get her killed.

What the hell was he going to do to keep her safe? And how was he going to do it while keeping his distance from her? All great questions with no answers. It was only one night, he reminded himself. One night of being under the same roof with Sloan Bishop. He could handle it. What could possibly go wrong?

Knowing Sloan? Damn near everything.

CHAPTER EIGHT

Sloan leaned back against the wall as she sat on her bed. Her computer positioned on her lap, she stared blankly at the screen. She needed two sources for the story. Two sources to confirm what Zahra told her. It didn't matter that she was there and saw it. Only part of the conversation was held in English. She needed to interview either Svensson, who she doubted very much would speak to her, or the interpreter.

She rubbed her face. How was she going to track him down? He'd left almost immediately after they'd gotten stuck. A boat came along side and got him and took him to God knows where.

She looked around her tiny room with its bare walls. Her gaze landed on Eddie's fedora. Svensson had let her have it after she'd put up a fuss.

She'd tagged along when Svensson and MacGregor went to Eddie's cabin. They said they had to check it to make sure he hadn't left a suicide note. If she hadn't been there they probably would have left a fake one.

Suicide. No fucking way! The argument Eddie was

having with the mystery man must have gotten physical. It wouldn't have taken much to grab Eddie and throw him over the railing to the deck below. Then whoever it was must have tossed him overboard to cover it up, like he was some kind of garbage.

Anyway, she'd asked Svensson if she could have the fedora since she and Eddie were good friends. MacGregor said 'no' it had to go to Eddie's family but she'd turned on the tears and Svensson gave it to her much to MacGregor's disgust if the expression on his face was anything to go by.

Eddie was dead. It still hadn't really sunk in. She'd written an article and sent it to her editor, but he had to hold it until Eddie's family had been notified. She'd stupidly thought if she wrote the article, it would put some distance between herself and what happened. It hadn't helped at all.

Tears filled her eyes. As much as Eddie was a pain in the ass in so many ways, he was a good person. Someone she really admired and looked up to. He was driven like no one she'd ever known, except maybe her father. Eddie had always wanted to be on top and would do anything to get there. He had a nose for a story and the killer instinct needed to do anything necessary to get it.

Sloan needed more killer instinct. Or, at least, she needed to know when to use it. Her mother always told her she would never be the reporter her father was if she didn't start toughening up and going in for the kill when she could. She swept the annoying tears from her cheeks. The problem was, when she'd gone in for the kill, it had cost her the best relationship of her life.

Her story had come out about a Coast Guard screwup that had almost cost a life. It was a training exercise that went wrong. One of the trainees thought they knew what they were doing and went rogue. He jumped into the water to "save" a fellow Coastie and ended up almost drowning them both.

It was a damned good story, and she was proud of it. Axe hadn't been her source, but she wasn't about to kill the story because people thought he was. He had no right to be mad at her because his fellow Coasties were assholes. That wasn't her fault.

She sighed. Either way, it was time to get off her ass and get her work done. The interview with Zahra was really good, and it was the proof that Sloan needed that this whole thing wasn't an accident. Talking to the interpreter would add credence to Zahra's story. She needed to get his name from Zahra. She knew his first name was Mohammed but there were fifty million Mohammeds in Egypt. She needed a family name to get started at least. Maybe Zahra had contact information for him. That would be the best-case scenario.

It just didn't make sense to her, though. Blocking the canal meant that no shipping was getting through. So, if no shipping was getting through, then there were people all over the world not getting the products that they needed. So, who gained from that?

She heard a sound in the room next door. Axe was back. She didn't want to admit, even to herself, the relief she felt when she'd seen Axe standing in the hallway. It was like someone had removed a thousand pounds from each of her shoulders. Now there was someone on board who would be in her corner. Well, maybe not in her corner, but at least he wasn't an enemy, or so she hoped.

On the other hand, it was also a form of torture to have him so close and not be able to spend time with him. She needed to bounce ideas off him. Talking with him had always helped her focus in on the most important parts of the story. He made her laugh too. He always made sure she took some time out to enjoy things like hiking or going for a bike ride.

And the sex, well it was good. Better than good. Her body ached to be with him.

Sloan tucked an escaped tendril of hair behind her ear. She needed to speak with Axe, and there was no time like the present. He needed to know what Zahra had told her and what she knew about Eddie's death. Then he could tell the FBI, and at least somebody would look into it. She got up off her bed, straightened her white shirt, and glanced at herself in the mirror. She wasn't looking great but there was no hope of fixing that. She redid her messy bun and added a bit of lip gloss. Then she opened her door.

Quietly, she stepped into the hallway. She locked her tiny cabin then moved directly toward Axe's quarters. She lifted her hand to knock, but hesitated and dropped her hand again.

She didn't like the way he had spoken to her earlier. Maybe he'd been so cold to her so MacGregor wouldn't be suspicious they were close. But they weren't close. Not anymore. And did Axe really care what MacGregor thought? The whole scene had stung, and heat crept up Sloan's cheeks at the memory. But if she didn't speak to Axe now, then how was he going to know what was really going on aboard the ship?

She raised her hand again and knocked loudly. There were some shuffling sounds from inside and then the door opened.

Axe filled the doorway and glared at her. "What do you want, Sloan?"

She swallowed. "Axe, we need to talk."

He ran a hand through his hair. "Now is not the time."

"I really need to talk to you about everything that's going on without MacGregor and his goons around here. We need to talk about Eddie."

Axe shook his head. "Sloan, I don't want to be involved

in any of your stories. Once was enough." He glared at her, and she winced. The pain morphed to frustration. She didn't deserve his doubts and mistrust. Understood them, yes. But protecting her actual source in the Coast Guard came with that price.

She huffed out a breath "This is different. Eddie is dead and I—"

Axe quickly put a finger up to her lips. She abruptly stopped talking and concentrated on the feel of his flesh against her mouth. *Stop it, Sloan. That bridge has burned.*

He glanced around and then pushed her back into the hallway. He closed the door and locked it after him.

"What?" she asked with a frown.

He turned and moved toward her so her back was to the wall and his face was inches from hers. Her heartbeat ticked up as it always did when he was this close. She licked her lips.

Axe spoke in a quiet voice. "If you're going to insist that we talk, we have to do it somewhere people won't listen in."

Alarmed, Sloan cocked her head. "You think your room is bugged?" she said just above a whisper.

Axe nodded. "I think there's a good chance."

Having him this close was making it hard to focus on anything other than him. She took a deep breath. Mistake. His scent; citrus and something wholly Axe, hit her and made her hot core tingle.

She cleared her throat. "So, you know there's something going on here then. Something not on the up and up."

He nodded. "Yeah, and talking about it in this hallway isn't helpful. Follow me." Axe grabbed her hand and took her on a long, winding path through the ship, down different hallways that seemed to turn back on themselves.

"Where are you taking me?" she asked as they turned yet another corner and started down a narrow corridor.

Axe turned and said over his shoulder, "Somewhere

where we can talk uninterrupted and the walls don't have ears."

"How do you know that they're listening to your conversations? Did you find a bug in your room?"

Axe held open the stairwell door for her. "No, but I haven't really had a chance to look. Rohan Patel, the Chief Mate, made me think it's quite possible that all the rooms in this place are bugged. He brought me down here earlier so we could talk."

They came out of the stairwell into a hallway. It was darker since there were no windows, and the overhead lights were about twenty feet up. The floors were made out of steel shaped like honeycomb The creaking and groaning the ship was doing with all the work being done to move her was significantly louder now. The fresh air was replaced by a stale smell mixed with diesel and cleaning products.

"Where are we?"

"We're heading to the engine room. Even though the engines themselves aren't on, it's pretty noisy because of the generators, and chances are good we can at least chat down there without too much being overheard."

They made it to the end of the hallway and down another set of stairs. Then they came to a door with an *Authorized Personnel Only* sign, and Axe pushed it open. He hustled Sloan through it and then turned around and closed it behind him.

Sloan blinked. All of the equipment was a shade of bright green that was almost painful to look at. The floor was solid in here and painted red. There were hoses and ducts sticking out in all kinds of directions. There were gauges and other types of equipment on the walls with various levers and knobs covering almost every surface. It was noisy, even with just the generators on. Sloan couldn't imagine what it was like when the engines were actually running.

Two men looked up from what they were doing. It appeared they were working on some sort of pipe. Sloan really had no idea. She didn't know anything about engines, and mechanical equipment was not her friend. It seemed to sense that she was in a hurry or needed something done quickly, and it immediately stopped functioning.

One of the men came toward them. He leaned in and said something to Axe. Axe nodded and said something back, and the man bobbed his head in return. He walked back over to the other guy, exchanged a few words with him, and then they went back to what they were doing.

Axe grabbed Sloan's hand and pulled her past the two men, deeper into the room. He stopped when they reached the far wall. There was equipment all around them with pipes and hoses and dials. It smelled like diesel and hot machinery. Her stomach rolled.

Axe stood in front of her, his lips compressed into a thin line and his arms crossed over his chest. "Now, what is it you need to tell me?"

Sloan swallowed. "I spoke with Zahra, the pilot that came on board to get the ship through the canal. She says that Captain Svensson purposely steered the ship erratically. She says he steered it in a zigzag pattern of some sort, which was bound to get the ship stuck since the *Sea Jewel* is so large. The ship should only have been in the middle of the canal, not going back and forth, side to side.

"Zahra also said that she warned the captain it was too windy to take the ship through the canal in the first place. Waiting until the next day was preferable. She told him the wind would make the ship more difficult to control and there was a greater chance of getting stuck. She says he ignored her and just kept going."

"So, the Egyptian pilot is saying that the captain deliberately ran the ship aground. Am I getting that right?"

Sloan nodded. "Yes. She says she tried to stop him, but he just wouldn't listen to her."

Axe narrowed his eyes. "Is there anyone who can corroborate her story?"

"Well, I can, to a point. I was there on the bridge for the start of the discussion that was held in English, but when it got more heated, she switched to Arabic and the interpreter translated it into Norwegian for Svensson. Obviously, I don't speak Norwegian or Arabic so I can't say what was said during the entire conversation, plus I was kicked out of the room before they'd finished. But I have no doubt the argument was heated. They were clearly fighting."

Axe frowned. "Patel said much the same thing. He thinks Svensson grounded the ship on purpose as well, and he thinks MacGregor and his men helped the captain do it."

"Helped how?"

Axe gave her a look that she could only describe as suspicious.

"What?" she demanded. She hated that her voice sounded defensive even to her own ears.

He impaled her with his gaze. "Are you going to use this in your story? I won't tell you anything if you're going to print it."

Sloan bit the inside of her cheek, trying to maintain her temper. She had made one error, and it wasn't even really a mistake. Or at least it wasn't her fault. "Look, I want this story, absolutely, but I'm not gonna run out and say anything just yet. Remember, I need two sources to confirm everything before I can put the story out. Currently, I don't have that. Plus, there is more going on here. If I'm going to write this story, I want the whole thing, not just part of it."

Axe leaned forward. "What else is going on? What haven't you told me?"

"Hm. This is a case of 'you scratch my back and I'll

scratch yours.' I'm not telling you anything else until you tell me what else you know." She wasn't giving in that easily.

Axe took a step toward her, pulse in his jaw jumping. The heat from his body reached hers. He was pissed off, but why should she give up the best story of her life to help him? They were no longer together. He had made that abundantly clear. She had to think about herself and her career.

"Sloan, there's more to this situation. It's vital that all this information does not get out just yet. We don't want MacGregor and Svensson and anyone else who's involved to be tipped off. The FBI is supposed to arrive tomorrow. They are only supposed to investigate what happened to O'Mara, but if we tell them everything, there's a chance they can push the boundaries a bit and find out what's really going on. So you can either tell *me* now, or you can tell *them* tomorrow. It's up to you."

Sloan clenched her fingers into fists. Axe was the most frustrating man she'd ever met. She wanted the story, but at this point, she wanted to know what happened to Eddie even more. "I'll make you a deal. You tell me what you know, and I'll tell you what I know. I promise not to write anything until I get the go-ahead from you."

It was a big fucking deal that she just gave him the authority to let her know when she could write the article. A huge fucking deal. But Eddie was worth it, and there was no way she was going to find out the whole story unless she had access to more information. She was smart enough to know that. Axe had access and other resources she could only dream of. She was damn sure not gonna let this opportunity get away from her. Eddie deserved justice, and he deserved to have the truth told. She would be the one to do it, and if it took her a little longer, she'd have to live with it.

"So, what do you say?" She stuck out her hand. "Do we have a deal or not?"

Axe looked down at her hand and then took another step forward until they were almost touching. He placed a hand on the wall behind her next to her head. His scent blotted out the other smells in the room. She had a hard time concentrating when he was this close. The urge to kiss him was overwhelming, and when he leaned down, she thought he was going to capture her mouth. Maybe prayed for it…a little.

"No deal," he said, his lips mere inches from hers. "I told you before I am done sharing anything with you. You screwed me before, and you'll do it again. Anything to get the story. Well, it won't be me you screw this time. Save your information, but you'd better be ready to share it with the FBI tomorrow. They don't take too kindly to people who obstruct their investigation." He turned and started walking away.

Sloan's breath caught in her chest. He'd been cold. Colder than she ever imagined him being. Icicles hung off his words. If he wasn't going to help her, then she was alone on the ship. She didn't trust the FBI to get to the bottom of things. No matter what, they could only operate in a country if they were invited to be there. If the Egyptians decided that Zahra was to blame for everything and Eddie was an accident, then the FBI would be sent home. She couldn't let that happen. She needed to know why they killed Eddie. She needed to know Eddie's killer would not go free.

"Axe, wait," she called after him.

He stopped and glanced back at her. She beckoned him. He came back slowly and refolded his arms across his chest. "What?"

Sloan reached into her back pocket and pulled out her phone. "Eddie didn't fall overboard. He was thrown and not into the water. He was thrown onto the deck from the flying bridge."

Axe's brow furrowed. "How do you know that? Are you sure?"

Sloan clicked through to the pictures and found the one she wanted. Then she turned the phone toward Axe. "Yeah, I'm sure."

Axe looked at the picture on her phone and then looked up at her. Sloan's heart started racing. The memory of being on the deck when Eddie fell was a hard one to swallow. She blinked rapidly, trying to keep the tears filling her eyes from coursing down her cheeks.

"I'm sorry. It's hard to lose a friend." Axe swallowed and looked back at the picture.

Sloan's stomach dropped. She'd forgotten all about Axe losing one of his best friends in a fire. He'd lost two, really, since the other wouldn't speak to him. She wanted to say something nice, but she couldn't think of anything that would make the situation any better. She wiped the tears from her cheeks.

"How did you come to have this picture?" Axe clicked the screen, and she heard the familiar whoosh of a text being sent. Then he handed the phone back to her. She noticed he hadn't asked permission, but at that moment, she didn't care.

All she wanted was to find Eddie's killer. No. That wasn't true. All she really wanted to do was climb into Axe's arms and stay there for a long while and have a good cry. She always felt safe in those arms, and safe was the last thing she was feeling these days.

She cleared her throat and wiped her eyes again. "I was on deck. It was so hot in the cabin I just wanted a breath of fresh air. The desert is cooler at night, so it was nice to get the breeze, even if it was warm. I was hidden halfway down the port side, leaning against a container, but I'd seen Eddie talking to someone.

"Then, they disappeared and I heard this god-awful

sound. A sound I'll never forget. Like a watermelon hitting pavement at high speed." She shuddered. "It's the type of sound that vibrates through your whole being. When I turned to see what had happened, I saw Eddie dead on the deck. Instinctively I hid around the corner out of sight, but I leaned back around and snapped the picture. I wouldn't want you to think I was a ghoul or anything. It wasn't like I wanted to take a picture of him, but it was just…instinct."

She took a deep breath. "It took me a few minutes to get myself together enough to peek back around the corner. When I did, I saw three men carrying Eddie's body away. He was definitely already dead.

"Then some minutes later, the alarm bell went off, and people came running. When I got myself together enough to follow the sound of people yelling, it was too late. The captain and several of the crew were all looking over the side. He said to me that Eddie had fallen into the water. But one of MacGregor's goons killed him and then threw him overboard to cover it up. I just know it."

A pained expression flashed across Axe's face, and then it was gone. She knew he hated senseless death. He'd seen a lot of it during his time with the Coast Guard. Human trafficking was one of the areas under their purview, and as a law enforcement officer, he was usually one of the first on any vessel. He'd told her that he'd seen some horrible things, but he never shared details. She liked to think it was because he didn't want her to have nightmares, but it could also have been because he didn't trust her completely. He was being so cold to her now, she was finding it hard to believe he ever cared about her.

"You saw someone throw Eddie onto the deck?"

"No. I heard Eddie hit the deck and turned to look. MacGregor and several of his goons were there seconds later.

I'm not sure which one of them threw Eddie over the railing to the deck below."

"Damn. We would've had them right away if you were a witness. As it is, it's going to take a while to build up enough evidence to do anything, and since we're in Egypt, God knows how that's all going to work. Honestly, though, that's up to the FBI. I'm just here to watch over his body until they show up. The rest of this is above my pay grade."

"You don't mean that." A knot cinched hard in the pit of her stomach. "You can't possibly mean you're not going to investigate?" Eddie needed justice.

Axe shrugged. "There's only so much I can do on my own, and it's not my job. I'm just here to watch over things until the FBI arrives."

"But you're not on your own. I'm here. I can help."

Axe glared at her. "These are dangerous people. By blocking the canal on purpose, they've proven that they're willing to go the extra mile. Eddie obviously knew some-thing, and now he's dead. Maybe he realized that the *Sea Jewel* was used to block the canal on purpose. Maybe that's all it took for them to kill him. Or maybe he knew something else, like who's behind all this. 'Cause God knows, MacGregor is not the mastermind, and neither is Svensson. Either way, you have to stop digging, or they'll kill you, too."

"You don't think they'd really risk another death on board, do you?" A shiver went down her spine.

"I think they'd risk whatever they had to. They didn't go into this thinking it was going to go easily. They knew there would be difficulties and risks. Killing Eddie shows you just how far these men are willing to go."

"Do you think Eddie knew something other than the ship was grounded on purpose to block the canal?"

Axe pinned her with his stare. "I don't know what Eddie knew, but whatever it was got him killed. I don't want to get killed, and I don't want you dead either. Until the FBI arrives, we're on our own, and that's not a good place to be."

Sloan heard him, but she was still stuck on another thought. "If Eddie knew something, beyond what we know, then it would have been in his room, wouldn't it?"

Axe shifted his weight, putting more space between them. "I guess. What do I know? I don't know anything about Eddie."

"I know Eddie." Tears filled her eyes again. She swallowed hard and blinked rapidly. "I knew Eddie, and if he had anything, he would have made notes about it. There was nothing in his room, though, I checked."

Axe froze. "What do you mean, you checked?" His voice was quiet and determined.

"Um, well, I played the hysterical female card and demanded to go with Svensson when he went to check for a suicide note. I think the original plan was for him to put one in Eddie's room, but he got spooked because I went along."

"You searched Eddie's room with Svensson there?"

"I didn't search it exactly, but I did take a good look around. His laptop was missing. I just assumed that MacGregor had that. There was nothing else to see."

"Did Eddie use some sort of recording device to do his interviews?"

"He used his phone. We all do now. It's just so much easier. I didn't see his phone either, come to think of it. Again, I assume MacGregor has it."

"Well, it seems like if Eddie found out anything, MacGregor has the proof, and it's already probably gone."

"Maybe." Sloan ran her hands over her face and leaned back against the bright green wall of gauges. "But Eddie wasn't stupid, and he knew MacGregor was up to something. He was the one who pointed out to me that half of the crew look like mercenaries. He was pretty sure they came from all over the world, but they've all had some sort of military training. If he really thought he had something big then he probably wouldn't keep it on his phone or his laptop."

"Where would he have kept it then?"

Sloan shook her head. "I'm not sure. Let me think about it. If I come up with something, I'll let you know."

Axe shifted his weight again so they were back to being mere inches apart. "Make sure you do. Sloan, I'm not joking. This is life and death here. Don't do anything stupid."

CHAPTER NINE

Axe ground his teeth as he moved through the ship toward the mess hall. He was hungry, tired, and generally pissed off. *Goddamn Sloan*. There was no way she was going to keep her nose out of this story, nor would she listen to reason.

He'd almost lost it in there and kissed her. Jesus. If only she didn't look so damn good. She had driven him crazy, just standing there. The fact that she was determined to find out what happened to her friend no matter how scared she was only made him want her more. But wanting her wasn't going to help either one of them, and it wasn't going to keep her out of danger. His only hope was that Eddie's death made enough of an impression to drive thoughts of doing anything crazy out of her head. God knew that his friend Andy's death had left its mark on him. He still had nightmares.

He shook his head as if trying to dislodge the memories. Thoughts of Andy always lead to memories of him, Andy, and Kyle. They'd been the three musketeers all the way through the academy and through their postings in the Coast

Guard. They'd finally ended up on the same ship. It was better than hitting the lotto.

Or it was until that one call and the fire. He couldn't save Andy. The fire had just moved too fast. He'd never seen anything like it. There had to be some sort of accelerant involved. Andy got caught way back in the main cabin, and there was no way to get through the flames to pull him out.

Kyle was just inside the doorway. Axe had reached in and pulled him out. That's how his arms became permanently disfigured but he'd been lucky and had no other injuries.

Kyle wasn't so lucky. He had second-degree burns over seventy percent of his body. Axe had been so grateful that he'd been able to save Kyle, but Kyle hadn't wanted to be saved. He hated his burns and all the therapy he had to go through. He resented the hell out of Axe for not being seriously injured. All these months later, Kyle still wouldn't speak to him.

Axe jerked the cuffs of his sleeves down. There was nothing he could do now for Andy or Kyle. All he could do was keep his head down and keep moving forward. He'd thought his time as a Coastie had been over and was seriously thinking of quitting before his time in Panama. Being with the Team RECON guys made being on a team feel right again. Kicking ass and taking names always made him feel good.

But those days were over, and he was back with his old crew. Sometimes he caught them staring at his burns. They had to be wondering how come he couldn't save Andy. Well, he wondered the same thing. There's no way the fire should have spread that fast. Axe swallowed hard. He fisted his hands and tried to regulate his breathing. Going over all this again was useless. He'd been through it a million times, and none of it made sense.

Axe rolled his shoulders and took the last corner before

entering the mess hall. He immediately clocked MacGregor and his goons in the far right corner. He grabbed a tray and went through the chow line.

He took a bit of everything and moved to a table on the left side of the room near the front. He set his tray down and moved a chair around to the end of the table so he was sitting with his back to the wall. There was still room to walk by, but Axe could see people coming in either direction. He wasn't going to leave himself open to MacGregor and his men coming up behind him.

He took a bite of his meatloaf. It wasn't half bad. He ate a fork full of mashed potatoes and wondered what the fuck he was supposed to do next. His orders were to watch over Eddie's body and gather some preliminary information on what happened for the FBI. He'd done that. The data said MacGregor and his goons were lying fucks that pretty much had the run of the ship. The captain was in league with them, and the Chief Mate was terrified of them.

Axe took a sip of coffee. Every instinct he possessed wanted to keep going and investigate fully but he was one guy and MacGregor was just as likely to kill Axe if he got in the way. Or was he?

Axe chewed slowly. If Eddie was killed because he knew something, it had to be more than the fact the ship had purposely blocked the Suez Canal. Both the Egyptian pilot and the interpreter knew that, and they were still alive. Or at least Zahra was. He had no idea where the interpreter was, but he mentally added the task of tracking him down to his list of things to do. If, of course, he was going to continue to investigate.

MacGregor didn't kill the pilot Zahra Nabil. She obviously knew Svensson was guilty so why not kill her? Was it because they needed a scapegoat? Maybe. That was one answer. Axe didn't think it was because they didn't want to kill a woman. Maybe they didn't want to kill an Egyptian woman and have the government send people to investigate.

Nope. That didn't work either because now FBI agents were on the way, and they weren't exactly known as lazy-ass investigators.

Axe swallowed the last bite of his food and followed it up with more coffee. He was missing something. Who was he kidding? He was missing almost every piece of the puzzle.

He stood up and put his tray in the dirty dishes pile and then left the mess hall. MacGregor and his goons were still in the back corner, but they looked like they were finished as well. They'd be on the move soon enough.

Axe made his way back to the deck and leaned against the railing. The lights of all the ships waiting to go through the canal were twinkling in the twilight. The number seemed to have doubled since this morning, and he knew by tomorrow morning, it would double again.

Noise from the banks reached him. The Egyptians were working around the clock to get the ship freed, but there was just no way. Even Axe knew enough about heavy equipment and sand to know that it was going to take a hell of a lot more than some diggers to get the *Sea Jewel* out. They were going to need tugboats, and lots of them, at the very least.

Axe turned from the rail and spotted Sloan moving along the narrow walkway ahead of him. Where the hell was she going? They were one deck down from the top, and there wasn't much else on the ship in the direction she was headed. Axe shrugged mentally and followed her. He'd warned her about wandering around on her own but, obviously, listening to him wasn't high on her list of things to do.

She came to an area of the walkway that jutted out from the deck above. It was an overlook of sorts that provided access to a lifeboat that could be brought up from below if there was a need to evacuate.

Axe hung back and stuck close to the wall. He didn't want Sloan to see him. She would get angry and out of sorts because he was following her, and then there'd be a fight about how she could look after herself. It was true most of the time, but sometimes, Sloan let her ambition get the best of her. Who was he kidding? She always let her ambition get the best of her.

Sloan leaned on the rail and looked out at the waiting ships. She seemed in no hurry to move. Maybe she was just getting some air. Axe stayed back and waited.

Ten minutes had passed, and she was still standing there. The sky was now dark, and the lights on board the ship had turned on. Sloan was bathed in a harsh bright light from above. The heavy equipment on the banks was still going, but it didn't look like they were making much progress.

Sloan paced back and forth on the little balcony. She was getting antsy. She always snapped her fingers and tapped her legs when she paced, like she had all this pent-up energy, and if she didn't do something to let it out, she might burst. Axe had always found it sexy as hell. He knew exactly how he'd like to help her get rid of her excess energy. He shifted his uniform pants to ease the binding issue he was having and tried to think of other things.

Another few minutes went by, and Sloan ran her fingers through her hair, a sure sign she was frustrated. Unease settled over Axe. Sloan was exposed. There was no roof above her. The area she was standing in was open to the containers on the level above. The area also jutted out from the rest of the ship. If someone wanted to get to her, she was a sitting duck. Axe didn't like her staying out here on her own, and he wasn't going to leave her, but it was time to pack it in. He made his way to the little balcony.

As he stepped into the area, a movement out of the corner of his vision alerted him, and he grabbed Sloan, pushing her against the wall and shielding her with his body. An oversize wrench smashed onto the deck with a loud clang, and Sloan let out a small scream.

Axe heard footsteps running and looked up, but the bright lights were directly overhead, and he was blinded. The stairs were too far and if he attempted to get up to the next level to find out who it was, they'd be long gone.

He looked down at Sloan, who was still pinned between him and the wall. "Are you alright?" He ran his gaze over her face, but she seemed uninjured. Just scared.

"Y-yes. I'm fine. What was that? Did somebody do that on purpose?" she asked, her large eyes filled with fear.

"Possibly, but it will be damn hard to prove. What are you doing out here anyway?" He wanted to distract her. There was no point in scaring the hell out of her. She was there already.

"I just needed some air. My cabin seemed to close in on me. I thought maybe being out here would help me sort some things out."

Axe tightened his hold on Sloan. "Did nothing I said earlier about being careful sink in? Sloan, you just can't wander around the ship. It's too dangerous."

Sloan pushed against his chest. "I am a reporter, and it's my job to investigate. Part of that is wandering around and asking questions. Sometimes I need to be outside. I'm not going to change that because you don't think I can take care of myself."

"Wandering around almost got you killed. If I hadn't been here, you would have been smacked in the head by that wrench, and you'd probably be dead right now."

Sloan paled. So much for not scaring her. Axe cursed under his breath. She pushed against his chest again, but he just couldn't bring himself to let her go. She fit perfectly against him. She always had. He missed her. And this, this had been a close one. He could have lost her permanently. A fucking nightmare was what it was. Someone was trying to kill Sloan, and Axe just wasn't fucking having it. No fucking way.

He swooped down and kissed her upturned lips. He hadn't planned on it. He just couldn't help himself. Sloan opened her mouth and deepened the kiss. She wrapped her arms around his neck and pulled him closer. He crushed her to the wall so her soft curves were pressed against the hard planes of his body.

He slid his hands down to cup her ass and rub her against him. He was hard as rock and desperate to be inside her. He kissed her fiercely, and she fisted her hands in his hair. She wanted him as much as he wanted her. He knew it, and it was driving him mad.

She lifted a leg over his hip and moved her pelvis to rub against him. He was losing control. Losing the ability to think. He needed to stop now before it was too late and they had sex on the walkway.

Axe broke away from the kiss. He dropped his arms and took a step back. His hard-on was painful against his zipper. He needed space if he was going to calm down again. *Stupid.* She was still a reporter. The one that made his life very difficult. Fucking her wasn't going to change that. No matter how good it would feel. "You need to be more careful, Sloan," he growled.

Sloan stopped straightening her clothing and glared at him. "If they're trying to kill me then they'll be trying to kill you too. We know the same information. So, you better watch your back, Axe."

Axe froze. That wasn't something he'd thought of until she mentioned it. They might take a run at him. Interesting. *Let 'em come.* He'd love a good fight right now as long as Sloan was safe.

He moved back to lean against the rail. The loss of Sloan's body heat was palpable to him, so he crossed his arms over his chest. It was too hard to be close to Sloan without touching her. Someone threatening her had put his protective instincts into overdrive, and all he could think about was that she was his and he would kill anyone who tried to hurt her. *Not helpful.*

He ground his teeth. "Somebody thinks you know something. Or at least, they believe that you're not going to give up until you do know something. Me, I'm less of a threat. I'm here for twenty-four hours until the FBI takes over the investigation. By that time, MacGregor and his boys will have all the evidence gone and all the 'witness' testimony sewn up. This will all be written off as an accident, both Eddie's death and the ship getting jammed in the canal."

"But what about Zahra? She knows what's going on, or at least she knows that the captain ignored her advice and brought the ship into the canal regardless of the weather conditions. Isn't the FBI going to ask her questions? Doesn't MacGregor consider her a threat?"

Axe hesitated. "She won't have to speak to the FBI. She had nothing to do with Eddie's death. They are only coming to investigate the loss of an American life. They have no authority to investigate how the ship got wedged in the canal.

"MacGregor could see her as a threat, but it's more likely he'll just keep selling it as the woman pilot made an error, causing the whole mess. That is if he's even asked about it. The local papers are saying the wind was a factor, and along with an inexperienced pilot, circumstances point to it just being an accident. Most of the international news is going with that as well. I even asked a couple of the other local reporters on board, and they are sticking to that story like glue. Zahra's career might take a hit, or she might be fired, but she should be left alone to live the rest of her life. Even if she complains, it's not likely people will listen."

Sloan nodded and let out a long sigh. "That's just depressing. I mean, it's better that she's alive, but still. It's not her fault what happened. Why should she have to suffer for it?"

Ax shook his head. "Life isn't fair." He knew that one cold. If life were fair, Andy would still be alive and Kyle wouldn't hate his guts. They would all still be best friends.

Sloan snorted. "Life isn't fair? That's all you got for me?"

Axe shrugged. He didn't have any answers. "Look, Sloan. There's not much I can do right now. I can get you back to your cabin and keep you safe overnight until the FBI get here and then it's up to them."

"Fine. I need to get off the ship anyway. I will find the interpreter and then write what really happened up on the bridge."

Axe's gut churned. Sloan was always going from the frying pan into the fire. The interpreter angle would be dangerous to pursue, but there was no point in arguing with her about it. Once she was off the ship, she was no longer his problem. Or, at least, that was what he was telling himself. Besides, if she was looking for the interpreter, then she wasn't investigating the real story; why the hell would someone wanted to block the canal in the first place? The answer to that might definitely be worth killing over.

CHAPTER TEN

Sloan followed Axe all the way back to their rooms. She was far more shaken by what happened than she cared to let on, although whether it was the wrench or the kiss that had her knees wobbly was up for debate. Having Axe's arms around her after he saved her life had been…heavenly. It truly was the only place she felt one-hundred percent safe. She'd needed his strength to keep her upright. Her legs hadn't seemed capable of holding her.

Then kissing him was divine. They'd always fit together perfectly, and the sex was to die for. It just wasn't fair that they couldn't work it out. She'd been upset when he'd broken off the kiss, but they'd have ended up having sex right there if he hadn't. A woman could only handle so much at a time, and Axel Cantor was like catnip and kryptonite all rolled into one.

Axe stood outside her door and waited for her to get her key. He spoke softly, "You need to stay in your room all night. Don't open your door to anyone but me. We don't know who is trying to kill you or why."

Sloan shot him a look. "Don't we? Not like MacGregor's

been discreet about his power aboard this ship. His goons are always walking around like they own the place."

Axe kept his voice low. "MacGregor may be behind trying to kill you, but we don't really know why, and we don't know that it was him up on that deck." Axe folded his arms across his chest and leaned against the wall. "But MacGregor isn't the only unknown factor on this ship. Svensson is involved in all of this as well. What we don't know is if he has his own people or if he's with MacGregor."

Sloan cursed silently. She'd forgotten about the captain. Axe was right. The captain was involved, and from what she'd seen, Svensson and MacGregor weren't the best of friends. There was tension between them. "Do you think the captain could have done this all on his own? Or…" She paused. "Do you think he's just another branch of this mess?"

Axe shrugged. "If I had to guess, I would say Svensson and MacGregor are working together, but they may not be friendly. So don't trust anyone who comes to your door. Don't open it for any reason unless I am there. Remember the room might be bugged, and chances are good they hacked your laptop by now."

Axe's voice for the entire conversation was just above a whisper. Sloan found herself leaning in to hear him. His closeness, the tantalizing scent of him was driving her crazy. She wanted to haul him into her room and spend the rest of the night screwing his brains out. A night of incredibly hot sex with Axel Cantor was just what she needed to put the world right. Too bad he was still angry with her for doing her job. He might have kissed her earlier, but she knew he hadn't forgiven her.

"Your cell phone works right?" he asked.

She nodded. She didn't trust herself to speak at the moment. If she opened her mouth she would invite him into her bed and that wouldn't be good for either of them.

"Good. Keep your phone beside you with my number on the screen. If anyone comes to your door, call me immediately. *Do not open the door*. Do not go anywhere on your own. If someone breaks in, scream as loud as you can. You see anything or hear anything out of the ordinary, hit my number, okay?"

Sloan bit her lip. "Do you really think they'll try again tonight?" A trickle of fear made its way down her back.

Axe hesitated. "It's unlikely, but there's no point in taking chances. I don't want…" his voice trailed off.

Axe's gaze locked with hers, causing her heart to thump against her ribs. She wanted so badly to wrap her arms around him and feel his body close to hers. She desperately wanted to continue what they'd started out on deck. She started to reach out to him but he straightened and moved away to stand in front of his own door. The moment was over. Whatever he felt, he was hiding it behind a blank look. He could always make himself unreadable to her whenever he wanted.

Sloan cleared her throat and willed the heat out of her cheeks as she unlocked her door. "Okay Axe," she croaked. "Thank you for saving my life."

Axe nodded. "Goodnight, Sloan."

"Goodnight, Axe." Sloan went into her room and closed the door. She leaned against it and breathed slowly, trying to get her equilibrium back. She wanted more from Axe. She never felt safer than she did when he was holding her. And now that someone was trying to kill her, that safety was all she craved.

She sat down at the little desk and stared at her laptop. What would she write? She could say that someone just tried to kill her, but she really had no proof. It could have been an accident, or at least that's what everyone would say. It was an accident that a tool fell. It's a big ship, and a lot of things can happen.

The thought that somebody had hacked into her laptop and read her emails set her blood on a low boil. This was her life. Her career. Where did they get off messing with her things? Sloan tried to dig up some righteous anger. She was a reporter, goddammit, and a good one. People mucking about in her space, in her stuff, trying to stop her from writing a story, that just wasn't going to fly.

But she just couldn't really muster the indignation she needed to write something passionate about what was happening on board the *Sea Jewel.* Fear sat in the pit of her stomach. Somebody had tried to kill her. In all the places she'd gone, all the times that she'd been in dangerous situations, none of the danger had been directed at her. No one had specifically wanted to *kill* her. She rubbed her face.

She was supposed to be a fearless and intrepid reporter. That's what everybody said. That's what her mother wanted. That's who her father was, and Sloan had always said she wanted to be like her father. Problem was, Eddie was dead already and someone had just tried to take her out. Her father would just keep going, pushing, pushing, pushing to get the story. She glanced down at her hands. A tremor went through them. She wasn't sure she could push like that.

She heard her mother's voice in her head. *"Your father would never hesitate. He just always went for the story. The story comes first. Sloan. If you want to get anywhere in life, you can't hesitate."*

It was easy to say if you were sitting at home reading and doing puzzles on the couch while drinking vodka. Sloan shook her head. There was no point going down that path. She knew where it led.

She opened her laptop and stared at the screen. She had no idea what to write. It seemed silly to write about the acci-

dent because that's all she could call it. She couldn't write
about what Zahra said because she only had Zahra's word
for it. Sloan was a witness to part of it, so she could put
something together, but she couldn't really say what she
wanted to. Plus, if they had hacked her laptop, then they
knew what she was going to say. And maybe they wouldn't
even let it out. Could they do that? Could they stop her
email from sending? Of course they could. Who was she
kidding? She slammed the laptop closed. There was no
point. She jumped from her chair, stalked to the bed and
flopped down.

She must have fallen asleep because she woke with a start.
Some sound had frightened her. She tried to figure out what
had woken her, but the sound didn't repeat. She sat up and
glanced at her watch. It was just after midnight. Great, now
she was going to be awake for the rest of the night.

She reached for her water bottle and noticed that there
was a note on the floor. That had to be what had woken her
up. The sound of the paper being slid under the door. Sloan
got up off the bed and went over and grabbed the paper from
the floor. The note read, *Meet me in container hold three at
two a.m.*

Just what kind of an idiot did they think she was? She
wouldn't fall for that shit. What, she was going to go stand
where they said so they could kill her since they missed
earlier? She looked at the note again. It was handwritten, and
it looked like a woman's writing. Could it be from Zahra, or
was it a set up?

Sloan went back over and sat on the bed. She studied the
note carefully. Well, it had to be someone who knew the
ship. The reporters from Egypt had never been on a ship
before and the guy from Saudi didn't really speak with her
but her guess was he wouldn't know where the container
holds were either. To be fair, she wouldn't have known if it

weren't for Axe taking her down to the engine room. They had gone all around the ship.

So far, MacGregor's men had been super careful. Would they handwrite a note? It seemed like it could be legitimate. But maybe that was the whole point, to make it seem genuine, and once they got her alone they'd kill her. Sloan leaned back against the wall. Well, she had two hours to decide if she wanted to go or if she wanted to stay.

Just shy of two hours later, Sloan shoved the knife she'd swiped from the mess into her waistband, and let herself out of her room as quietly as possible, locking the door after her. *Nothing ventured, nothing gained.* She was going to the meeting as much to silence her mother's voice in her head as to find out what the possible source had to say.

She moved swiftly down the hallway. She paused in front of the elevator door but decided to take the stairs. Quietly she accessed the stairwell and then started her descent. It didn't take long to reach the designated walkway in the bowels of the ship.

She had contemplated going through all the back hall-ways like Axe had done, but chances were she'd get lost. It was just better if she took the most direct route. She could only hope MacGregor's men weren't watching the security cameras. She knew there must be some aboard the ship. Hopefully, they weren't where she was going.

She scanned the walkway. It was narrow and poorly lit from the fluorescent bulbs two levels up. There was no one around. Sloan walked toward container hold three her foot-steps echoing quietly on the honeycombed flooring. The ship groaned and swayed. Sloan's belly rolled. The smell of diesel fuel and stale seawater wasn't helping.

Container hold three wasn't so much of a room as an area. She stood on the walkway and looked around. A faint sound came from in front of her. She inched a few feet farther along. The light was dim as some of the bulbs were out, casting long shadows. Sloan squinted. Someone was standing by the containers a bit farther down the walkway, but they were in the shadows and she couldn't make them out.

She walked slowly forward. The individual turned and faced her. Sloan squinted, but she still couldn't make out who it was until the person moved into the light. Zahra. Sloan hurried to where Zahra was standing. "Why didn't you sign your note? I thought it was MacGregor, and he was trying to kill me again."

Zahra's eyes got big. "MacGregor tried to kill you?"

"No. Well, sort of." Sloan sighed. She didn't want to frighten Zahra, but at the same time, she wanted to be honest. "I was out on one of the observation decks, and a wrench fell from above and almost hit me. If it had hit me on the head, I would have been dead. I can't prove that it was MacGregor."

Zahra reached over and put her hand on Sloan's arm. "These types of things happen fairly frequently on these big ships. It could have been an accident."

Sloan studied Zahra's face. Did she really believe it was an accident? Or was she trying to make herself feel better? Either way, it didn't really matter. "I'm sure you're right."

"So, what's going on? Why are we meeting like this?"

"I saw more articles today saying it's my fault that the *Sea Jewel* is stuck and blocking the canal. It's simply not true. I want the truth to be out there. MacGregor finally let me email my family today. They are embarrassed, and they think it's my fault. It's not fair."

"I get that. It must be very hard on them." She slowly leaned back against a rust-colored container. "If you tell me what really was said during your conversation with Svensson, and I can back it up with an interview with the interpreter, then I can print the truth."

"We don't need the interpreter. I can—"

"I didn't mean I needed him to interpret for me. What I need is his witness statement. You all spoke in multiple languages, so I need confirmation as to what was said. You can tell me, and I know the part that occurred in English, but I need the interpreter or Svensson to confirm what was said in Arabic and Norwegian."

Zahra shook her head. "You misunderstand me. I don't need the interpreter because I can prove Svensson got the ship stuck on purpose."

Sloan straightened. "How? What proof do you have?"

"The ship has logs. A computer logs every movement. Every direction or input that is given is logged to the ship by a software. The computer will show that Svensson manually made those turns. He manually…" Zahra made a back-and-forth motion with her hand.

"Zigzagged," Sloan said.

"Yes! Zigzagged up the canal and then turned to catch the wind. It will all be in the computer. Even if an outside force was used to turn the ship, the computer will log that movement."

Excited by this information, Sloan paced back and forth, tapping her fingers on her thighs. "So, the computer logged everything that happened when the ship entered the canal, everything that Svensson did, every movement of the ship?"

Zahra nodded vigorously. "There is always a log kept of everything that happens aboard the ship. Paperwork is filled out but also the computer automatically logs all data. The captain's actions will be there."

"I don't follow you? What do you mean, his actions?"

Zahra's brow wrinkled in concentration. "Any input given to the ship is recorded. If the captain tells the ship to turn right or left, to speed up or slow down, all of that data is logged in a computer program. So, all of the zigzag directions Captain Svensson gave will be in the computer."

This was exactly the break Sloan needed. If this were true, the proof of what happened to the ship would be in the system. Sloan stopped pacing and stared at Zahra. Her heartbeat ticked up. "This is incredible. We can prove what Svensson did! Did you mention this to anyone else?"

A guilty look flited across Zahra's face and she paused before nodding. "I did tell someone but I think they already knew. Anyway," she brightened, "they won't tell anyone."

Sloan wasn't sure she believed that but there wasn't much she could do about it now. A thought hit her. "Can the captain erase those logs?"

Zahra shook her head. "No. No one on board the ship can access those logs. It's the company's way of keeping track of what their employees do. That way, if there is a mistake made, they can discover how it happened."

Sloan frowned. "The parent company, Pacific Overseas Express must already know that Svensson did this on purpose."

Zahra frowned. "I hadn't thought of that but, yes, they should know that it was not my fault. That it was Svensson's fault. Why aren't they saying anything?"

Sloan swallowed. "Zahra, even if they know what really happened, they don't want the world to know that their captain was responsible for it. This blockage is gonna result in multimillion-dollar, if not billion-dollar, lawsuits. If they point out that their captain did it on purpose, then they are responsible for the blockage. It's better for them if you're blamed."

Zahra leaned back against the container. Her shoulders slumped. She covered her face with her hands. A small sob escaped. "They aren't going to tell the truth. I'll never clear my name."

Sloan reached out and squeezed Zahra's shoulder. "I will do everything I can to get the real story out. Zahra, don't give up hope. Now that I know the software has this information, maybe I can find a way to get it. There has to be somebody at Pacific I can speak with. Just please don't give up hope."

"But how? How will you prove it wasn't my fault? You just said the company won't give you the data. Someone will have to speak with you, and why would they do that?"

Sloan stared at the crying woman. She was right. It was not going to be easy, but she couldn't let this woman's life be destroyed by these people. "I need to get off this ship and find the interpreter. He knows the truth. Svensson had Patel kick us all out of the room before your argument was over. They're going with weather and inexperience."

She nodded. "The government, if they have to accept blame, would like to blame me. They don't like that I am a pilot. But why do they want to accept blame? Won't that mean they will have to offer money to those stuck waiting to get through the canal?"

Sloan nodded. "I'm not sure if they will blame you officially. Once the ship is unstuck, then I imagine some report will be written about weather conditions, and that will be that."

Zahra shook her head. "It is useless. With the story being all over the internet that it's my fault, even some of my own family doesn't believe me. My father, my brothers. They all think it's possible that this catastrophe is my fault. I have brought embarrassment and shame to the family."

"We will figure this out, Zahra. These people killed Eddie. I'm not going to let them get away with that. We will make the truth come out. I promise. But you have to promise me that you will stay strong. Don't give in to the pressure. I know it's hard, but you did nothing wrong, and we're going to prove it." She squeezed the other woman's shoulder again.

Zahra said, "I hope you're right, Sloan. I really do. I will be strong. But please figure this out quickly."

Sloan nodded and then froze. There was a clanking sound. Zahra froze as well. The women exchanged glances. Sloan fingered the knife tucked in her waistband. It wasn't much, but it was the only protection the two of them had. The clanking sound happened again and then footsteps. Someone had started down the stairs at the far end of the walkway.

The two women looked at each other, and then Zahra nodded at Sloan before taking off down another walkway to the right. Sloan turned and started back to the stairs closest to her. Her heart was pounding, and her mouth was dry. There was another clanging sound and more footsteps. Sloan froze. There was nowhere to hide. She was in the middle of the walkway. She took a few steps and stood in the shadow caused by a burnt-out bulb.

The ship groaned. Sweat trickled down Sloan's back. Someone was walking on the walkway above her. She looked up but couldn't see anyone in the darkness. Freezing in place, Sloan tried to stay calm and breathe but her lungs were having problems sucking in air.

The footfalls stopped and then there was a flurry of movement and a small scream. Zahra Nabil suddenly came sailing down from above. Her eyes were wide with fear and her mouth formed a silent *O* as she fell passed Sloan to land with a sickening thud on the floor several stories below.

Sloan was paralyzed. She couldn't take in what had just happened. Footsteps sounded directly above her. She wanted to scream but her throat had closed. Her knees began to shake, and her stomach heaved. Someone had thrown Zahra off the walkway above her and they were still there.

A cold sweat broke out across her entire body. She glanced down and saw Zahra's body on the floor below. Her neck and right leg were twisted at awkward angles. She closed her eyes and bit her cheek in an effort not to vomit.

The person above started walking toward the far end of the walkway. Sloan pulled the knife from her jeans, then turned and headed in the opposite direction. She moved as quickly as she could without making any sound. She came to the stairs and started up.

There was a loud clang and the ship groaned again. Then more footsteps. Multiple people were moving around. It was hard to tell where these ones were coming from. The sound echoed. Sloan scurried up the stairs as fast as she could. Sweat had made her grip slippery, and in her haste, she dropped the knife. It disappeared down the stairwell, but she didn't try to retrieve it. She didn't stop running until she was in front of Axe's door.

Her hands were shaking as she raised them to knock. She gulped in air. "Axe," she whispered as she knocked on his door. She still couldn't get her voice to work. "Axe?" He had to answer. He had to be in there. What if something had happened to him? What if MacGregor's men got to him first? A sob escaped her throat. "Axe?" She was on the edge of losing it. What the hell was she going to do now?

The door opened and she fell into Axe's arms and buried her head in his naked chest. "Oh thank God," she sobbed.

"What is it? What's wrong?" Axe held her away from him and checked her out head to toe. "Are you okay?"

She shook her head and tears streamed down her face. "Z-Zahra's d-dead."

"What? How?" Axe stared at her.

Sloan tried to speak but she just couldn't get the words

out. Axe closed his cabin door and locked it. Then he guided her to the bed and sat her down. "Okay tell me what happened," he said as he reached for his long-sleeved uniform shirt and put it on. Sloan realized he already had his uniform pants on. He was probably sleeping in them.

Sloan tried to wipe her tears with the backs of her hands, but they just wouldn't stop falling.

Axe pulled her close and wrapped his arms around her. He kissed the top of her head and wiped away her tears. "It's okay. You're gonna be okay," he crooned.

Her body relaxed against his chest. She gulped in air like she'd been drowning. Slowly her tears stopped, and Sloan was able to gather herself. She straightened and wiped her face on some tissues Axe had given her.

She finally looked up and met Axe's gaze. His face was blank but his hands were fisted in his lap and his blue eyes had gone ice-cold. She reached out and he took her hand.

"Tell me what happened." His voice was soft, and it sent a shiver across her skin.

"Zahra sent me a note to meet her." She wasn't going to tell him she didn't know who the note was from originally because that was opening the door for all kinds of recriminations she just couldn't handle at the moment.

Sloan threw the used tissues in the trash can. "We met in container hold three, on the walkway. She told me that she could prove Svensson had blocked the canal on purpose. There's software on board that logs all of the input the ship receives. So Svensson's directions will be logged. They'll show he was zigzagging and blocked the canal on purpose."

"Okay. Then what happened." Axe was watching her closely, his gaze getting colder by the second.

"I explained to her that the owners of the *Sea Jewel* wouldn't want that information to come out but that I would work on finding a way to get them to admit it."

Axe frowned. "How did she take that news?"

"She was sad and angry. She really wants...wanted," Sloan corrected with a shaky breath, "to clear her name." She shook her head.

"We were just wrapping up when there was a sound and some footsteps. Zahra took off one way and I went the other. I found some shadows to hide in and the footsteps ended up being directly above me. Then—" tears started to fall again and Sloan had a hard time forming words. "Then Zahra was suddenly falling from the walkway above me. She hit the floor a couple of stories below. She died instantly." Sloan took a deep breath and closed her eyes.

Axe stood up and moved over to lean against the wall. His hands were balled into fists. The pulse in his jaw was jumping and his eyes had gone from icy to scorching. She flinched from his gaze.

"We talked about you staying in your cabin. Do you remember that?" Axe's voice was hard. "Someone tried to kill you earlier, so we said you were going to stay in your cabin all night." He swallowed. "What the fuck were you thinking?" he growled. He pushed off the wall and was towering over her.

Sloan's heart thudded in her chest. In all the times they'd fought, even the worst blow ups they'd had, she'd never seen Axe so angry as he was at this moment. She felt the rage coming off him in waves. "I—I— Zahra wanted to meet…" Her voice died in her throat. The thunderous look on Axe's face was enough to silence her.

"Of all the stupid, dumb ass, dangerous things to do, you go out and risk your life for a story." His voice broke on the last word. His knuckles were white, and his body practically vibrated. He ground his teeth.

"I…It was important to meet her. She had news. I—"

Axe's eyes drilled into her very soul. "Did anyone see

you? Do they know you were there?" he ground out the questions, voice as cold as his gaze.

"I—I'm not sure. I tried to be quiet but then I got so scared I ran up the stairs."

Axe just stood silently staring at her as she sat on the bed. Sloan stood up. "Look, maybe it was a mistake to meet her, but I needed to hear what she had to say. I knew she wouldn't have sent the note if it wasn't really important. And it was important." Why couldn't he see why she had to go?

"The story is everything, is that it, Sloan? Worth risking your life over. Worth risking *my* life over. It's not like they don't know you're gonna run and tell me everything and I won't leave you on your own."

Sloan suddenly felt ill. All the blood drained from her head, replaced by fear and wooziness. She sat back down on the bed and lowered her head to her knees. Her voice was muffled as she groaned, "I'm sorry Axe. I didn't think of—"

"No, you didn't think. You never do Sloan. It's always about the story. You were the best relationship I've ever had, and you destroyed it because of a story. You just keep on pushing. Nothing is ever enough for you. It's all about your next big headline."

"That's not true." She was on her feet again. "I met Zahra because I cared what happened to her. I want the truth to come out."

"Yeah, as long as it has your byline attached to it." He pushed off from the wall and stood in front of her. "What's to stop MacGregor or one of his guys from bursting in here and killing us both, huh? We know what Zahra knew that means we're just as much of a danger to them as she was."

"I'm sorry, okay? I didn't think about that part but—"

"Sloan, you never think." He took a step closer. "You could have been killed. You still might be. What the fuck, Sloan? Seriously. What. The. Fuck!"

She blinked. Axe was right. She'd come in close contact with death twice already on this ship. What the hell was she thinking meeting some anonymous person like that? She was thinking it was her job. "I'm a reporter. It's my job to gather the facts of the story and if sometimes that puts me in a bit of danger, so be it," Sloan said with a whole lot of bravado she didn't remotely feel.

Axe's eyes blazed as he stood staring down at her. His jaw moved as if he was grinding his teeth. He took a step back. "If you want to risk your life, so be it. There's the door. You're on your own. I won't risk *my* life to protect you if you're not willing to stop being stupid and taking unnecessary risks."

Sloan stood there with her mouth hanging open. Was he really kicking her out of his room? Did he truly not care if she left? Her knees wobbled. She was terrified to be out there on her own.

"You wouldn't," she whispered.

"Wouldn't what, Sloan? Stop protecting you? How am I supposed to keep you alive if you go ahead and take huge risks without telling me? Why should I try to protect you when you won't protect yourself?"

The truth of his words hit her. Hard. He was right. She was asking him to risk his life for her and she wasn't bothering to do anything to protect herself. "Axe I—"

There was a loud pounding on Axe's door and Sloan let out a small scream. Axe dove for his backpack and pulled out a gun. He tucked it behind his back and moved in front of Sloan so as to block her from the doorway. "Who is it?"

"Patel. Chief Mate."

Axe moved forward and unlocked the door but he kept the gun by his side. He opened the door a crack. "What is it? What's going on?"

"Zahra Nabil is dead. MacGregor and his men have all

left the ship. I wanted to check and make sure you and Ms. Bishop were safe."

"Yes, we're fine. What do you mean MacGregor left? Isn't there a sandstorm starting out there?"

"Yes, but a small craft came along side and they all went down the pilot stairs and got off. I sent a message to the Port Authority but there's not much they can do in this storm."

"Understood. Do you need any help?"

Patel shook his head. "No, we have it under control. As long as you two are fine...do you need anything?"

Axe shook his head. "No thanks, we're good. Let me know if you need some help."

"I will...and thanks." Patel nodded and then walked down the hallway out of sight.

Axe closed the door and turned to face Sloan. "MacGregor and his boys are gone. You should be safe now. You can go back to your room."

Sloan blinked. She didn't want to go back to her room. She'd seen a woman die tonight. A good woman who had done nothing wrong. It had been stupid to meet Zahra. She understood that now, but she couldn't unsee what she'd seen. All she wanted was to be with Axe. "I don't want to go back to my room. I want to stay here with you."

Axe's face was unreadable as he stared at her. "Sloan," his voice was like gravel, "staying with me won't change anything."

She shook her head. "I don't need it to change anything." *Liar liar.* Axe threatened that he was done with her. She just couldn't live with that. Not once, not even when they'd had their last huge fight, did she ever think he would give up on her. And now he had. She needed to get him back. She'd pushed him too far and she needed to find a way to get back to where they were. "I just don't want to be alone."

Axe shook his head. "Sloan, it's too late for that. I...just can't…be around you if you're going to take these kinds of risks. You could have been killed." His voice broke. "I wouldn't be able to live with it if you got yourself killed over a fucking story. I…can't be a part of that Sloan."

Tears started down Sloan's cheeks. "I won't take stupid risks again. I won't." She took a step toward him so they were inches apart.

"Yes you will, Sloan. Go back to your room. You'll be safe there. It's already morning. The FBI will be here as soon as this sandstorm lets up."

She'd lost him. Her heart was shattering and her mouth went dry. She'd finally really lost Axe. *No! No fucking way.* She reached out and put her hands on his bare chest. She went up on her toes and kissed him. Hard. She wrapped her arms around his neck and kept kissing him but he stayed still. He refused to kiss her back. His arms hung limply by his sides. She pressed her body to his determined not to give up.

Finally Axe's arms snaked around her waist and his mouth opened. She immediately deepened the kiss, pouring her soul into every movement. His tongue matched hers and he pulled her tighter against him.

"Fuck, Sloan," he mumbled as he broke off their kiss and started undoing the buttons on her blouse. She ran her hands down his chest and grabbed his belt buckle. She had it undone in seconds. This is what she needed. Spending the next few hours in Axe's arms, blotting out the memory of Zahra's death.

Axe pushed the blouse off her shoulders and her bra soon followed. He rained kisses down her neck, taking a moment to suck on the hollow at the base before moving down to suck her right nipple.

"Axe," she moaned and threw her head back. He sucked her nipple harder and then switched to the other side. His leg was pushed between hers and she rubbed her hot center up and down his well-muscled thigh.

Sloan undid his pants and pushed them down his hips. He stopped what he was doing and slid out of his pants and then his black boxer briefs. Sloan shimmied out of her jeans and thong. His eyes darkened as he looked at her naked. "Sloan," he growled, "you will be the death of me." He captured her lips in a scorching kiss and moved her back until she hit the bed. Then he gave her a slight push and she fell back. He immediately positioned himself on top of her, capturing her lips once more.

Axe moved his way down her body, stopping to suck her nipples, and then plant kisses across her belly. Sloan sunk her fingers into his hair and pulled him back up. She needed him inside her now. She wanted to feel that delicious friction that would have her pushed over the edge into oblivion.

"Now Axe," she moaned as she opened her legs and wrapped them around him.

"Sloan, I—"

She kissed him. Hard. "I need you inside me now, Axe." His eyes turned a deep blue as she rubbed her hot core against his cock.

"Sloan," he growled again as he buried himself inside her.

She moaned with pleasure. He pulled almost all the way out and then sank all the way in again. "Axe…more…faster." She arched her hips and matched his strokes as he increased his speed. "Yes, yes," she mumbled as he slammed into her. A minute later she climaxed squeezing his cock inside her. Axe joined her seconds later and then collapsed on top of her while they both tried to catch their breath.

"Axe, I—"

There was another banging on the door. "Chief Cantor?" a voice called.

"Yes, what is it?" Axe snarled.

"Mr. Patel has asked if I could bring you up to his office."

Axe cursed. "I'll be there shortly. I know the way."

"Yes, sir," the voice said and then there was the slight sound of footsteps receding.

Axe rolled off Sloan and stood up. He grabbed his clothes and started pulling them on.

Sloan sat up. "Axe, are you sure it's safe? What do you think Patel wants?"

"Don't know." He picked up his gun from the desk where he'd laid it and tucked it into the waist band of his uniform pants. He put on a navy T-shirt and then pulled on his boots. His cell phone dinged. It was on the table next to the bed. Sloan glanced at the screen. It was a text from Nick Taggert. It just said, "Here," and that was it.

Axe grabbed his phone and then turned to her. "I need you to be gone when I get back, Sloan."

"What?" She blinked. "I want to stay here and wait until you come back."

"The sex didn't change anything, Sloan. What I said stands. I am truly sorry you lost your friend. Seeing someone die is hard no matter what, but I can't care about what you want anymore. It just costs me too much. Be gone before I get back." With that he turned around and headed out of the cabin, closing the door behind him.

Sloan sat there stunned. How could he just walk away like that? How could he leave her? Tears started rolling down her face. She had to face the truth. The man she thought would always be there had just walked out the door and it was all her own fault.

CHAPTER ELEVEN

Axe opened his email one more time, but still nothing new from Bertrand or anyone else. Nick had just sent the one text saying he was here.

After coming back from Patel's office Axe had grabbed a shower. He needed to get Sloan's scent washed off him before it drove him crazy.

She'd been gone when he'd gotten back just like he asked. He wasn't sure if he was happy about that or not. No, he wasn't happy about it but it was the way things had to be. He couldn't take her carelessness any longer. She was always jumping head long into things without a thought for anyone or anything including herself.

He regretted being so harsh but she'd scared the hell out of him. She could have been the one thrown off the walkway. Even now just the thought of it made him crazy. He glanced down at his hands which were gripping the back of the desk chair so hard the knuckles were white.

His stomach rumbled for the umpteenth time, and he glanced at his watch. It was almost nine. The FBI were originally due in about an hour, but the sandstorm had delayed their arrival. It looked like it might be closer to two or three p.m. before they would get on board the ship. Axe wanted to get up to the mess, have breakfast, and get back down to his stateroom. Sand got everywhere during a storm. He didn't want to eat any with his breakfast if he could help it.

He opened his door and stepped out into the hallway at the same time as Sloan. One look was all he needed to know she was not doing well. Her eyes were puffy and the circles underneath were darker. The fine lines around her mouth had gotten deeper.

He couldn't stop himself from asking, "You okay?"

"Is that your way of telling me I look like shit? Thanks." Sloan brushed away a stray hair and hooked it behind her ear.

That would teach him. He needed to keep his mouth shut. "Nope. Just asking if you were okay but it's none of my business."

He started down the hallway and Sloan caught up to walk beside him. It was taking everything he had not to reach out and comfort her. She was hurting and he wanted to brush away the pain, but it wouldn't do him any good and for once, he needed to put himself first.

Sloan hit the elevator button, and the doors opened. They both stepped in, and then she hit the button for the floor with the mess hall on it.

The elevator was small, really only big enough for three or four people. Sloan's scent hit him hard. It just added to his current struggle to keep his temper in check. He was totally pissed off that he was even in this situation. If he was still back on the *Fitz* everything would be fine. Axe had known the moment he'd first kissed Sloan that there was no way he was going to leave her unprotected on this ship. Seeing her this morning just made it all the harder to let her go. She was exhausted, and he was willing to bet her nerves were raw. It was the moment she needed him most, but he just couldn't. He was done. He needed to be able to sleep at night. She was willing to throw him under the bus time and again. Eventually, he had to smarten up no matter how much it hurt.

The elevator dinged and the doors opened. *Saved by the bell.* Her scent and the memories of a few hours ago were getting to him. Just the thought of her could make him hard.

Axe stepped back and gestured for Sloan to leave the elevator. Without looking at him, she exited and he followed a few seconds behind. He needed to get his shit together. He had to forget how great the sex was or the wrong head would take control.

He needed to adjust his thinking. Sloan was an amazing person and a great reporter. She just couldn't be *his*. He needed to be able to trust his partner and know that she would have his back. Sloan just couldn't seem to come through on that score which made him incredibly sad because they fit together in almost every other way. They both liked to be outdoors. They had similar political views. Hell, they even liked the same movies and laughed at the same jokes. He was even willing to admit she was a hell of a reporter. He respected her work just not the way she went about it.

Sloan was always a handful. He loved that about her. It just made her hard to be around.

They walked into the mess hall and grabbed trays. After filling their plates with all the breakfast offerings, they found a table and sat down.

The sound of the wind picked up, and the ship shuddered slightly. Axe made an attempt to be civil. They still had a few more hours on this tub together and Sloan was in a world of hurt. "The storm is in full swing now."

Sloan nodded. "It's my first sandstorm. It's weird. I didn't even think of sand as something that could be dangerous in that way."

"It's not pleasant, for sure. Sand gets in everywhere. If you end up in one, make sure your mouth and nose are covered. Your ears and your eyes as well. It's like being attacked by a steel-wool pad. The stuff hurts like hell if you're stuck out in it without the proper covering, and it takes a week of showering to get it out of your hair and other spots."

Sloan's smile was tight. "Sounds lovely. Glad we'll be inside."

"Don't worry, you will still chew some before it's gone. Like I said, it gets in everywhere."

They ate the rest of their meal in silence. When they were both finished Axe cleared their trays and then came back to the table. "I have to go see Patel. He asked me for help earlier. He wants to be as prepared as possible for the Egyptian investigators and he thought it might help to have a member of U.S. law enforcement look over the scene."

Sloan just nodded.

Axe paused. He hated to do it but duty called. "Sloan, is there any way Zahra could have jumped off the walkway?"

"None whatsoever. She was determined to prove her innocence."

Axe pulled out his chair again and sat down. "Tell me what she told you again."

Sloan glanced at him but didn't maintain eye contact. "This software will show all of the input that Svensson made, so it should show that he made the ship turn sideways purposely. She also said the software can't be accessed from on board the ship. It's used as a precaution so the owners can keep track of what the captains, crews, etc. are doing all the time. They need to know if it's someone's fault."

"Zahra thought this software would exonerate her."

Sloan nodded. "She was upset and sad that her family didn't believe it wasn't her fault." Sloan corrected herself. "At least her father and brothers didn't." She sighed. "Axe, there's no way she would kill herself, knowing the proof was out there. She wanted to clear her name and her family's reputation."

Axe drummed his fingers on the table "Did she say how she was going to access this software?"

Again, Sloan shook her head. "Well, that was sort of the problem. I think she thought the company would look at it and see that it was Svensson's fault. I pointed out to her the chances of Pacific admitting it was their fault for blocking the Suez Canal and causing billions of dollars of damages was pretty slim."

"What did she say when you pointed that out?" Axe asked.

"She was very upset, but I promised her that I would help her prove her innocence. I meant it, and she knew that. Despite what it looks like and what it sounds like, I'm telling you right now, Zahra wasn't giving up." Sloan was adamant.

Axe studied her. She was exhausted, and her emotions were raw. She needed sleep, and more importantly, peace of mind. He hadn't helped with any of that. Guilt washed over him. "If it's any consolation I agree Zahra didn't kill herself but I'm not sure that matters."

Sloan leaned back in her chair and rubbed her eyes with the heels of her hands. "This whole thing, it's a puzzle that's missing too many pieces. I understand that MacGregor is part of it. He was brought on board with his goons to work with Svensson to make this happen, or that's what it seems like. But who's running the operation, and why did they want to block the canal?"

Axe shook his head. Sloan was right. They still had no

idea who was behind any of this or why they wanted the canal blocked. He didn't point out that it could be terrorism on a global scale. Sloan was too likely to run with the story and he, or someone, had to check it out first. Whatever was going on, someone needed to investigate, and quickly, before all the evidence and witnesses disappeared.

CHAPTER TWELVE

A few hours later Sloan knocked on Axe's door. She wanted to run from this man. Hide under her covers and never come out but he'd made an effort to be civil at breakfast so she could do the same. Besides she needed someone to bounce ideas off and Axe was always so good at helping her with that.

Axe opened the door and his expression went flat. *So much for being civil.*

"Sorry to bug you but I have a couple of questions." She held up her hands. "Don't worry I won't quote you or even say an 'unnamed source,' I just need to bounce some ideas around."

Axe stared at her, his expression blank. Finally, he stepped back and let her enter his room.

Sloan walked in and immediately started pacing. "So, why do you think MacGregor and his goons left?"

"They knew the F.B.I. were coming and they had too many dead bodies to explain."

Sloan winced. "But why now?"

Axe sighed. "I thought we just established that. Because

the FBI were coming."

"Yes." She nodded. "But they could have left at any time. They've known the FBI were coming for a while, so why did they leave during the storm?"

Axe cocked his head. "You think leaving wasn't their original plan?"

Sloan paused and bit her lip. "I think they had planned to face the FBI. You said it yourself, they all had their stories straight and there were no witnesses besides MacGregor's guys, so what did they have to worry about? Eddie's death was bound to be written off as an accident. They didn't know I saw what really happened."

"Are you sure about that? Someone did try to kill you."

"True but… I don't know. My instincts tell me they planned to stick it out, otherwise why bother to get their stories straight?"

Axe nodded slowly. "I get where you're going with this. They originally planned to hold to their story and, without any evidence, they could assume Eddie's death would be ruled an accident. The whole thing would be over and done with, and they'd get away scot-free."

"So"—Sloan sat down at Axe's desk—"what changed their minds?"

"Zahra's death," Axe stated. "I don't think they meant to kill her. If she'd really been on their shit list, they'd have killed her earlier, like right after the ship got stuck. It would have made more sense to just remove her from the scene and kill her elsewhere, just like the interpreter."

Sloan had been resting her head in her hands, but she shot off the bed at Axe's pronouncement. "The interpreter is dead?"

"No, sorry. I don't know. What I'm saying is, it would have made more sense to take care of Zahra at the same time as they took the interpreter off the ship. If she'd disappeared, no one would have been surprised, right? The Egyptian government has been saying it was weather conditions, but the inexperienced pilot didn't help the situation. Zahra going into hiding would make sense. Her family is getting death threats as it is. But MacGregor didn't kill her, or even remove her immediately, which says to me they thought they could control her."

Sloan tapped her leg as she paced. "Or at the very least, control the narrative. Zahra's death changed that." She let out a sigh. Her heart hurt for Zahra and her family. It was all so unfair.

"Agreed."

Sloan had the distinct feeling Axe already knew something, and he wanted her to catch up. She tapped her leg and then stopped. "They didn't kill Zahra on purpose, or let me rephrase, they didn't plan on killing her here on the ship. Too many dead bodies to explain. Eddie found out something, so they killed him but made it look like an accident. They couldn't do that with Zahra, too. So once she was dead, they had to leave, or risk being arrested."

"As you said, they wouldn't be able to control the narrative in the same way."

Sloan stopped moving. "With the FBI coming on board and two dead bodies, it was going to be a shit show for MacGregor."

Axe rubbed the stubble on his cheek. "I'm thinking it would be easy to discover in the autopsy that Zahra didn't kill herself. There will be bruising where whoever it was picked her up and…" he stopped speaking.

Sloan knew it was because she'd gone pale. Just the memory of it had her hands shaking.

"Anyway," Axe continued, "MacGregor isn't stupid. He would have known that, so leaving was the best way out for them. Put distance between them and this ship."

Sloan rubbed her forehead. "Won't the FBI want to speak to them, though? Won't they track MacGregor and his men down?"

Axe shrugged. "I'm sure they'll want to speak to MacGregor and his men, but how much effort will they put into tracking them down? I'm not sure. You have to remember, Sloan, they are just here to investigate Eddie's death. That's it. Whether Svensson blocked the canal on purpose or not has nothing to do with their investigation. They will try to find MacGregor, but he's not going to the top of the Most Wanted List."

"Shit. So, MacGregor and his goons get away with killing Eddie and Zahra" Sloan blinked back tears.

"I didn't say that," Axe corrected. "I said the FBI would do their best to track them down, but it isn't going to be their top priority." He stared at Sloan for a good long minute. "If you can find out what Eddie knew, then I'm guessing you can bring down MacGregor and whoever is behind this whole thing."

Sloan stared at Axe. Was he actually telling her to investigate MacGregor? To poke at something that would be very dangerous? He'd just yelled at her for her risky behavior. He'd even dumped her over it and broken her heart. "I can't believe you just said that."

A ghost of a smile flitted over Axe's face. "Me either, but let's face it, you were going to investigate anyway. I'm just telling you what direction to start in. Find out what Eddie knew, and you'll go a long way in solving this puzzle."

Axe moved so he was resting his backside on the small desk in the room and his legs were out in front of him. His eyes narrowed. "You will have to be very careful, though. They made a run at you once already. MacGregor won't miss twice."

A shiver went across Sloan's skin. Was a story worth

risking her life over? Probably not but she'd already lost Axe so she had very little left to lose. Besides justice for Eddie and Zahra was different. That *was* worth risking everything for.

A thought suddenly occurred to her. "What about Svensson? MacGregor and his goons leaving has left him holding the bag, hasn't it?" She started to sit down on the bed but thought the better of it. Too many memories of the last time she was on that bed. She turned and leaned against the spot on the wall Axe had vacated.

"Not necessarily. We think Svensson blocked the canal on purpose, but we're the only ones accusing him at this point. Zahra's dead, and the interpreter is gone somewhere. Rohan Patel knows the truth, but I don't think he'll talk. He didn't like MacGregor and the hired security, but he seems loyal to Svensson. With Zahra dead, there's really no proof except for the software. It's not like Pacific is going to yell from the rooftops that their captain went rogue and blocked the canal on purpose." Axe shook his head. "No. The *Sea Jewel* blocking the canal will be declared an accident, and in the end, weather and Zahra's lack of experience will be blamed, if not officially, at least in the court of public opinion."

"But that's not fair. That's not what happened." Sloan slammed her fist on her thigh.

"You're right. It's not fair, but I think that's what's going to happen."

"No way! I'm not letting Zahra go down for this. It's not fair to her. It's not fair to her family. They deserve the truth to be out there."

"Agreed. When the FBI guys get on board, which should be in about twenty minutes now that the storm is over, we'll tell them what we know. We'll walk them through it step by step, but ultimately, it's up to them."

Axe straightened. "Sloan, I want to be honest about this with you. Chances are good, even if they can prove it, no government wants to yell from the rooftops that the canal was blocked on purpose. It just gives ideas to all kinds of crazies out there. This whole thing is a political hot potato, and chances are very good the truth will get buried for many reasons, all of which are above my pay grade."

Sloan put her hands on her hips. "Two minutes ago, you were telling me to keep investigating, and now you're telling me there's no point?"

Axe straightened. "No. I know you're going to keep investigating because an unsolved puzzle is just too much for you to walk away from!" He ground his teeth and glared at her.

Sloan looked away. He wasn't wrong and she hated him for that but she hated herself more for wrecking things because of it.

Axe sat back down on the desk. "I am saying you may never get to publish the story you want to publish. If you find out the truth, then at least one person knows it, and that's better than no one at all. You are going to have to pick your battles on this one. I…wouldn't want anything to happen to you."

She looked up to meet his gaze. There was pain there, and a lot of hurt. She'd done that to him but he'd done the same to her. Maybe Axe was right. Maybe they just weren't good together.

Sloan took a deep breath. It was all so unfair. Her and Axe breaking up. Eddie and Zahra's deaths. None of it made any sense and, because of circumstances, the truth might never see the light of day.

She really needed to find the interpreter because if he backed up her story, she could blow this wide open. The hell with those in power. She could write it and spread it all over the web before they even knew it was there, but she really needed to get off this ship to do it. Plus she needed to get away from Axe. It was too much being this close to him and not being able to touch him. To talk to him like she wanted to. To be his girlfriend.

"I want to get off the *Sea Jewel* as quickly as possible. Can we go see the FBI and just tell them everything in a hurry? There are things I need to do. I really want to get this article out."

Sloan looked down at the floor. The weight of Axe's stare settled on her shoulders. He was thinking she was up to something, and he was right. She was. She was also running away. This was going to hurt for a long time but the sooner she got used to the idea they were through the sooner she could start healing and she couldn't do that standing three feet away from him.

"Look, you were saying I should investigate, and I need to get off this ship to do that."

Sloan braced herself for the lecture from Axe about being careful and not pushing things, but none came. He merely nodded. "I'll do what I can to help, but once the FBI arrives, I have to go back to my ship."

The fact that Axe didn't yell at her about going full tilt after a story broke her heart. He'd always told her to be careful. Always. The fact that he didn't even say a simple 'watch yourself' or something meant it was well and truly over.

Axe cleared his throat. "I can ask around and see if I can help you find the interpreter. I'm assuming that's one of the threads you're going to chase. I have a few contacts in country, but I wouldn't hold my breath. If MacGregor and his crew wanted the guy gone, then he could be dead already."

She gave herself a mental shake. She needed to focus on the story. It was all she had left. It was exactly what she'd been afraid of—the interpreter was already dead. But she held out hope.

She couldn't give up yet. Zahra deserved better.

Axe's cell phone beeped. He glanced down at the screen. "They're here."

Sloan nodded. "Let's go."

She moved into the hallway, and Axe followed her out. He locked his door behind them. They made their way to the elevator, and Axe hit the UP button.

"Where are we meeting them?" Sloan ran a hand over her hair. She knew she looked a mess, but it was hard to care. She'd pulled her damp hair back into a messy bun again and she was wearing a light blue blouse with a faded pair of jeans. It was as good an outfit as any.

The elevator doors opened. Axe gestured for Sloan to get in. He got in behind her, and as the doors closed, he hit the button for their floor. "Rohan's office."

"You don't think he'll tell them what he knows?" Sloan asked. Axe had said he had doubts, but she hoped he was wrong.

"I think he'll tell them about MacGregor and his men, but I don't think he's gonna throw Svensson under the bus, if that's what you're thinking. It doesn't help him any. As the second in command, why didn't he stop Svensson? The captain drove the ship into the canal against advice from the pilot. Why didn't Patel step in? Why didn't he stop the captain from doing something with the ship that would endanger people's lives and, quite frankly, world trade?" Axe shook his head. "No, he's not going to say anything. It will cause way too many questions to be asked."

Sloan sighed. "I want to believe that you're wrong. I want to believe that he's going to tell the truth because it's the right thing to do. He seems like such a nice guy."

The elevator doors opened, and they stepped out. There was a group of men at the end of the hallway, standing by Rohan's door. They were all wearing jeans and FBI jackets.

There were four of them, but she surmised there would be at least one more inside the office.

They approached the group of men. Axe stopped in front of them. "Who's in charge?"

"That would be me."

Axe turned to follow the voice that came from his left, inside of Rohan's office. He immediately smiled. "Preston! What are you doing here? I thought you were stuck behind a desk back in DC."

The attractive blond woman in front of Rohan's desk smiled. "Axel Cantor. I should have known you'd be on board. Who else would be involved in a mess like this?"

She offered her hand. Axe reached out, and the two shook while smiling at each other. They hung on a beat or two longer than was necessary to Sloan's way of thinking, and there was something in their smiles that made blood pound in her ears.

Sloan took an immediate dislike to the other woman. She was taller than Sloan, and her blond hair was pulled back into a neat bun. She had big green eyes and a bright smile. There was no doubt in Sloan's mind that men flocked to this woman.

Preston, what kind of a name was that? She exuded confidence and authority. A cool exterior with an air of complete control. It would be an aphrodisiac to some men, and by the look on Axe's face, he was one of them.

Axe turned to her. "Sloan Bishop, freelance reporter, meet Saige Preston, one of the best agents in the bureau."

Sloan did her best not to roll her eyes as she offered her hand and Preston shook it. There was a wariness in the other woman's eyes at the mention of Sloan's profession. Well, that was fine because Sloan was wary, too. If she didn't miss her guess, Saige Preston and Axe had dated at some point. They might even have been lovers. Either way, it had ended on a good note.

Unlike her own relationship with Axe. *Dammit.*

Sloan fisted her hands and tried not to grind her teeth. Jealousy wasn't pretty in any fashion. Besides, she didn't want Axe to have the satisfaction of knowing she was tied in knots over his "friend," Preston.

Saige Preston turned to Axe. "I understand you were put in charge of the investigation."

Axe nodded. "Yeah. The *Fitz* is stuck in the canal too. They asked me to come over and keep an eye on the situation."

"OK. Then why don't we go find us a quiet place to talk, and you can fill me in on what's going on?"

"Sounds good. Let's head to the mess hall," Axe said.

Preston looked at him, surprise written on her face, but Axe gave a slight shake of his head. "I'll follow you," the blonde responded.

Great, they have their own code. Sloan sighed to herself. This interview was going to be long and painful. Watching them interact was just feeding the green-eyed monster. She needed to get a grip. She and Axe were through, and even though he'd helped her, and screwed her, they were not getting back together. He'd made that perfectly clear. He didn't trust her, nor did he really support her career, at least not until today. She couldn't be with a man who wasn't behind her one hundred percent. Why had he told her to investigate? That was setting off faint alarm bells, but she wasn't sure why.

Axe turned to Sloan. "Why don't you stay here and answer whatever questions these gentlemen may have for you?"

Sloan ground her teeth. She was being dismissed. He

didn't even want her in the same room. He must be afraid she'd write about it even though she'd given her word. *Fine.*

He was right. She would write about all of it, but not yet. Not until the investigation by the FBI was underway. She wouldn't quote Axe in the article or anything. She wouldn't even use him as her anonymous source. She couldn't help it if people made that leap. It wasn't her fault that's what happened with the Coast Guard story, and it wouldn't be her fault now either. Sloan bit her cheek. She would not give Axe the satisfaction of fighting with him. She had another source to question.

"Fine," she said through gritted teeth.

Axe and Preston went out the door and stopped to speak to the men in the hallway. Sloan turned to Rohan Patel still sitting behind his desk. "How are you doing?" she asked him.

"I am doing well. I have already spoken with the FBI and told them all I know."

"Did you tell them about Svensson?" she asked in a low voice.

Rohan shook his head. "There's no point. They are here to investigate Mr. O'Mara's death."

"Of course there's a point. They could go to the authorities and insist on a real investigation. The US has the power to make that happen. Who knows what the Egyptian government is going to say really happened?" Sloan hissed in a harsh whisper.

Rohan hesitated before he said, "I know, and it's awful, but it doesn't matter what I say. The company's never going to admit to the truth, and neither is Svensson. With MacGregor and his men gone, there's no one here to question what really happened. The company will let everything die down and then quietly retire Svensson. I'll be lucky to keep my job as well. If I say anything that may cause trouble, I'll be fired. I need this job. Involving the FBI doesn't help anyone, and there's no guarantee they will investigate properly."

"But, surely, the FBI will track down MacGregor and his boys. They were the 'witnesses' to Eddie's death. They have to speak to them. Then they can dig and find out what was really going on with the *Sea Jewel*."

Rohan shook his head and whispered, "I would very much like to have your faith in the system, but I have seen far too much to think like that. The FBI will carry on with this investigation, and everyone will cooperate but, in the end, no major revelations will come out. You will see. Mr. O'Mara's death will be labeled an accident."

Rohan leaned forward and lowered his voice even more, causing Sloan to have to lean closer. "You must understand, this is a political nightmare for all concerned. No one wants any nastiness to come out. The ramifications will be felt across the globe. It is sad that this is the case, but it's most expeditious for everyone if Eddie's death is an accident and the weather and Zahra are to blame for the ship being stuck."

He was saying what Axe had said. She could dig and find the truth, but the chances of clearing Zahra's name and getting justice for Eddie were slim. It just didn't suit the higher-ups to have the truth come out.

Rohan stood up. "Now, Miss Bishop, I believe these gentlemen would like to speak with you. I will leave my office, and you may hold your interviews here." Rohan gave her a look, which she took as a reminder to be discreet. He was telling her not to tell the FBI all she knew. Her stomach rolled. He was putting her in a tough spot. Rohan got out from behind his desk and walked out of the room.

Sloan looked at the FBI agents as they entered the room and began pulling chairs up to the desk. Did she tell them the truth, or did she keep it to herself? Which one would help Eddie and Zahra more?

CHAPTER THIRTEEN

"Jesus, Axe, you really get involved in the shittiest messes, don't you?" Saige said as she leaned back in her chair. "Are you sure about all this?"

Axe grimaced. "I'm sure, unfortunately. I'll give you my notes from the interviews with MacGregor's men, but it was all a cover-up. They killed O'Mara because he knew something, although I have no idea what. They threw him off the flying bridge, and he hit the deck. They hid it by throwing his body overboard. Sloan got a couple of pictures." Axe dug out his phone and clicked away. "There you should have them."

Saige leaned forward again and pulled out her phone. "Does Sloan Bishop know all of this? Is she going to print it?" she asked as she checked out the email. "Jesus. Those are some brutal pictures."

"Yeah, they are and, yes, Sloan knows everything, but… she hasn't put it all together just yet. She's not going to print anything until she gets a bit more of the story. She needs to speak to the interpreter to make sure that what she thinks was said was actually said. She needs verification."

Saige's eyes narrowed. "What do you mean she hasn't put it together yet?"

"Sloan knows the canal was blocked on purpose, but she really hasn't thought about the why. I've been encouraging her to stick with investigating Eddie's death and interviewing the interpreter. Either one of those threads could lead her to the truth, but my guess is she won't find out before we—or maybe, you—do."

"I'm only here to investigate O'Mara's death."

"Yeah, but now that you're here and know more is going on, someone has to say yes to investigating the rest."

Saige shrugged. "You'd think so, wouldn't you? What do you think is really going on?"

Axe ran a hand through his hair. "At first, I thought global terrorism. Holding the world hostage for money or a show of power, but no one has claimed responsibility, or if they have, some government has managed to keep it super quiet. What's the likelihood of that?"

"Very slim. The terrorists of today like to be loud and proud about everything. It's all out there on the Internet."

"Exactly. So, I think someone wanted the canal blocked for a specific reason."

Saige sighed. "I'm with you, but what?"

"Why do you block something? To stop something else from getting through. I think there is a ship on this end of the canal that somebody didn't want to get through to the Mediterranean."

Saige studied Axe. "All this to block one ship? Isn't that extreme?"

"Hell, I don't know if it's one ship or fifteen ships, but the only thing that really makes sense is someone doesn't want something to get through. Think about it. If it was just one ship, they could sabotage it. But what if it's multiple ships? How many ways can you cripple a ship before it becomes obvious something is going on? By blocking the canal, everyone is held up. Makes it hard as hell to determine the actual target."

"I see what you mean. Like a mass shooter event where one person was the target and the rest were collateral damage."

Axe shook his head and grinned. "Saige, your brain always goes to the darkest places."

"Yes, but that's an advantage in my job." She winked.

"True enough."

"You've put a lot of thought into this. Do you think they'll let you run with it?"

Axe raised an eyebrow. "Me? This is way outside my purview. I was thinking you could take it and run."

Saige shook her head. "The Egyptians won't let us anywhere near it. We're only here because the world is watching. There's no way in hell they'll let the FBI take the lead in this type of investigation."

"It's not like the U.S. Coast Guard has any jurisdiction either."

"No, but didn't I hear something about Panama and Ecuador? Something about a vaccine?"

Axe grinned. "That was a one-time thing, and drug interdiction—which is what we thought it was—is part of our job."

Saige's phone went off, and she glanced at the screen. "I've got to go. The Egyptian medical examiner is here. We need to take a look at O'Mara's body and process it before we let them have it." She stood up. "I'm not sure if I can pursue any of this, Axe, but I'll run it up the flagpole."

Axe stood up. "Uh, just don't do it in any of the offices or your room if you're staying on board. MacGregor had them all bugged, or at least the Chief Mate thought that was the case. He still could be listening."

"Good to know." She smiled. "Take care, Axe. I'll keep you in the loop as much as I can. Let's do drinks when we're both back stateside."

Axe smiled. "I'd like that."

Saige turned and walked out of the mess, and he watched her go. They'd been on a few dates when he was taking a hand-to-hand combat course in Virginia, and he'd liked her, but their schedules were crazy, and once it was over, they hadn't reconnected. Someone to keep in mind when he was back home and managed to exorcise Sloan's ghost. But she was a damn hard act to follow.

First, though, he needed to get back to his ship. He'd seen an email notification pop up on his phone while he was speaking with Saige. His CO had new orders for him.

He headed back down to his room and gathered his things. Twenty minutes later, he was standing on deck, reading the latest email. Schwartz had told him to get back pronto and then sent two more emails requesting updates. Axe had written the report earlier, but the storm had caused issues with the Wi-Fi, so he had just hit send on his report when Sloan came up and stood next to him.

"Hey," she said as she dropped her backpack at her feet.

"Hey," Axe nodded. So, you're finally getting off this tub." Axe glanced down at the bag and then up at her head. She was wearing a fedora.

"Eddie's. I just wanted a reminder of him, you know."

Axe understood completely. "Yeah. It looks cute on you." She smiled. "Thanks."

His heart lurched. She did look cute. So fucking cute it was killing him. He hated the idea of Sloan out there poking around in this mess without him to protect her, but he'd done the best he could to limit her exposure. And he just had to draw a line in the sand. He couldn't protect her if she wouldn't protect herself.

His gut churned. The fact that he wasn't being totally honest with her, bothered him, but if he gave her his theory, then she would start charging around like a bull in a China shop. It was better this way, or so he told himself. He needed her out of harm's way, and out of his life, if he was ever going to find any peace.

Axe quickly reviewed Sloan's exposure. MacGregor had Eddie's laptop and phone so chances were good she wouldn't turn anything up there. The interpreter was another matter. He was worried she would track the man to the ends of the earth. He just hoped that either MacGregor had lost interest because he had bigger issues to deal with, like the FBI, or he just didn't care anymore. His job was finished. Either way worked for Axe. Hell, the interpreter could be dead, which also worked, although Axe hated to think that might be the case.

As long as Sloan was as far away from trouble as he could make her, then it was all good. She would hate him when she figured it out, if she hadn't already but he would rather that than have her killed. His chest ached a bit, and he rubbed it absently.

"So, what's your plan?" Sloan asked.

"I am going back to my ship. You? What's your first step?" He clenched his jaw and tried to keep a neutral expression on his face.

"Well, I got the interpreter's full name from Rohan, so I will start looking for him. Unfortunately, his name is Mohammed Gamal. It's one of the most common names in the country. More than a million men are named Mohammed Gamal." She sighed.

Axe wanted to shout for joy. It should take her a while to find him, if she could at all. It limited her exposure to danger so much more this way. Pangs of guilt hit his gut, but he refused to give in. She was safer if she was tucked away looking for Mohammed Gamal. And he had to stop worrying about her anyway. It was over. He needed to move on. How the hell he was going to do that, he had no idea.

"On the bright side, I already called the company that supplied him, and I am meeting with Gamal's boss first thing tomorrow. Hopefully, he will have an idea where Gamal is now."

Axe's joy dissipated. "Ah, is Gamal on a job somewhere?"

"No, that's the thing. He came off the ship and was supposed to go immediately onto another ship, but because the canal is blocked and nothing is moving, he decided to take vacation. I'm hoping his boss or his co-workers know where he went. I really will be pissed if he took off for the U.S. or Europe or something."

Axe said a quick prayer that Gamal had done just that. The U.S. would be perfect. Then he would know for sure Sloan was out of danger. MacGregor wouldn't bother going all the way to the States to kill Sloan. Or, at least, he hoped not. "Well, good luck with it. Let me know if I can help." He might not be with Sloan anymore but he had to know she was safe and walking the earth somewhere. He just couldn't lose anyone else.

"Thanks, Axe, I appreciate it." She glanced at him from beneath the brim of the hat. "Thanks for saving me from the wrench."

He swallowed hard. Leaving her while she was still in danger no matter how minor the threat was killing him but if he didn't go now, he never would. "Yeah. Me, too. Take care, Sloan." He reached down and gave her a quick hug and then took off down the stairs to the platform. His boat had better be there because Sloan staring at him with those big eyes was too fucking painful. He rubbed his chest again.

"Your boat is here, sir," one of the crew members said.

"Thanks." Axe threw his stuff on the RHIB and then

jumped on board. The boat took off and sped away from the *Sea Jewel.* It took everything in his power not to turn around and look for Sloan on deck. She'd ripped his heart out already, and now she was working on his soul.

Ten minutes later, Axe yelled to the ensign driving the boat, "Um, where are you going? The ship is back that way." They'd passed the *William Fitzgerald,* and Axe had thought with all the traffic, maybe the ensign was just swinging around or even going for a short spin. Life on board a ship can be dull sometimes and getting out was a nice break. Now they were well past his ship and still moving at a good clip.

"My orders are to deliver you to the *Miracle Girl,*" the ensign yelled back.

"What? What's the *Miracle Girl*? Why am I going there? Did Schwartz tell you to take me there?"

Axe studied the ensign. He didn't recognize him, which wasn't necessarily unusual. The *Fitz* was a fair size, and he might not cross paths with everyone on board. Still, with MacGregor lurking somewhere, maybe he'd been too relaxed. The kid didn't seem particularly dangerous. He looked like he'd barely graduated high school but looks could be deceiving.

Axe shifted his weight over his feet so he could spring up if he needed. He opened the zipper on his backpack and shifted his weapon to the top. Then once he was sure the kid wasn't paying attention, he tucked his gun into the small of his back under his T-shirt.

He sat back and studied the kid. The ensign's uniform looked legit, and nothing about him triggered Axe in any way, but he'd had his head up his ass about Sloan, so maybe he wasn't the best judge of what's what at the moment.

The RHIB circled around another large container ship and then made a beeline for a midsize yacht that had seen better days. The closer they got, the more the *Miracle Girl* looked like it was a miracle she was still afloat. The yacht had to be forty years old. She was in desperate need of a paint job, and the wood probably hadn't seen polish in decades.

Axe studied the boat more carefully. She had what looked like a state-of-the-art communication system, but it was half covered by old canvas and a solid layer of dirt. As they swung around behind the boat, Axe realized the furniture was all ripped and patched with duct tape, but the equipment, like the anchor chain and ropes, only looked old on the surface. A closer inspection revealed they were shiny and new under all that dirt. The *Miracle Girl* looked bad, but underneath the veneer of neglect, she was actually a fully operational, fast as hell boat. Someone was trying to go incognito. Was it MacGregor? Axe was about to find out.

The ensign pulled the boat up next to the *Miracle Girl* and turned to look at Axe. "Uh, here you go, sir." He glanced at the boat again and then back at Axe. "Are you sure you want to board that tub? She looks like she might sink at any moment."

"Yes, she does, but sometimes looks are deceiving." Axe stood up and grabbed his backpack and slung it over his left shoulder. He let his right hand hover not far from his gun.

"If you say so, sir." The kid shook his head. "Better you than me," he muttered.

Axe moved to the edge of the launch. The waves were still high from the storm. He was going to have to throw his bag and then jump. He wasn't happy, but he didn't have a choice. He started to pull his gun out when a voice said, "Well, that's a hell of a welcome. Leave it in there."

Axe turned to the left in time to see a shadow detach from the inside cabin and move out onto the deck. "Son of a bitch! Tag, man, I am so happy to see you."

Nick Taggert stepped out into the bright sunshine. "Back at you, Axe." He offered his hand. Axe tossed over the backpack. Nick dropped it on the deck and then offered Axe a hand up. Axe made the jump, and the other man helped him land it safely.

"Damn good to see you, Tag." Hands still clasped, the men did a shoulder bump.

Axe stepped back and gave Nick the once-over. He looked good. A hell of a lot better than he had in Panama. His dark hair was a bit long still and he was sporting some stubble, but his blue eyes looked bright and watchful. Pain didn't lurk there like it used to. Axe was glad to see it. "You look good. Tanned, too. How long have you been here?"

Nick grinned. "Not that long at all. I'll explain in a minute, but the tan is from Morocco mostly. Been spending all of my downtime there."

"Morocco? Why?"

"Carolina is there now."

Axe smiled. "So that's how it is. Well, you look good, so it all must agree with you. You don't look like you're in pain anymore."

Nick moved his upper body. "I'm not. Carolina has helped me get back into shape so I'm all good. But enough about me. Let's go inside out of this heat." He turned and walked into the main cabin. Axe grabbed his backpack and followed.

"Hey, Axe Man," a voice called from his right.

As Axe's eyes adjusted from being out in the bright sunshine, he realized the room was full. "Well, shit, the gang is all here." Elias Mason was sitting on the sofa to his right. Next to him was Finn Walsh. Directly across the room, Cain Maddox sat on the opposite sofa.

"'Bout time you got your sorry ass over here," Elias said. "We hear you got yourself involved in quite a mess. We leave you alone for a couple months and all hell breaks loose."

"Funny." Axe shook his head as he dropped his backpack

in the corner and went to greet every man in the room. He finally gave a shoulder bump to Cain and crashed down beside him. He looked at the men across from him and over at Nick, who was leaning against the counter in the galley.

Axe's shoulders dropped down from his ears, and he took a deep breath, the first since he'd seen Sloan on board the *Sea Jewel*. These were his people. His team. No matter what happened now, he knew he wasn't on his own.

Elias was rubbing his leg and Finn was making an origami llama by the looks of things. He was also rolling his shoulder so he must still be struggling with his recovery from where he'd been shot. Cain still had a haunted look. There was obviously a lot of pain lurking behind his cool exterior. Axe wasn't in the best of shape either. He was still trying to figure out how to move forward after the fire. They were still Team RECON, as in reconstructed; Humpty Dumpties trying to put themselves back together again. The only one who looked like he was doing better was Nick. His back was healed, and he seemed happy. Maybe there was hope for the rest of them.

No matter what, they were all, in their own way, trying to get over the trauma in their lives. Thank God, Bertrand had decided to take the risk and make them a team. It was unorthodox, but Axe had no doubt it had saved their lives. None of them were any good at anything else in life besides being in the Coast Guard. They would all be lost without it. The fact that they were all here together again was like winning the lottery, or finally getting to go home. It just felt right.

Nick grabbed a chair from the table and put it at the front of the room. He sat down on it backwards, blocking the walkway into the galley. "To bring you up to speed, Axe, as soon as I got your email, I got on the phone to Admiral Bertrand. He immediately okayed me coming. He told me to grab the rest of the team. Turns out he was wary about this whole thing to begin with. Something just didn't sit right with him about a ship accidentally being jammed in the canal. So, he was happy to send us."

Axe cocked an eyebrow "I thought he was still pissed about the Panama thing."

Nick shrugged. "He's gotten over it. He got a lot of good press with the higher-ups for Panama. We've proven ourselves to be good as a team, and he wanted people who he could trust on this.

"Officially the U.S. Coast Guard has no jurisdiction, but the death of the American O'Mara gave Bertrand the opening he needed for you to explore a bit, Axe. When I got your distress call, he immediately told me to get the team together and get over here. He wants us to keep a low profile and find out what's really going on with the *Sea Jewel.*

"If things go well, maybe he'll make us official. If they don't, we all just go back to our normal jobs. Either way, he doesn't lose, and for him, it's also political. Saving the Tarchuarani was a big political win for him. He's looking to move up. Having us as a group under his wing gives him an advantage when it comes to getting things done.

"So, when did you guys arrive?" Axe asked. He leaned back into the sofa and put his boots up on the coffee table in front of him.

"Bertrand had us on a plane within a couple hours after I spoke to him. We got in last night. He had this boat waiting for us. He thought we might need to be on the water, but with the sandstorm, we opted to take some rooms at a local hotel. We just got into place maybe an hour ago."

Finn ran a hand through his hair. "I feel like I've got sand everywhere. I'm still chewing it. It's gonna be weeks before I get it out of my hair."

"Nothing like a little sandpaper scrub to get you all buffed and shiny." Elias grinned.

Axe snorted. "Well, I'm damn glad to see you all. This shit is unbelievable."

Cain turned to Axe. "Why don't you fill us in? We're lacking a lot of detail."

Axe nodded then preceded to lay out all that had transpired in the last twenty-four hours. When he finished, he couldn't believe it had only been maybe thirty hours since he set foot on the *Sea Jewel*. Once again, his relief at seeing his friends, his teammates, was overwhelming. Now he felt like they could actually make a difference, and maybe they could get justice for both Eddie and Zahra.

"So do you think that it's some kind of terrorist thing?" Nick asked.

Ax shook his head. "No. I think if it was a terrorist thing, we'd have heard something about it. Some group would be all over the Internet saying they did it, or they would've already hit somebody up for money or the release of prisoners. The CIA or the Department of Defense or someone would have heard increased chatter, and this wouldn't have been such a surprise. I think this is worse."

"Worse how?" Cain shifted on the sofa so he could see Axe better.

Axe took a deep breath. "This is gonna sound weird and kind of farfetched, but honestly I think someone did this to keep something on this side of the canal. They didn't want something to get through."

Finn leaned forward on the sofa. "You think someone blocked the Suez Canal to stop some ships from getting through? Seems like a big fucking deal to stop one ship. I mean, couldn't you have blown it up or sunk it some other way?"

"Crazy, right?" Axe shrugged. "The thing is, if it was one

ship, maybe it would be extreme, but what if you wanted to stop a few ships from getting through? You can't blow them all up or sink them in some sort of accidental way. If suddenly there was a rash of accidents by the Suez Canal, the whole world would pay attention. It would be obvious."

Elias grinned. "But blocking the Suez Canal isn't obvious at all."

The general laughter in the room did Axe's heart good. It had been a while since he'd had a laugh. "It is obvious, but it's almost so obvious it's a distraction."

Nick grabbed the sides of the chair and leaned back. "So, what you're saying is somebody really didn't want some ships to get through to the Med and you think what they did was lodged the *Sea Jewel* on purpose to block it, but did it in a way that everyone is paying attention to the blockage, not to the reason behind it."

Axe nodded. "If you think about it, it's rather ingenious. You get a ship. You drive too erratically and block the canal. Everyone is paying attention to the block. Did the ship lose power? Was it the weather? Was it pilot error? And now they're all wondering how will it get free. Will the heavy equipment work? Do they need more tugboats? When is the tide high? They're also all talking about the consequences. Cargo is not getting through and it's jamming up world trade, but nobody is looking at the specifics."

"Meaning someone is hiding the reason they did this in plain sight," Cain stated. "Makes sense."

Finn ran a hand over his face. "So, do you have any idea who's behind it or what ships they wanted to block?"

"Nah, I got nothing. With MacGregor possibly tapping all the offices with listening devices and possibly also getting into my laptop, it didn't seem wise to start doing research."

Nick reached over and grabbed a bottle of water off the shelf next to him. "With the number of ships lining up daily, it's going to take a heck of a lot of research to get this figured out."

"Agreed," Axe nodded. "I was hoping Bertrand might have an idea or could put some people on it."

Nick frowned. "I don't think the Admiral wants to put anyone else on this. He's sort of out on a limb. We're doing this on the down low. He's not going to want to pull in resources and draw attention to it."

"So, we're going to have to start doing some research?" Elias groaned. "I hate research."

Nick smiled. "I have a better idea. I have some friends I can call. They are ex-Navy and in the security game now. I worked with one of the guys when I was on a joint training mission with the SEALs, and I did a favor for them when I was working out of Hawaii. They operate a big firm out of New York. Callahan Security. I'll give Mitch a call. I'm willing to bet he can pull together the list of waiting ships and their owners faster than we can."

"So, what are we going to work on then?" Finn asked as he placed what looked like an origami elephant on the coffee table in front of him.

Nick got up off the chair. "A couple of things. We're gonna work on finding out about MacGregor and his guys. We need to know who they are, what they're up to, and where they are now. With that storm, they might have left the *Sea Jewel*, but there's no way they're out of the local area already. I'm sure the FBI already made calls to the Egyptians about stopping them on any kind of public transportation, like the airports or trains.

"I think they're still here somewhere on one of the many ships that are waiting to go through the canal. I mean, if they went into Port Taofik, they'd show up on someone's radar. The smartest place for them is on one of the many ships out here. It's not like anyone is going to search every ship, and even if the Egyptians decided to do just that, it would take weeks to get through every nook and cranny. Being out here is the best place for them to be."

"I agree," Axe said, "but if that's the case, how are we going to find them?"

Nick grinned. "Oh, I think we'll find them. They can't have gone too far. It's another thing I want to talk to Mitch about. Rumor has it his brother has a girlfriend who is a hacker. I have an idea how we can track them, but I'm going to need their help. In the meantime, start combing the Internet and make a note of anything that's occurred as a direct result of the canal being blocked."

Cain raised his eyebrows.

Finn asked, "Can you be more specific?"

"Not really." Nick shrugged. "Any event that's canceled because of lack of supplies or an event that's moved because of the blockage. Anything that stands out to you that its occurrence can be linked to the blockage. I think if we concentrate on that, it won't take long to find the man or woman behind this mess. No one is doing this for something that's small potatoes."

CHAPTER FOURTEEN

"Another dead body? This time a woman? What the hell is going on?" Omar paced back and forth in his hotel room.

There was a long sigh on the other end of the line. "The situation became difficult, and an extreme action had to be taken. It's regrettable, but sometimes these things do happen."

"Regrettable? Who is going to believe two deaths on board the ship is merely coincidence? Is the FBI really on board to investigate?" He drew a harsh breath. "What kind of a mess are you getting me involved in?"

"Mr. Balik." The man's voice sharpened. "It is you who involved us in this matter. It's true that it's taken an unfortunate turn, but things are still under control. Your name has not been associated with either death, or the incident in general. You need to remain calm and let us handle the situation."

"But the FBI? They're going to investigate—"

"They are on board to investigate the American's death. They have no jurisdiction over the Egyptian woman's death, nor does the Egyptian government want them here any longer than absolutely necessary. I have it on good authority they will be asked to leave in a matter of days. The situation is under control." There was a pause. "How are things on your end?"

Omar smiled. For once, things on his end were going well. They'd hammered out the last of the new deal last night. They were going to sign the paperwork tomorrow and have a celebratory dinner afterward. One more day. That was it. One more day, and then his life would change drastically. He couldn't wait to see the look on his father's face when he announced the deal had been signed. He had another surprise in store for his father and it was a big one. "Things on my end are good."

"Glad to hear it. I'll be in touch when things have calmed down." The line went dead.

CHAPTER FIFTEEN

S loan sighed as she lay back on the hotel bed. It was nice to be off the ship. Nothing was moving, no odd clanging or groaning from the cargo containers, and the bed was ginormous in comparison. It was the little things that made life good sometimes. Port Taofik wasn't huge, but it had a couple of restaurants and some decent stores to get anything she needed.

If only she were there with Axe. She'd been crushed when he'd left her on the deck of the *Sea Jewel* with nothing but a hug. She'd watched his boat until it was out of sight and then she borrowed some binoculars from one of the crew and watched some more. He hadn't gone back to the *Fitz* like he'd said he would. He'd gone past it. She surmised he was going to meet Nick Taggert and the rest of the team. He wouldn't share that with her even if they were still together. She only knew the guys because they'd asked her to write the articles on the Tarchuarani in South America.

Axe always drove her crazy. Just the thought of being with him was enough to get her all hot and bothered. She'd wanted him so much on the ship that morning, she just couldn't wait to feel him inside her. But now that was unlikely to ever happen again.

As much as she hated to admit it, maybe he was right. Maybe it really was better this way. They had fought like cats and dogs when they'd been together before. He didn't support her career either. Of course, he'd been right that she hadn't really supported his either. He'd been harsh with his criticism saying she would sacrifice everything for her career, even him. But, if she wanted to get to the top, didn't she have to sacrifice things?

She just needed to move on. Find someone who supported her choices and understood how important her career was to her. Axe obviously had no problem with that if his interaction with Saige Preston was anything to go by. He was flirting with her only hours after breaking up with Sloan.

She pushed those thoughts from her head. They weren't helpful. She glanced at her watch. It was almost time to go meet Charlie Philips. She wouldn't be in this mess if it weren't for Charlie. Of course, she wouldn't have had the story if it weren't for Charlie either. The man had been a friend of her father's, and he'd gone out on a limb for her so she could be on that ship. He couldn't have known it would turn into the nightmare that it became.

Sloan got up and threw some water on her face and then brushed her hair. She was taking Charlie out to dinner as a way of saying thanks for getting her on the ship. *The New York Times* had picked up some of her articles from her time on board, and she managed to sell a few more to other papers, too.

She walked into the restaurant that Charlie had recommended and immediately came to a stop. Leave it to Charlie to pick a place that was "authentic." She snorted. It was a tourist hell with every stereotype imaginable on display. There were low benches with cushions and low tables in front of them. The cushions were all done in red, as were the tables. The walls had varying pictures of scenes from around Egypt, and the wait staff were wearing what looked like costumes from a bad mummy movie.

Sloan scanned the restaurant and found Charlie. She walked over, gave him a quick hug. "Hey, Charlie." She sat down across from him. "Quite the restaurant you got going here."

"Yeah, they go in for the tacky Egyptian thing to attract tourists, but the truth is, the food is amazing."

Sloan smiled and picked up a menu. Charlie Philips was in his late 60s with thinning white hair and long sideburns. He had jowls like an old hound dog, and his neck was as big around as Sloan's thighs. He had a large belly and a permanent tan. He'd been in Egypt so long he probably wouldn't ever go back to being pale. But the thing about Charlie that always struck her was his sparkling blue eyes. They exuded intelligence and interest, and they literally glowed when he told a story. He was also the nicest man Sloan had ever met. He'd been like a second father to her.

She smiled at him again. "So, what's good here?"

"Everything. If you're okay with it, let me order."

"That's fine with me. You choose what you think I'll like. Are you still enjoying life in Cairo? How long are you in Port Taofik?"

"Cairo has changed, but I'm too old now to go anywhere else so I'm adapting. I'm here until the *Sea Jewel* is unstuck. The story is a good one, and everyone is interested."

The waitress came over and took their orders. Charlie also ordered a beer, but Sloan stuck with a soft drink. Things had rocked too much in her world of late, and she just wanted to go to bed without feeling crappy.

"How was it aboard the ship? That turned into a hell of a story."

Sloan filled Charlie in on what had happened aboard the *Sea Jewel*. She trusted Charlie to keep it all to himself. Plus, she didn't mind maybe sharing a byline with her old friend. "Now I have to find the interpreter to back up Zahra's story."

Charlie leaned back against the wall and uncrossed his legs. Sloan was finding it difficult to sit so low on the floor so she could only imagine how Charlie was doing it.

"You know, Sloan, finding the interpreter could be dangerous. If MacGregor is as bad as you say, he might be out for the interpreter, too."

"I know. That's why I have to find him first. I can't write the article until I have a corroborating witness."

"That's not exactly true." The waitress arrived and put the beer down in front of Charlie and the soda in front of Sloan. Charlie took a swig of beer and then continued speaking, "It really depends on the type of article you want to write. You just sat here, telling me Zahra's story. That's a human-interest piece. One I think millions of people would want to read. You personally interviewed her. She expressed her fears and her joy and all the things that make a human-interest story so appealing. You connected with her. Don't underestimate that. It's what makes a great story."

"But I'm trying to write a hard-hitting news story. I need at least two people to back up my facts."

"Why?"

"Why what?" Sloan asked.

"Why do you want to write a hard-hitting news story?"

Sloan blinked. "Well, because this is news, and it's news the world should know."

"Yes, it's definitely news the world should know, but why do *you* have to be the one to write the story?"

"Well, because I was there." What was Charlie driving at?

Charlie took another sip of his beer. "Sloan, I love you as if you were my own daughter but, sometimes, I think you're a little dense. The reason I brought you out here was because I thought you would connect with what Zahra had to say. I thought you might see the value of human-interest stories. You're a really good writer and a damn fine reporter, and that's what would make you so good with the human-interest angle. The problem is you keep trying to do hard news. There's nothing wrong with that, but it's not where you shine and, honestly, I don't think it's where your heart is."

Sloan was floored. She'd had no idea that Charlie thought she was better at human interests than news. Maybe he was right, but she wasn't ready to give up on the dream of being like her father, who'd won every award, including a Pulitzer. She needed to live up to that.

"I want to be like my father. I—"

"Your father was an asshole, Sloan. I know you idolize him but, really, he was just an asshole. He was an excellent reporter and I loved him like a brother, but he wasn't a nice person, and he wasn't kind, and he wasn't a good father. That's why he was such a great reporter. He went for the kill every single time…period. He asked all the hard questions all the time, but don't ever mistake that he was a good person. Sloan, *you* are a good person. This drive to be like your father is going to cost you so much more than you know. You have to ask yourself is it worth it?"

Sloan had difficulty breathing. No one had ever said anything bad about her father. Not once. And here was his best friend telling her that her father had been an asshole. She'd didn't know how to react. "But not every good reporter is an asshole. I wouldn't necessarily have to be an asshole to be good. I *am* good. My stories are good."

Charlie nodded. "Your stories are good, but they're good because you connect on a human level. Anyone can write the facts but putting those facts together in an entertaining way that captures people's imagination, that's what makes somebody good. Your father did it by being a bully, by not caring who he hurt. That's not who you are, or at least, that's not who you should want to be."

Sloan took a gulp of her drink. Charlie was giving her a whole lot to think about, and she wasn't loving how she was feeling about it. She knew in her heart of hearts she was great at the human-interest story. It really was the thing that made her happy. When she took a step back and looked at her best published stories, she knew Charlie was right.

He was also right about the cost. Going for the kill had cost her Axe. Her stomach rolled. Just like her father going for every story had cost him his wife and child. Axe had nailed it. He'd said she'd sell her soul for the story. Turns out she *was* just like her father only now she wasn't so sure that was a good thing. Losing Axe was a heavy price, and one she was pretty sure she didn't want to continue paying.

The food arrived, which provided a good distraction. She shut down that line of thinking and tried to keep the conversation light. And it turned out Charlie was right. It was excellent. After stuffing herself beyond belief, Sloan finally leaned back from the table. "So, you don't think I should try and find the interpreter?"

Charlie wiped his mouth with a napkin. "I think you don't have to find the interpreter to write a good story. I think you can write a great tribute to Zahra Nabil without bringing the interpreter into it and putting yourself in danger."

Sloan sighed. What he was saying was true. Maybe it was okay if she just wrote the human-interest story instead of the news story.

Charlie drank the last sip of his beer and put the bottle down on the table. "Besides, you're missing the most important part of this story."

"What do you mean? What's the most important part of the story?"

"The *why*. Why did Svensson, or whoever, block the canal on purpose?"

Sloan blinked. *Son of a bitch.* It had been right there, staring her in the face, and she'd missed it. She'd been so intent on proving Zahra's innocence, it hadn't occurred to her to ask why the canal was blocked in the first place. Another puzzle piece clicked into place. Axe. He encouraged her to pursue the interpreter angle because he knew it was less dangerous. He *knew* it would keep her away from the real story. Heat rose in her cheeks. "That asshole!" she said through clenched teeth. He said he was done protecting her because she refused to protect herself but really he just wanted her off the scent of the real story.

Charlie raised an eyebrow, but she just shook her head. She needed to calm down and concentrate. She reviewed the reasons someone would block the canal and agreed with Charlie that it had to be someone wanting to stop some sort of shipment from going somewhere. Charlie cocked his head. "I think based on the fact that the ship blocked it from this end, we can guess that it's something that was behind it, so that means going from here to the Mediterranean. The captain, or whoever, could block the canal, but he couldn't guarantee how long the canal would be blocked. So holding it up for even just a day had to matter."

Sloan started tapping her fingers on her thigh. "If someone holds up shipping so something doesn't make it to the Mediterranean, who benefits?" She paused. "That's not the right question. The right question is, who does it hurt if the shipments don't get through?"

Charlie pointed at her. "Now you're thinking."

"Well, all the goods that are going to Europe will be held

up, so whoever was receiving them either has to wait or they have to find a new source."

The waitress came by, and Sloan handed her the cash for the meal. Charlie slowly unfurled his legs and got to his feet. Sloan followed suit.

Charlie smiled down at her. "Now, my girl, you are on the right track. It's going to take a lot of digging, but I have no doubt you can find out the answer. Call if you need some help." Someone called his name and Charlie looked up and smiled at an attractive middle-aged Egyptian woman.

"Who's she?" Sloan asked.

"A friend," Charlie said and then gave her a look. "It's none of your business, young lady."

Sloan laughed and gave Charlie a hug. "Thanks for the pep talk. You've given me a lot to think about. I'll be in touch about the story." She turned and walked out leaving Charlie to chat with his 'friend.'

The hotel was only a ten-minute walk away, so she decided to stay on foot. By the time she got back to her room, she realized how exhausted she really was. Charlie had been right. Searching for the interpreter not only could be dangerous, but would be like looking for a needle in a haystack. And in the end, she already knew what he was going to say. No, the more important story was the why. She needed to investigate the why. And the rest of what Charlie said, about changing the focus of her career and the cost if she kept going like she was, well, she'd have to continue to think about that.

CHAPTER SIXTEEN

A xe sat down on the couch in the salon in the same place he'd left a couple of hours ago. They were all gathered because Bertrand was on the phone, and he wanted to speak to them as a team, or so Nick had said.

"We're all here, sir." Nick straddled the chair once again, resting his arms on the back.

"Good. Gentlemen, I appreciate you mobilizing so quickly. I know I didn't give you much notice. Your speed is appreciated." There was a pause. "This canal business is delicate. The Egyptian government is not pleased that the FBI is there, but they felt they had no choice but to 'invite' them since the death happened on the ship that was blocking the canal. Political pressure was brought to bear."

Bertrand cleared his throat. "Cantor, the report you emailed, set off alarm bells all the way up the line. Everyone is on edge about this situation. Having the canal blocked is wreaking havoc around the world. The thought that it could have been done on purpose has all of Washington in an uproar. I have assured the higher-ups that you wouldn't have sent out a distress signal if it wasn't serious."

There was a pause, and Axe realized he needed to say something. "Sir, we are now sure the canal was blocked on purpose. It has been confirmed by several sources." Great. Now, he sounded like Sloan. "I even have some photos of equipment that we think was used to help wedge the ship."

Bertrand swore long and loud. "Do you know who is behind it?"

"No, sir," Nick cut in, "but we have some leads to follow. We don't think it's a terrorist organization, and it doesn't seem like it was done for political reasons."

"Well, that's something at least." Bertrand sighed.

Nick glanced around the room before he spoke. "We're following up on a few things. I don't want to get into it yet until we have a firm grip on what's happening, sir."

Bertrand grunted. "Fine. I want everything in a very detailed report. I have to run this up the flagpole."

"Yes, sir," Nick responded.

"Gentleman, I don't have to remind you how delicate this situation is. The Coast Guard has no authority whatsoever there. You need to tread lightly. No blowing up warehouses. No piles of dead bodies. No involving the Navy of any country. Do I make myself clear?"

"Yes, sir," the whole team said in unison. Axe grinned, and Elias had to cover his laugh with a cough.

There was a loud sigh on the phone. "What I am about to tell you is off the record. The top brass at Homeland liked what you guys accomplished in Ecuador. It gave them inside information, and they were able to turn it into some sort of bargaining chip.

"Because of that success, they were happy to send Cantor over to the *Sea Jewel* when they found out he happened to be in the canal. They are willing to give me latitude on this and let you all run with what you've got but, make no mistake, if you fuck up, you'll be up for court martial so fast it will make your head spin. You all are out there on your own. There's only so much interference I can run. So, again…don't fuck up. Don't even think about fucking up. It's not just your asses on the line. Remember that.

"On the other hand, if this goes well, they are inclined to let me keep you as a unit permanently. They see a lot of applications for this unit, and Homeland likes the idea. A lot. It gives them trained operators at the ready. Makes them feel like one of the big boys at the table along with the CIA, FBI, Navy, and the rest. So, one final time, do not fuck this up."

"Yes, sir," Nick replied. "Thank you for being so candid. We appreciate it."

Bertrand grunted in reply. "Is there anything I should know before I go?"

"Ah, we do need a bit of help with something," Nick responded.

"Christ." It came out as a sigh. "What do you need?" Bertrand demanded.

Nick rolled his shoulders. "We need a list of the ships that are waiting to enter the canal on both sides. We need to know where they're coming from, where they're going, and who owns them. I have some…friends I can ask for this information if it's okay with you."

There was a moment of silence. "Why do you need it? What is it you're looking for?" Bertrand asked.

Nick glanced at Axe and gave him a nod.

Axe leaned forward on the couch. "Sir, it's Axel Cantor. I think the group that jammed up the canal were guns for hire. Someone doesn't want something to go through the canal." Axe proceeded to fill in Bertrand on his theory.

"And you want to find the correlation. I get it. Do you have anything else to go on? Any clue as to what links the ships?"

Axe's heart hammered against his ribs. Admitting to his

boss that this was all a hunch scared the hell out of him. This man held Axe's entire career in his hands. "Uh, no, sir, but I am confident we'll know it when we see it."

Axe glanced around the room. Nick nodded again. Elias did the same. Cain and Finn both smiled slightly to show their support. His team was behind him. He eased out a pent-up breath, and the vise around his chest eased a little.

Nick stood up. "Sir, we're confident we can figure this out with a bit of help and some resources."

"Okay, Taggert. You can ask your friends. Just...don't fuck it up." Bertrand ended the call.

Axe leaned back on the couch. "Well, that went better than I thought it would."

"Yeah, I didn't know the old man liked us so much," Finn commented as he grabbed a bottle of water off the coffee table.

"I'm not sure he does. He just likes to look good and, so far, we've made that happen. You heard him. If we don't screw this up, we get to permanently be a team." Nick looked around the room. "I don't know how you all feel, but that sounds good to me."

The knot in Axe's gut unfurled a bit. Being with this team was the only time he'd truly relaxed. It had been the time he felt the most normal since the accident.

"So, let's not fuck this up," Cain said in a quiet voice. Axe glanced over at his teammate. Cain wasn't much of a talker, and he kept pretty much to himself, so it was good to know he needed the team too. There were nods all around. No one wanted to go back to their regular assignments.

Nick glanced at his watch. "It's close to dinner time. We have one more call to make, and then we'll figure out food." He reached over and tapped his phone screen. A few seconds later, there was ringing and then a receptionist answered the phone. Nick gave his name and made his request.

Less than a minute later, the phone was taken off hold. "Nick Taggert! Jesus, it's been a minute. How the hell are you?" A loud boisterous voice filled the salon of the yacht.

"Mitch Callahan, I'm doing well. Thanks for taking my call."

"Seriously? We almost got our asses shot off together during a training exercise. Of course I'm going to take your call. What's up? Are you looking for a job? I could sure use someone with your skills."

Nick grinned. "Nope, still with the Coast Guard and not looking for work, but thanks for the offer. Business must be booming."

"Yeah, it's booming alright. I can't keep up, and good help is hard to find. Seriously, if you ever think about getting out and want a private gig, call me. I need people I can count on."

"I'll keep that in mind. You're on speaker by the way, and my team is here with me. I need a favor."

"We owe you one for Hawaii, so that's fair. Where's here and what's the favor?" Mitch asked.

There was a squeak and then a soft thunk. Axe grinned. He'd know that sound anywhere. Callahan had just leaned back in his chair and put his feet up on something, most likely his desk. Axe liked the guy immediately.

Nick sat back down on the backward chair. "We're on the Suez thing and need a bit of help."

Mitch whistled. "I do not envy you that mess. Is the USCG helping to dig the *Sea Jewel* out?"

Nick paused. "Not exactly."

"Forget I asked," Mitch said. "What do you need?"

"It's…complicated. My team and I are operating sort of outside the normal lines of communication. The admiral that pulled us together wants this done on the down-low."

"Right." Mitch was silent for a second. "I heard you were

involved in something sketchy in South America. You off saving the world again?" Nick waited a beat and then Mitch said, "Don't answer that. I probably don't want to know. So, what can I help with?"

"I'm gonna provide you a little bit of background. This is Axel Cantor. He's going to explain."

"Hey Mitch, it's Axe. I was on the *Sea Jewel* because an American died on board the ship. There were a group of men there acting as some sort of security force. We're thinking mercenaries, former special ops guys, but from all over the world. I can't really get into details as to why they were there, but they left during a sandstorm. We know they haven't gone far, so we're thinking they're on some of the ships that are out here waiting to go through the canal, but we need to track them. Taggart says that if anybody could figure this out, you and your brothers can."

"You don't ask for much, Axe." Mitch laughed. "There was a group of mercenaries on a container ship, and now you want to find out where they went."

Nick nodded. "That about sums it up, Mitch."

"Give me a second." Music played in the background as Mitch had put them on hold.

Elias took a swig of his water. "You got some idea on how you're going to track these guys, Tag?"

Axe leaned forward. "You're thinking about tracking their cells, aren't you?"

Nick had opened his mouth to respond when Mitch came back on the line. "Nick Taggart, Axel Cantor, and the rest of you gentlemen, meet my brother Gage Callahan."

"Gage, we spoke before in Hawaii," Nick said.

"I remember, and thanks again for your help."

Nick said, "I've heard a lot about you from your brother and others. I know some of your former colleagues."

Gage laughed. "I don't know if that's a good thing or a

bad thing, but I'll take it either way. My brother tells me you're looking for some help tracking some men down. What do you have in mind?"

Nick nodded at Axe. "Hi, Gage, it's Axe Cantor. We were wondering if you can track cell phones for us but, here's the thing, the cell phones were on the *Sea Jewel* up until this afternoon. Now we need to find out where they are, and we don't have the numbers."

"I'm guessing these are burner phones. Mitch tells me you're trying to track a bunch of mercenaries in the Suez, so that's a logical assumption."

"Yeah, that about sums it up. We need to see if we can find where MacGregor and his goons have gone." Axe leaned back on the couch again.

"MacGregor? Hamish MacGregor?" Mitch asked.

Axe raised his eyebrows in surprise. "Yeah, you know him?"

"Fucking animal. I came across him in the SEALs. He was working with the SAS at one point, but they kicked him out. The man has no morals. He's a serious gun for hire, and he doesn't draw the line at anything. Last I heard, he was working for Silverstone."

"Fucking Silverstone," Nick growled. "Why is it every time there's a shitstorm, Silverstone is in the middle of it?"

"That's a damn good question," Gage growled "I've had a few run-ins with them myself, and I know our other brother Logan has tried a couple cases against a few of their members before they were with Silverstone. He used to be with the JAG Corps. Nothing sticks to these guys. They're like fucking Teflon. They have some serious pull."

Nick crossed his arms over the back of the chair. "Do you think that means some government might be involved in this?"

Axe hadn't thought of that. Their last run-in with Silverstone had involved a rogue government plot. Was some government trying to wreak havoc on the global shipping industry?

"Not necessarily," Mitch responded. "The last I heard, Silverstone expanded internationally and are taking on all kinds of clients. Like I said, good help is hard to find. I keep running up against these Silverstone types, and I won't hire them. They're dangerous, and you can't trust them. They can always be bought by the highest bidder."

Gage cleared his throat. "Back to the question at hand. Can we track these Silverstone guys that were on the *Sea Jewel* even if they're using burner phones and we don't have their numbers? The short answer to this is yes. Here's the long answer.

"I'm sure you guys use burner phones, and I know we certainly use them in our business, but the truth of the matter is they aren't really anonymous. Since 2005, the United States has mandated that all cell phones have GPS trackers in them. We can grab the data and find out what cell numbers were on the ship, and then we can go looking for those cell numbers in the surrounding area."

Axe spoke up. "If you don't mind me asking, how do you do that?"

Gage cleared his throat. "My better half is a computer expert. As she explained it to me, she'll triangulate all the calls in the area and find the ones that fit the location of the *Sea Jewel*. Then she'll look for those numbers in the surrounding area. The thing is, once she has the numbers from the *Sea Jewel*, she really only has to look for a similar grouping. MacGregor's guys will all be together at this point, so it won't be hard to find them. If you want to know which number belongs to which man, it's a little harder, but not impossible.

"All cell phone calls are really just data, ones and zeros

that are read by a computer. This data is collected all the time. It's been collected for years. There's a publicly traded company here in the US that has this data. They can pull up every cell phone call that's been made in the last so many years." Gage gave a quiet snort. "Now, it's time-consuming and very labor-intensive so they don't do it unless it's a dire emergency. They wouldn't go back through the data and download the actual call for me.

"With the numbers in hand, however, I can make some calls and backtrack the numbers to see when they first showed up, then follow their movements all around the globe. By seeing what other numbers they interact with in what locations, it becomes easy to figure out who uses each burner phone. This is the system law enforcement and intelligence agencies are now using to track down criminals and terrorists." The sound of something hitting wood sounded through the phone, as though Gage had rapped his knuckles on the table.

"That's some scary shit. Sorry, this is Finn Walsh. Anonymity is well and truly dead."

"Yes, it is," Gage agreed. "Burner phones aren't really anonymous, but the reality is no one's coming looking for you unless you're a terrorist or a major drug lord. It's just not feasible to track down every criminal. It would take way too long and way too many people. The expense would be astronomical."

"You can do this without any…issues?" Nick asked. "We wouldn't want you to do something that would put you in a difficult position."

"We can do this. You're not asking for conversations. You're asking for locations. Much easier."

Mitch chimed in, "This makes me so damn glad I'm out of the 'saving the world' business. I'm having a hard enough time just saving my clients. I don't envy you guys. Being the front line against terrorism is an uphill battle. We'll work on it asap and get back to you as quick as we can."

Nick cleared his throat. "Um, we need one more thing."

Mitch chuckled. "Why am I not surprised? Shoot."

"We need a list of the ships waiting to go through the canal and who owns them."

"Shouldn't be too much of an issue," Gage said.

"Thanks, guys. We owe you one," Nick said as he stood up.

Mitch laughed. "I would have said we're even, but you asked for two things so, damn straight, you owe me. Next time you're in town, the beers are on you."

"Agreed." Nick clicked off the call.

Finn stretched his arms above his head. "I don't think I'll ever look at a cell phone the same way."

Elias stood. "Yeah, Uncle Sam's spying ability is scary as hell. Glad we're on the right side of it."

Axe and Cain also got to their feet.

Nick looked around the room. "Maybe we should discuss something now. We're out here on our own. If we succeed, we're golden, and we get to keep this team together. If we screw up or cause an international incident, we will be the scapegoats and our asses will be court-martialed. Bertrand will do everything in his power to help us but, let's be honest, the higher-ups in Homeland Security aren't likely to listen to him. They'll need people to blame, and that will most likely be us."

Elias snorted. "That's a cheery thought."

"I just want you guys to keep it in mind. We don't want to do anything that's going to kill anyone's career." Nick ran a hand through his hair.

They all nodded.

"Now, who's hungry? I'm making steak." Nick moved the chair out of the way and started toward the galley. He called over his shoulder, "Elias, you guys keep going on the research from this afternoon. We'll check in after dinner and see what everyone turned up."

Axe still hadn't gotten out of the salon since he stepped on the ship. He'd hunkered down there when he was doing research earlier. He grabbed his backpack and headed down the stairs. After passing Nick in the galley, he went down another set of stairs to the berths.

The third door on the left had an empty bunk. He entered the room and threw his backpack in the corner. He immediately sat down on the bed and put his hands over his face. Fatigue washed over him. He hadn't relaxed really since he'd seen Sloan on the *Sea Jewel*. He was tired and hungry. He was also…sad.

He missed Sloan.

There was a hole in his chest where his heart used to be or at least that was what it felt like. Leaving her was the right decision but it just sucked.

After what Bertrand said, there was no way he could connect with Sloan again. If she wrote an article that blew the lid off this and mentioned Axe, he'd be the one dead in the water. The best he could hope for was Sloan was distracted in her search for the interpreter. The longer she was out of the way, the better it was for everyone concerned.

CHAPTER SEVENTEEN

S loan sat up in bed. She couldn't sleep.

How could he? How could Axe point her away from the true story? She'd gotten caught up in the drama of Zahra's innocence and missed seeing the bigger picture. She knew how. He wanted to keep her safe as long as he could. He knew she would jump headlong into the story without thinking about the consequences and he was trying to keep her safe from herself. Well, he was gone and what she did was not his business anymore.

Flipping back the covers, she crawled out of bed and started pacing in the hotel room. The big navy-colored T-shirt she had on was an old one of Axe's. She couldn't bring herself to throw it away, even though they weren't together any longer. Now it was like salt in her wound.

It was only just after ten, but she was exhausted and really needed a good night's sleep. Sadly, her brain wouldn't let her relax enough to make that happen. She was just too incensed.

The fact that he wanted her out of the way, steering her to chase down the interpreter, meant he thought digging around and trying to find out who hired MacGregor to block the canal was dangerous. She resented being pushed out of harm's way like some errant child. Where did he get off making decisions about her safety without consulting her? And to think she'd been so impressed with him being supportive. She should have known better. *Asshole*.

She was pursuing this story no matter what anyone said.

Sloan tapped her fingers on her thigh as she continued to pace. He was probably right. It would be dangerous, but she didn't care. She was a good reporter, and she craved this story. She was going to damn well figure it out and write about it. To hell with the consequences.

Charlie's words came unbidden into her mind. Did she really want to write this story? Wasn't it better to tell Zahra's story? And what about Eddie? He would want her to go for it. To follow the story no matter where it led but what about *his* story? He was a great reporter and a good guy. She could write a great piece about him.

She sighed. The thing was she could write Zahra and Eddie's stories later but if she wanted to get the scoop on this story, the story of the canal blockage, she had to do that now. She went over to the desk and flipped open her laptop. Who benefited? That was always a good place to start. She needed to figure out who was getting something from the canal being blocked.

Maybe she should ask Charlie for help. Then again maybe not. He'd been pretty clear on what he thought her strengths were, and chasing this story wasn't part of them.

She pulled up a few of the financial papers. Assuming this was a business thing, which seemed likely, figuring out what new deals were being made might provide a clue.

She flopped down hard into the chair in front of the desk. She could look in the newspapers for days and still not figure out who was behind this. There had to be a better way.

She leaned back and looked around the room. Her gaze landed on Eddie's fedora. What would Eddie do? She sighed and rubbed her face with both hands. She seemed to spend her entire existence as a reporter wondering what other people would do. First her father and now Eddie. What should *she* do was the real question.

She stood up again, grabbing Eddie's hat off the desk. She plunked it on her head. "Okay, I'm an ace reporter. I know what I'm doing. I'm not a fraud," she said. Sometimes it helped her imposter syndrome feelings if she said those words aloud. She paced the length of her room once more.

"What do I do? How do I determine who benefits from the canal blockage?" Sloan liked to talk to herself. It helped keep her thoughts straight. Of course, she only did it when she was alone. She'd never hear the end of it if she talked to herself in front of other reporters.

She needed a list of what ships were waiting to go through the canal at both ends. Then she needed to find who owned the ships. She could get the first from the Suez Canal Authority but the latter would take some digging. Charlie was just going to have to help her whether he liked it or not. She was tired of men telling her what to do and not being supportive. Screw them. They would bend to her will this time.

She went back over to the desk and sent an email off to Charlie, saying what she needed. He was bound to have some intern or other who could help with this. She'd even share the byline if he contributed to the story.

That done, she went back to pacing. Blocking the canal was dicey business. They would have had this planned and the equipment all lined up well before the *Sea Jewel* got to the Suez. What if it had gone wrong and only blocked part of the canal? The ships coming from the opposite direction would have the right of way. No, they knew that, so that's why Svensson had to block the canal at the narrowest point. He zigzagged to cover what he was doing. It wasn't like he could turn a hard right and no one would notice.

How did they know Svensson would cooperate? Did they pick him randomly? Sloan shook her head, making the fedora wiggle a bit. No. They needed a big ship to make sure they blocked the whole thing. They must have chosen the ship first and then coerced Svensson into it. Was he a victim? She needed to know more about him. Maybe it was blackmail.

Sloan walked over to the laptop and sent another email to Charlie requesting background on Svensson, including his financials. Money troubles were often the reason behind people doing stupid things. Sloan frowned. Charlie was just trying to look out for her. She knew that deep down. What he'd said had stung, but she knew he loved her like the daughter he'd never had. He was only trying to help. Why did the men in her life think she needed help?

That was a question for another time. She just didn't have the energy to tackle it right now.

As Sloan stretched her arms above her head, she knocked off the fedora. She had bent down to pick it up when she noticed a piece of paper sticking out of the inside. It had been tucked under the inner band. She plucked the paper out, and then plunked the hat back on her head. She unfolded the paper. It was Eddie's handwriting. There was a phone number and a name. Then there were a couple of questions like Eddie was trying to work the problem but then they were crossed out like he'd eliminated them. Under that was a statement that made Sloan gasp.

Could it be? No. That wasn't possible. Was it? The blood raced through her veins as the implications of Eddie's note hit her like a freight train. That would change everything. Every. Single. Thing.

CHAPTER EIGHTEEN

A xe looked up from his screen and rubbed his eyes. It was just after midnight, and his vision was starting to blur. "Sorry, guys, but I'm packing it in. I can't see straight anymore. I need to crash."

Nick looked up from his place at the galley table. "I'm with you." He ran a hand through his hair. "I'm not getting anywhere, and my brain has gone foggy. Let's pick it up in the morning."

Axe turned to check on Elias who was beside him on the couch, but Elias was already asleep. He usually burned the candle at both ends so Axe wasn't surprised to see him passed out already. He'd probably been to at least one all night poker game this week before Nick had called. Axe nudged him. "Elias, wake up, man."

Elias sat up. "I was just resting my eyes."

Axe snorted. "Right. We're calling it a night. Go get some shut-eye."

Elias shut his laptop and stood up. "Night, Axe. Night, Tag," he mumbled before he disappeared down the stairs.

"Where are Cain and Finn?" Axe asked.

"Cain's on overwatch duty, keeping an eye on everything out there, and Finn crashed a while ago. He's next up for overwatch." Nick stood and stretched his arms above his head as he yawned.

"Glad to see your back is better," Axe said as he closed his laptop.

"Me, too," Nick agreed. "I wasn't sure it would ever go back to normal It still feels a bit different, but the scar tissue has calmed down, and I'm back to one hundred percent." He glanced at Axe's arms. "How are your burns?"

Axe fisted his hands. He hated talking about his burns. Blood rushed through his veins as he tried to control the anger that churned in his gut. Nick was asking as his team leader, as his Master Chief, not to be nosy. Axe knew it, but it didn't make having the conversation any easier.

"They're fine," he growled.

Nick just stood there, staring at him.

Axe stood up slowly and unclenched his fists. "Really, Tag, they're fine. They don't hurt, and they don't interfere with my ability to use my hands and arms in any way. They're just…a reminder that I screwed up. That's all."

"Axe, you—"

"Hey, Finn," Axe said as Finn came into the salon area. "Your turn to be on watch?"

Finn nodded. "Yup. Just going to make some coffee before I go up. You guys want some?"

Axe shook his head. "Nope. I'm headed to bed." He nodded to Finn and then walked by Nick, avoiding his gaze. He didn't want to talk about what happened, and he didn't need to hear a lecture about letting things go and moving on. This wasn't something he could let go of. It was literally burned into him.

Axe opened his eyes and glanced at his watch. It was seven a.m. He'd slept longer than he'd thought, and it was good sleep. He thought he would toss and turn all night, but exhaustion had overwhelmed him, and he'd crashed hard. He rolled off his bunk and went directly into the shower. Ten minutes later, dressed in jeans and a white long-sleeved T-shirt, he made his way to the galley. Something smelled good.

"Hey, Sleeping Beauty," Elias called as Axe came up the stairs.

"Morning." Axe looked around. Cain was cooking what looked like eggs and home fries at the stove. Elias and Finn were sitting at the galley table, drinking coffee. "Where's Tag?"

"He's keeping an eye on things topside," Cain said as he stirred the home fries in the pan.

"Is that really necessary?" Axe asked as he made his way over to the coffee pot. He grabbed a mug and poured himself a cup. It was strong and black, just the way he liked it.

Finn shrugged. "I think it's less about security than just keeping an eye on what's generally going on. A fleet of tugs arrived overnight. Rumor has it they'll try to move the *Sea Jewel* today."

That was news to Axe, and it shouldn't have been. He was the one with all the contacts. He'd built up a network of people who supplied him with information over the years. He'd become something of a legend for it. So how come no one had told him?

He pulled his cell out of his back pocket and checked his email. They did tell him. Yesterday. He'd just forgotten to check his phone. Shit. He leaned against the counter, his phone in one hand and coffee in the other. Scrolling through his email, he found he'd missed quite a few things.

Axe took a sip of coffee. "It looks like today is a trial run.

If they can't free the *Sea Jewel* today, they'll go for it tomorrow night. More tugs are on the way and will be here then. It's also a full moon with a very high tide. It's the best chance they'll have to free the ship. If that doesn't work, they have a group of Dutch advisors on standby, and our Navy has offered a team of dredging experts."

"So, the whole thing could be over in forty-eight hours," Nick said as he entered the galley. He went over and sat down next to Finn.

"Looks like it," Axe agreed. "The general consensus of my sources seems to be, if the tugboats don't get her out in the next two days, then it's going to be weeks before she'll be free. Dredging takes a while."

Cain pulled down five plates and started plating up the food. "How reliable are your sources?"

"Reliable. The ones I'm hearing from are in the Egyptian Navy, and they have friends that work for the Suez Canal Authority."

"How do you know these people?" Elias held out his empty coffee cup.

Axe grabbed it and refilled it. "These guys were over in Bahrain for a training exercise. We drank some beers together. They're good guys." He handed the cup back to Elias. "Tag, you want coffee?"

Nick shook his head. "I've already had my quota for the morning."

Cain handed everyone a plate then sat down at the table next to Elias. Axe remained standing, eating at the counter. The food was good. Cain always added something to the eggs that made them taste better than when Axe made them.

"You know what all this means, right?" Finn said between bites. "Whoever blocked the canal is on a deadline. It's been blocked for four days. Say it takes two more to move the *Sea*

Jewel. That's only six days. Is that enough time to do whatever it is that they wanted to do?"

Elias swallowed. "Do you think they'll do something else to sabotage the removal efforts? Is that what you're getting at?"

Finn nodded.

"I don't think so." Axe swallowed his last bite of food. "MacGregor and his team wouldn't have left if they thought they might have to stop the ship from being freed."

"I thought they left to avoid the FBI." Elias got up and put his dirty plate in the sink.

Axe nodded. "They did. But think about it. If you were paid to do a job, would you leave before it was finished? Silverstone wouldn't let you get away with that shit. They could have stayed a couple of extra days if they needed to. It would take a while for Zahra Nabil's autopsy to come back and reveal she was murdered. It would be risky but it would still be doable. They had time, but they left. I think there's a ninety percent chance they accomplished their objective, and it doesn't matter now when the *Sea Jewel* is freed."

Nick put his fork down on his plate. "I agree with Axe. They don't care about the *Sea Jewel* any longer, which means whoever wanted the canal blocked either accomplished their goal or made it a foregone conclusion that it would happen."

Cain took a sip of coffee. "Are we any closer to knowing what the goal is or who's behind this?"

"Bertrand sent an email already, demanding to know our progress. Thankfully, Mitch Callahan sent the list of ships through and texted that he wanted us to call him in"—Nick glanced at his watch—"twenty minutes."

"Wait, isn't it the middle of the night back in New York?" Elias asked.

"It's twelve-thirty a.m. We're seven hours ahead. Mitch said he has the information for us, and he wants to discuss it." Nick stood up and gathered the rest of the plates and then took them over to the sink. "Axe, it's your turn to clean up."

Axe nodded and started gathering the dirty pots as the other men filed out of the galley to the salon and then onto the deck. Axe filled the sink with water. Sloan had always made fun of him for doing dishes by hand. Then laughed when he tried to justify it by saying he never felt like the dishwashers got them as clean.

Sloan. God, he hoped she was safe somewhere far away from here. He didn't want MacGregor to even be tempted to try anything with Sloan. It had damn near killed him to leave her standing on that deck. He had longed to go with her and make sure she was safe. But if she wouldn't take care of herself, then how could he?

Really what he wanted to do was take her to a Caribbean Island where they could spend their days at the beach and their nights in bed. But that wasn't going to happen. Those days were over. Sloan was his kryptonite. Dangerous as hell for him to be around. She had the ability to destroy him. She'd already ripped his heart out once with the whole article about the Coast Guard screw up. He just couldn't let her get that close ever again.

Axe pulled up his sleeves and stared at his scars. They were ugly. The skin was all mottled and still quite reddish. He didn't really have to worry about Sloan. These scars were enough to scare any woman off. Damn good thing no one could see the ones on the inside. Everyone would go running for the hills.

Twenty minutes later, the men were all seated in their usual spots in the salon. "Mitch," Nick said, "thanks so much for getting back to us so quickly. What have you got for us?" Nick sat down in his chair backward.

"Hey, Nick. I'm assuming all the guys are there, too."

"Yes, they're all here."

"Good. We emailed you the list. Good luck with that. There's a shitload of ships. Let us know if you want some help. As for the cell phones… We pulled the information you wanted. There was a total of forty-four cell phones on board the *Sea Jewel*. We got the crew and passenger list, so we know there were thirty-four crew members including MacGregor and his men. There were six reporters, the pilot, and Axe. That leaves two extra cell phone numbers."

Axe leaned forward. "Did you manage to trace which cell phones belong to MacGregor and his people?"

"Hi, guys, it's Gage. We traced the ones that were registered in people's names. There were twenty phones registered to crew members. And, of course, the eight that were registered to the reporters, the pilot, and you, Axe. That leaves sixteen burner phones, but among those, there were six that, when we looked at the calls, we realized they were being used to call back to countries that correspond to crew members' places of residence. So, they're calling their girlfriends or their bookies or someone that they don't want to use their regular phone to reach."

Nick leaned forward in the chair. "So that's ten phones you think are linked to MacGregor?"

"Possibly. We tracked eight of those numbers to a ship in the Gulf of Suez. We believe those are MacGregor and his men."

"Gage, it's Cain. What about the other two phones?"

"Our assumption is that Svensson, the captain, has one, and the other is probably an extra someone brought on board for some reason. Maybe one of MacGregor's men left it behind."

Nick asked, "You have the location of MacGregor's men though, right?"

"We know that eight cell phones that were on the *Sea*

Jewel are now on the *Green Leaf.* We're assuming those belong to MacGregor and his men."

Axe's blood started to thrum. It was always this way when he was on an op. The closer he got to his quarry, the more his body came alive. He smiled. "That's great work."

Nick agreed. "Axe is right. We owe you guys for sure on this one. Great job."

"Thanks. Happy to help. We'll keep digging and see if we can turn up anything else on MacGregor and his men."

Mitch's voice filled the room. "Good luck, boys. Let us know if you need anything else. My bed is calling."

"Thanks again, Mitch," Nick said and then clicked off the call. "So, what do you guys think?"

Axe stood up. He was getting restless. "I think we need to call Saige, the FBI agent on the *Sea Jewel*, and confirm with her that she needs to speak with MacGregor and his men, so they are officially wanted for questioning. Then we need to loop in Bertrand so we have the proper permission to aid the FBI in the apprehension of suspected criminals who may have been involved in the murder of an American citizen. After that, we need to go get those bastards on the *Green Leaf*."

CHAPTER NINETEEN

"Charlie, I need to find him. He needs to know this." Sloan spoke into her cell as she walked down the narrow street.

"Sloan, I understand what you're saying, but if Axe is not on his ship, I'm not sure how I can help." He let out a long sigh.

"I need the list of ships. I think he's with his other team. That's my guess, anyway. I know the team leader is here. I saw a text on Axe's phone and when he left the *Sea Jewel*, he didn't go back to his ship. He went further down the gulf. My guess is the whole team is here.'

"Who is this team?" Charlie asked.

Sloan hesitated. Charlie was first and foremost a reporter, and the existence of Team RECON, as they called themselves, wasn't something they wanted blasted all over the place. "It's just a group of guys that has worked together in the past. They're a good team and good at solving problems. This is a problem. I am sure they're all here now, and I need to find them."

"Can you tell me what's so important?"

"I figured out something. About what happened on the *Sea Jewel*. I'm afraid Axe is in danger."

Charlie was silent for a second. "You think he's on a boat in the Suez Gulf? I can hit up the Port Authority and ask about the boats that arrived in the last twenty-four hours. Will that help?"

"Yes, that would be very helpful. I just can't shake the feeling that Axe is in trouble. He really needs to know this information and he won't take my calls."

"Sloan, this sounds like it's getting more dangerous. You need to be careful."

"I'm trying. I don't want to attract any unwanted attention. I just need to find Axe. This information could change everything. As it is, I am worried he's put himself in danger without knowing it."

CHAPTER TWENTY

O mar's cheeks hurt from smiling. He was tired of the
Germans. He wanted to go celebrate on his own
terms. The waitress finally brought the bill, which the
Germans insisted on picking up. *As they should.* They were
getting a great deal on the finest Turkish textiles available.
And he was getting rich. Not rich from his father's deals, but
rich from his own. This deal gave him what he craved most, a
seat at the table. He was now a force to be reckoned with,
and his father was going to have to give him his due.

Omar felt a small pang in his chest. Going after his
father's position as the head of the company had always been
the plan, but he imagined doing it with his father's blessing.
Now with this deal, it was his moment. He could point to all
the work he did and the outcome that was vastly more favor-
able than anything his father had done lately. He'd already
spoken to a few members of the board, and they'd agreed to
back him. The elder Balik was being too cautious these days,
and the board was getting tired of his conservative ways.

Still, his father was an intelligent and powerful man and
Omar would be a fool to underestimate him. Hakan Balik

would be floored that he was being usurped by his son. He would also be enraged, and his father could be a vindictive bastard. Omar would have to be very careful if this coup attempt was going to be successful.

He'd earned it, though. All the work and abuse he'd taken from his father over the years had culminated in this deal, and Omar was not going to miss out on his chance to run the company. After all, wasn't it his father who drilled into him not to miss out on any opportunity presented to him?

Twenty minutes later, Omar was back at his hotel and heading up to his room when he noticed a very attractive woman at the bar. He slowed his step and made a decision. One more drink wouldn't hurt. He smiled. It was finally his turn to celebrate.

He walked up to the woman. "Can I buy you a drink?"

CHAPTER TWENTY-ONE

Axe hit ignore on his phone and attempted to put Sloan out of his head. She had to stop calling. Talking to her now was not going to help him. He needed to focus. This raid was going to be hard enough as it was. Having her living in his mind was a distraction that could get him killed. He slipped his cell back into his pocket. "So, what do you think Tag, do we have enough men?"

Nick was leaning against the stove. He'd studied the plans for the *Green Leaf*. "Realistically? No. But if we grab Saige and two of her guys and we pull a few more off the *Fitz* if Bertrand agrees, then we should be okay."

Axe tapped the blueprint in front of him. "I think if we come on board here, it's probably the best approach."

"Cain, Elias, do either of you have an opinion? You two are the experts in maritime security response. Put your MSRT training to good use."

Cain was seated across from Axe, and Elias was on Cain's right. The two men looked at each other and then back at the blueprint. "Axe is right." Cain pointed to the same location that Axe had indicated earlier. "It really is the best spot to breach the ship if we're doing it at night. We're gonna need to spread out quickly and move from bow to stern on both sides of the boat. It's not massive, so that helps. But it is going to have hidden compartments and stuff. We just have to expect the unexpected."

Elias leaned forward. "MacGregor will have someone on deck, watching. That's the hardest thing to avoid. We need to make sure we're not seen, otherwise MacGregor has the advantage, and it's going to get ugly fast."

Axe grunted. "I know. I've been thinking about that. What's the most inconspicuous vehicle that we can use here? What will they not expect to see anyone come out of?"

"Well, there're lots of other container ships in the area, but none of those can get close enough. The *Green Leaf* is behind us and off to the port side. Too far away from the *Fitz* if we need help, not that Admiral Bertrand would let Schwartz bring the *Fitz* over to come to our aid, but the *Green Leaf* is too close to the bank of the canal to have anything big approach it. It wouldn't take much to run aground over the edge of the canal. If we use any kind of a RHIB, they're going to keep their eye on it." Finn turned and poured himself another cup of coffee.

"Agreed." Axe nodded. "I was thinking more along the lines of a tugboat."

Nick's eyebrows went up. "A tugboat? You mean get one of the tugboats that are trying to move the *Sea Jewel*?"

Axe shook his head. "No. I'm thinking we get a local tug, a small one. Not these major ones they are bringing in, but a local job. No one will think twice about seeing another tugboat, and if we just drive it slowly and weave our way around the other ships, then MacGregor, or whoever he has on deck watching, is really not going to pay any attention to it. The thing is, I do think we're going to need a couple guys in the water to go up over the side. They're gonna have to take care of whoever is on overwatch and then everybody can swarm off the tug."

Elias nodded. "Axe is right. We're definitely going to need at least two in the water and, ideally, two boats. I don't like having everybody in one boat."

"How about an old fishing boat?" Finn asked. "We're in the Gulf of Suez, just up from the Red Sea. A lot of fishing that goes on here. There's gotta be a fishing boat around we could use. Even if it stands out, we could pretend to be lookie-loos. There's been enough of those that have approached the area to get a good look at the *Sea Jewel*, circled around and then left again. As long as they don't get too close to anything, the Suez authority doesn't seem to mind. So, I say we grab an old fishing boat and put some of us on that as well."

"I like it, Finn." Axe smiled. "It gives us the advantage of having two different vessels converging on the *Green Leaf*, plus the guys in the water. If we're lucky and fast, we should be able to get everybody rounded up before they even know what's coming. Of course, with MacGregor, it could all turn to shit very fast. These guys are hardnose, and they're not playing by the rules. I think, at this point, they don't really expect us to come, but the last thing we want to do is get in a situation where they know we're there before we want them to." Axe felt his cell vibrate in his pocket. *Damn it, Sloan.*

Nick took a sip of his coffee. "Axe is right. Even if we plan this to the *nth* degree, there's still a lot that could go wrong. Do you think there's any merit in trying to get them all up on the deck first so it's easier to round them up?"

Cain shook his head. "If we lose our element of surprise, then it's just going to be an 'us against them' battle. That's something we want to avoid. They know that ship and we don't. They're also gonna be prepared for shit to go down because they came here to cause trouble. We're working from a deficit. We have equipment but we're supposed to be low key. Plus, we don't have the type of support we'd normally have. It's our five tier-one operators against their eight highly trained team members on their turf.

I know we'll have a couple of FBI people and some other Coasties off Axe's ship. None of those people are trained the way we are. And they sure as hell are not trained the way MacGregor and his boys are. I'm afraid it'll be lambs to the slaughter. Honestly, the most we can ask of them is to gather all of the auxiliary crew and keep them from getting in the way."

"I agree with Cain," Elias said. "It's better if we're stealthy through the ship into the bunk areas, grab them, and bring them up on deck. It's going to be a fight, but that's better than them knowing we're coming and us trying to run them up on deck. If we're good and we're quiet, we should be able to get a good number of them before anybody knows what's wrong."

Axe glanced at Elias. "You don't think we're going to get all of them, do you?"

Elias shook his head. "I think if we had twice as many of us who were trained properly, we'd have a good chance. Like Cain said, it's their turf and they're bound to have some surprises in store for this type of situation. We would if the tables were turned. As it is, I think we'll get some of them, but some of them are going to get away. Realistically the odds are in their favor.

"They can go over the side of the ship and swim for it. The *Green Leaf* isn't a big container ship that's high off the water. It's a small commercial vessel. Yes, it's got some storage, but it's maybe thirty feet off the water. We could make that jump and survive, and so can they. Then they swim for the next boat over. There are so many boats out there at the moment, it would be easy. This isn't exactly a wide body of water. Hell, any one of us could swim for the bank and make it. Regardless I think we need to look for MacGregor and whoever else we can get. My main concern is that someone is going to get hurt."

"Elias is right," Nick agreed. "We'll be lucky to get out of this without anybody getting hurt."

"Do you think we shouldn't do it then?" Axe leaned back in his seat.

"I think we don't have a choice. They are our best lead to finding out who is behind all of this," Nick said as he set his mug down on the counter next to the stove. "I think if we roll up with the FBI and go on board in broad daylight, then MacGregor and his men will disappear, and we'll never find them. Going in in the dead of night is the best approach. Elias is just being realistic, and I think that's a good thing. Even if we can get a few of them, it'll be worth it. Somebody will know something, period. Now, whether they tell us or not is a different story, but I'm guessing if we apply the right pressure, they will. Remember, these men are mercenaries. They might be very skilled operators, but that doesn't mean that they're loyal to one another. My guess is they can be bought or bribed, even threatened into telling us what they know. Besides, that's probably not gonna be up to us. I'm guessing the FBI will step in once we have them in custody."

Axe's phone went off again, and he pulled it out of his pocket to decline the call if it was Sloan. "And speaking of the FBI… it's Saige." He answered the call. "Hey, Saige. We were just talking about you." He was just thankful it wasn't Sloan again.

"Axe," Nick said, "tell her we need them over here no later than seven p.m. We'll go over all the details with them then."

Axe nodded and conveyed the info to Saige. A minute later, he disconnected the call.

Nick turned to Finn. "See if you can find us a fishing boat and a tug that we can borrow."

"Sure, Tag. I'm on it." Finn left the galley and went into the salon.

"Cain, you and Elias go over the blueprints for the *Green Leaf* one more time. I want this solid so we know exactly what we're doing and no surprises."

Cain nodded. He and Elias leaned forward and stared at the blueprints again.

———

Axe glanced at his watch. It was just past midnight. They were planning the raid for four a.m. He tried to go back to sleep, but it was hopeless. He rose off the couch in the salon and walked out on deck. He'd given his room up to Saige. She and her men needed some shut-eye before the raid, too, and it seemed only right to give her the bed. She'd laughed and told Axe he should treat her as he would any colleague, but she would take the bed anyway.

Sloan had always poked a bit of fun at him for being chivalrous as well, but he knew she enjoyed it. Everyone liked to be looked after now and then.

Axe leaned against the wheelhouse and stared out. It was a calm night. Not too much of a breeze and a clear sky. He'd like it better if there were more clouds, but it was a hell of a lot better than a sandstorm.

There was a small craft approaching the old yacht. Axe watched as it got closer. He assumed it was a lookie-loo out to see all the ships, albeit at an odd time of night. Then the craft came closer. Could MacGregor have found out where they were? Did he know they were coming for him and decide to come get them first? All these thoughts blew through his mind at the speed of light as he straightened and stared at the approaching launch.

Cain came down the stairs from the flybridge. He was on his cell. "Yeah, Tag. It's approaching fast." Then he hung up and came to stand beside Axe. "You got a weapon on you?" he asked in a quiet voice.

Axe said, "I never leave home without it."

The door behind them slid open, and Nick appeared on deck. He stood on the other side of Axe. "Elias and Finn are sleeping. Do you think we should roust them?"

"I don't think MacGregor would be this obvious. I'm not sure what this is, but I doubt it's anything too serious," Cain said in a quiet voice.

The launch was about one hundred feet away now. Axe squinted. It was hard to see in the dark. The boat's running lights didn't help the situation. He thought it looked like there were two people on board the launch, but there could be more that were hidden.

Cain moved toward the bow of their yacht, and Nick walked to the stern. No need to stand altogether and provide any potential assassins with an easy target. The boat swung alongside, and Axe looked over the rail. The driver said something in Arabic and made a gesture that he took to mean lower the ladder so someone could board the yacht.

Axe started to shake his head when he saw another figure emerge from the darkness of the back of the boat.

Sloan peered up at him.

"*Jesus fucking Christ!* Sloan!" Axe growled. "What the fuck are you doing?"

"Axe, you need to let me up. We have to talk."

"Now is not a good time."

Sloan put her hands on her hips. "Now is the only time. I have information that you need."

Axe glared down at her. He wanted to throttle her, but at

the same time, he found himself checking her over to make sure she was in one piece.

"Hey, Sloan," Nick said as he lowered the ladder. He looked over at Axe and cocked an eyebrow.

Axe shook his head slightly. He had no fucking clue why she was here. He was well aware that her presence was jeopardizing not only the night's mission, but them being allowed to stay together as a team. Bertrand would have a shitfit if he knew there was a civilian on board, let alone a reporter. Axe's blood pressure skyrocketed as Sloan made her way onto the yacht.

The Egyptian pilot waved and steered the craft away from the old yacht. Axe turned to Sloan. "What the fuck, Sloan?"

She pointed to the salon. She walked over, opened the door, and disappeared inside.

Cain and Elias joined Nick and Axe on the deck.

"What's going on?" Elias asked.

"No fucking clue," Axe growled.

"I think we're about to find out," Cain said.

CHAPTER TWENTY-TWO

S loan did her best not to whirl around and scream at Axe, but it was damn hard. She hadn't forgiven him for pushing her to look for the interpreter when, clearly, he had realized the better story was staying here and figuring out why the canal was blocked in the first place. She refused to blame herself for that. As a reporter, she should have known better, but after suffering the trauma of someone trying to kill her and someone killing both Eddie and Zahra, she was not as clearheaded as she should have been. And he knew that.

She stood in the middle of the salon as Nick and Cain filtered in with Axe. She held up her hands. "Don't bother yelling at me for blowing your cover. You weren't that hard to find. Once you take out container ships, there aren't that many boats that arrived in the last twenty-four hours. No one wants to sit and wait for the canal to open if they don't have to." She said a silent thank you to Charlie who'd used his contacts to track Axe down.

Nick gestured to the couches. "Maybe you'd like to take a

seat and tell us what's so important that you needed to come out here rather than call or send a message."

Sloan ignored the offer of a seat. "I did call. Repeatedly. Someone didn't bother to answer their phone." She stood with her back to the galley so she could take in the whole room and glared at Axe.

"I came because I discovered something that could be the key to unraveling the whole mystery." Sloan grabbed a bottle of water off the coffee table and opened it.

"And you wanted to share that with us rather than write the story?" Axe asked. His voice held a note of skepticism.

It took everything she had not to walk over and punch Axe in the nose. She was out here trying to save his ass while he was busy being one. "I will write the story, but I thought it was more important to let you all know you're in danger first," she said through clenched teeth.

"Why don't you tell us what's going on?" Nick said in a calm voice.

Sloan drew a deep breath and then let it out. Being pissed off with Axe wasn't going to help her get Nick and Cain to believe what she was going to tell them. "I was working on another article when I dropped Eddie's hat. A piece of paper tucked inside fell out. On it, Eddie had written a name, a phone number and several questions which were crossed out. At the bottom was a statement. At first I couldn't believe it but I asked one of my sources for help and he confirmed that the number belonged to a burner phone, of course, but the only calls the owner made were to another burner in Germany.

"I studied the call history and realized the calls started just when the *Sea Jewel* began its voyage. The calls continued sporadically until today and were made in roughly the same area that the *Sea Jewel* traveled through. At first, I wasn't sure what it meant, but then I remembered something. Mac—"

"MacGregor and his men didn't board the *Sea Jewel* until the last stop before they started into the canal." Axe swore. "They weren't around at the beginning of the trip."

"Exactly. I guess it could have just been a mistress in Germany, but my gut says otherwise."

Cain looked over at Axe. "So, do you think it was a spare phone Svensson had? And he was actually the shot caller on board the *Sea Jewel*?"

Sloan cut off Axe before he had a chance to reply. "That's what Eddie wrote on the paper. He wrote the name of the person who he thought was in charge on the *Sea Jewel* and it wasn't Svensson." She took a breath. "It was Rohan Patel."

The look of shock on Axe's face was just a teensy bit satisfying. Okay, it was hugely satisfying if she were being honest. She'd dug up a vital piece of information Axe hadn't figured out yet. Score one for her!

"Son of a bitch!" Axe was on his feet. "Are you sure?"

Sloan nodded.

"Patel is the Chief Mate on the *Sea Jewel*. Jesus, he had me totally snowed. He pretended to be scared of MacGregor. He even let MacGregor order him around."

"Yeah, he was good," Sloan agreed. "He played it like MacGregor had his office bugged and he was being watched by MacGregor's goons." She took a sip of water. "He also showed you the pictures of the propulsion equipment that they used to turn the ship." She frowned. "I'm not sure why he did that."

Axe pulled out his phone and quickly clicked on the link Patel had given him. It didn't work. "Fuck! He did it to throw any suspicion off him, and it worked beautifully. That whole bit about the offices being bugged was to make sure we didn't communicate with the outside world. The pictures were to make sure I sided with him. By making MacGregor the bad guy, it meant Patel could run things without being watched.

"I was such an idiot. I fell for the whole thing. It makes sense looking back. Patel would have had to help MacGregor's guys get off the ship during the sandstorm."

Sloan piped up. "He also said he'd worked with Svensson for a long time, but this was his first job for Pacific Overseas Express. He'd never been to sea for them before. I'm not even sure his real name is Rohan Patel."

Nick stood up suddenly. "Did Saige speak to Patel about coming here?"

Axe froze. "I have no fucking clue. Do you think MacGregor would come after us?"

"Depends." Nick grunted. "If Patel knows we exist and that we know where MacGregor and his boys are, then it might make sense to slow us down. There's no way in hell he wants to be stuck on the *Sea Jewel* with the FBI if they know he's the shot caller behind the whole blockage."

"Right," Axe agreed. "I'll go ask Saige if she or her guys spoke to Patel—" The sound of gunfire ripped through the salon. Cain had gone back up top, and now he was shooting at someone. *That answered that question.* There was the sound of return gunfire, and then all hell broke loose. Axe took a step toward Sloan, but there was more gunfire, and then the sound of shattering glass on deck.

"Incoming!" Cain screamed on deck, then fired his weapon again. "Shit!"

After another crash, closer this time, the salon burst into flames. Sloan was on the other side of the wall of fire. Nick was with her.

"Nick!" Axe yelled. "Take care of Sloan!"

Nick nodded.

Axe took one last look at Sloan and then started toward a flight of stairs. There was another loud crash behind him, and the galley burst into flames. Another burst of gunfire ended abruptly, followed by the sound of a body hitting the water.

The sound of breaking glass continued. More firebombs were being tossed onto the boat.

Sloan screamed and stepped farther away from the flames, only to hear another crash behind her, and the whole front of the salon went up in flames as well. Fire danced along the deck outside as well as up the curtains to the ceiling. She turned toward where she'd last seen Axe, but he was gone.

Nick came and grabbed her by the arm. He pulled her into the far corner. "Cover your head and face," he yelled over the sound of the crackling flames.

"Where's Axe? Where's Cain?" she yelled back.

Nick shook his head. "Don't worry about them now. Turn away and cover your head."

Sloan's heart pounded. Her lungs hurt. She coughed and did as she was told. *Axe.* He better be okay. He had to be okay. She coughed again and jumped after another loud crash. She squeezed herself into a tighter ball and felt a cool breeze on her back.

Nick was suddenly standing beside her again. "Okay, Sloan, we're going out the window and over the side. Follow me. Keep your hand on my shoulder, and I'll help you when you get to the window."

Sloan nodded and coughed some more. When she turned, a wave of heat blasted her face. The whole room was in flames. The walls, the curtains on either side of the doors to the deck, the ceiling—everything was all engulfed. Even the deck outside of the salon, where Cain had been, was ablaze. Panic clawed its way up from her chest to her throat. She wanted to scream, but she wasn't capable of making a sound.

The stairs to the deck were blocked by flames. Axe was certain Cain would have gone into the water by this point. He stumbled on the step and looked back toward Sloan in the salon. He started in her direction, but Nick was helping her cover her head. As much as it killed him to leave her, the wall of flames between them guaranteed he'd never reach her. He trusted Nick to help Sloan, but every nerve in his body jangled with the need to go to her.

"Stay in the mission, asshole," he chided himself as he pivoted and went down the stairs to the sleeping quarters. One thought was on repeat in his head, sounding with each step he took away from Sloan: Nick was with her, and he would see that she got out. Elias and Finn needed to be woken up along with Saige and the other men from the FBI. He had no intention of letting them all burn to death.

"Elias! Finn! Saige!" he bellowed as he pounded down the stairs and started banging on doors. There was another crash and a scream. Saige's door opened, and she sprang into the hallway. Fire lit her room.

"Molotov cocktail through my window," she gasped. The flames were swiftly engulfing the small stateroom.

"Your men. Get them." Axe reached past her and slammed her door again. It wouldn't stop the fire, but it might buy them precious seconds.

"They're already in the engine room with Elias and Finn. I just came back for my gun." Saige went a few steps down the hallway but then started to cough. The smoke was getting thick and fire licked along the ceiling. Axe headed past Saige down the hallway to the engine room. Finn and Elias were at the door on the other side of the room The other two men were a few steps away. He ushered Saige in and closed the door hoping to stop some of the smoke from coming in.

"Finn! Elias! We gotta go!" Axe yelled.

Elias glanced at Axe. "We can't get this door open. I think MacGregor's men jammed it with something."

"We can go back this way." Axe gestured behind him. He turned and opened the door. His eyebrows were singed by the rush of flames from the corridor. He slammed the metal shut again only then noticing the intense heat from the metal door. *Dumbass!*

Finn shook his head. "There's no going that way. Once the Molotov cocktails hit the deck, there was no going that way. This whole boat is on fire. We have to get this door open."

"What's on the other side?" Axe demanded as he approached the group.

"It's the door to the jet ski storage."

Axe immediately understood. Finn was right. The only way off the boat for them was through that door. There was no doubt in his mind that that fucker MacGregor also knew the same and that's why the door was jammed. "What do you think he used to jam it?"

Elias shook his head and started coughing. "No fucking clue" he croaked, "but if we don't get it open soon, we're all going to be crispy critters."

Axe glanced behind him. The door to the engine room was still closed, but the amount of smoke billowing in and the sound of the flames meant the fire was near. The lights went out, and the emergency lighting clicked on.

Nick moved forward and held Sloan's hand in place on his shoulder. She was glad he did because it was so hard to see. Her eyes were watering, and she was having difficulty catching her breath. She wasn't sure she could follow him on her own.

They made it to the broken window on the other side of the salon. Flames licked around the entire frame. Nick took her hand and pulled her alongside him. "Sloan, I need you to ignore the fire and go out the window."

"What?" How was she supposed to do that? The fire was spreading across the floor now, too.

"Step over the fire and slide out the window. I'll help. Then just jump off the side of the yacht." He was yelling now. She had a hard time seeing him, but a breeze came, and the smoke cleared a bit.

The look in his eyes left her chilled to the bone. She either jumped now, or they died.

She turned and reached over the flames to grab the windowsill. She jumped and swung her legs through the window. Her feet hit the deck outside, and she slid. She let go of the windowsill and grabbed onto the rope railing, but she had too much momentum. Her flip-flops slipped under the railing and slid off the side of the yacht. The rope railing snapped, and she plunged overboard. Pain cracked in her skull as her head smacked the edge of the deck. Her vision swam. Flames and smoke were mixing with the black sky above, and then darkness closed in.

The shock of the water closing over her head was profound. It stopped her from passing out, but she opened her mouth in surprise and inhaled. She started to choke. She kicked as hard as she could. If she didn't break the surface in the next few seconds, she was going to drown. Her heart pounded. Her lungs screamed for air. Sloan flailed around and tried to swim upward. No way was this how it ended for her. No. Fucking. Way.

Finally, she broke the surface, choking and coughing up water. Breath wheezed in her throat as she struggled to draw air into her lungs. She needed something to hold on to stop from going under again. She coughed and choked some more as she searched for help.

There was a splash beside her, and Nick was suddenly there. He steadied her. "Are you okay?"

She just nodded while she coughed up more water. He grabbed her arm and pulled her away from the yacht. She looked up. The whole boat was in flames. There wasn't a part that wasn't bright orange. Axe. She resisted Nick's tugging. "Axe?" she choked out.

"He'll figure out a way out. You have to move away. It could blow at any minute. There are fuel and propane tanks on board."

Sloan stared at the flames. There was no way off that yacht. It was a burning mass, just floating there. No one could survive that. Anyone and anything on board would be incinerated. Her heart shattered. She couldn't breathe, but this time it was as if her lungs had frozen. Her vision started to narrow.

Saige looked at Axe. He knew that look. It was a look of fear. He'd seen it once before. It was the same look on Andy's face when he realized he wasn't getting out. Axe's stomach lurched. His hands opened and closed reflexively. He was not going to let this happen again, no way in hell. "I have an idea, but you're not gonna like it."

Finn turned and looked at Axe. "I don't like any of this, so I'll take whatever you got."

Axe nodded. "We could try shooting it, the door I mean."

"Jesus, Axe," Saige exclaimed, "there's enough metal in

here, if we start shooting at that door, it could bounce off anything and kill us all."

"I know it's metal, and a hell of a lot of things could go boom in here if a ricochet hits them, but I don't see we have other options." Axe clenched his hand tight around the butt of his weapon. "If we all shoot by the lock and make the hole big enough maybe, we can see what's blocking the door from opening and move it.

"Well, I don't know about you, but I'd rather go by bullet than burning—" Elias broke off as a coughing fit overcame him.

Axe looked around the engine room. One by one, everyone nodded. They all drew their weapons. "You two." Axe pointed to the FBI guys "Get behind that engine block. Saige, you go behind the other one."

Elias and Finn took up positions behind other equipment in the room, hoping to fend off any ricochets. Axe moved behind the second engine with Saige. "Everyone ready?"

Axe held up his fingers and counted down from three. When he dropped the last finger, everyone started shooting. Several pieces of metal ricocheted near Axe's head, but mostly their bullets went through. Finally, there was a hole big enough to see through. Axe yelled for everyone to stop shooting and then broke into coughing. The air was so thick with smoke it was hard to see. Axe stepped from behind the engine and went over to the door. Everyone followed. There was always someone coughing now that the smoke was brutally thick and the ceiling above them was on fire.

"Can you see anything?" Finn croaked

Axe shook his head. "I can't see a damn thing." Axe dropped to his knees and coughed. His lungs were screaming out for more air. He reached over and tried to push his hand through the hole, but it was too small. He looked around, trying to get an idea what he could use to make the hole bigger. There. A fire extinguisher in the corner. It was too small to battle the fire but it would be a hell of a club. He crouched low and scooted over and got it. He came back and then started smashing at the hole with the end of the fire extinguisher.

The air and every piece of metal in the engine room was hot, and the smoke was so thick Axe's lungs burned with every breath. Everyone else was crouched low, head to the floor so they could breathe what little oxygen was left in the room. If he didn't get this door open soon, they were done for. Finn didn't seem to be able to stop coughing. Elias shot Axe a meaningful glance. *Get us out of here or we're done.*

No. It wasn't going to end like this. His teammates were not going to die in a fire. It was his fault they were in danger. He should have seen through Patel. He should have known they were in danger. That MacGregor would be gunning for them.

Axe gave it everything he had with the fire extinguisher, slamming the canister on the door one last time. Then he dropped it on the floor. When he stuck his hand through the hole the jagged edges of the metal bit into his flesh. He reached around, searching to see what was blocking the door. There it was! He found the smooth cylinder of a metal pipe. Someone had jammed it through the door handle on the other side. He tried to move it, but it was wedged tight. He worked on it some more, but nothing. No progress. *Fuck!* He coughed. His lungs were on fire. He tried to see how everyone was doing, but the smoke was too thick. He could hear them, but his vision was blurred by the smoke.

He was not giving up. No fucking way! He stuck his arm through the door again and worked the metal pipe. He kept wiggling it again and again until, finally, it dropped to the floor. He pulled his arm back through and opened the door. He fell onto the deck next to the jet skis and coughed.

He tried to suck clean air into his lungs, but even here there was smoke. He yelled, his voice hoarse. His heart hammered. No one came out of the engine room. He wiped his eyes and yelled again. Still nothing. He got to his hands and knees and had started to crawl back into the room when, one by one, everyone came out. Axe closed the door behind Elias. Smoke billowed out of the hole they'd shot into the metal.

"All right everyone," he rasped, "get in the water and swim as far as you can."

Elias was sitting on the floor next to Axe, coughing. They watched as the others jumped in the water and started swimming away. Elias turned to Axe. "Your turn."

Axe shook his head. "I made that mistake before. I'm not leaving anyone behind. You first."

There was a loud crash behind them as the ceiling gave way, and now the whole engine room was on fire. It wouldn't be long before there would be a huge explosion. Elias stood up, squeezed Axe's shoulder, and then dove into the water.

Axe was only a second behind. He swam for all he was worth, his lungs screaming for air, but the water felt good after the heat and smoke. He surfaced and came around the side of the yacht. The whole thing was on fire. Sloan. His heart stuttered. She had to be off the yacht now because if she wasn't, it was too late.

Sloan struggled to stay afloat. She couldn't seem to catch her breath. Darkness was closing in. Suddenly someone wrapped an arm around her, and she was being pulled away from the fire. She wanted to fight. She wanted to be next to the yacht in case Axe made it out. He was going to need help. She just didn't have the strength. She started coughing once again.

"Sloan, honey, stop fighting me. The yacht is going to blow. We have to get away."

Sloan froze and then fought to turn around. The arm released her, and she whipped around. "Axe!" she yelled and threw her arms around his neck. They both went underwater and came up sputtering.

"Honey, we have to get away from here. Now." Axe gently removed her arms from around his neck. "Can you swim?"

Two minutes ago, the answer would have been no, but now she could swim the Nile and back if she had to. *Axe was okay.* Sloan nodded.

Axe pointed out a tender that was a few hundred feet away. They turned and started swimming for it. They were only about ten feet away when a loud boom rang out and debris started falling from the sky. The fuel in the engines had exploded. Sloan turned to look at what was left of the yacht. It was completely gone except for the shell of the hull below the waterline, and that was on fire. Anyone or anything that had been on that yacht had been incinerated.

CHAPTER TWENTY-THREE

"Are you sure you're okay?" Axe asked as Sloan walked out of the hotel room's bathroom. He took a second to admire her long legs sticking out from underneath one of his old Coast Guard T-shirts. Damn, she looked fine. Then again, she always did to him. It didn't matter that she had dark circles under her eyes or that she had a bruise on her cheek. She was gorgeous. He was just so goddamn thankful she was still alive.

"I was cleared by the medical staff before they released me, just like you were, so please stop asking me." She glared at him as she walked across the room and then sat on the bed. "How's Saige?"

The team had stayed in this hotel before getting on the yacht, so they'd come back after being released from the hospital. Nick had rented rooms in the small hotel for all of them. Axe knew Saige was supposed to be on the second floor of the five-story inn. "She'll be fine. The doctors decided to keep her overnight as a precaution. She has some minor burns, but she'll make a full recovery."

Axe ran a hand through his hair. He was exhausted, and

he smelled like smoke. All he wanted to do was take a hot shower and crawl into bed. And that was just what he would do as soon as he got the energy to get off the chair in Sloan's room and walk to his own.

He handed her one of the phones Nick had sent up. All their equipment had gotten drenched, so nothing worked. While Sloan had been in the shower, Axe had programmed his new number into her phone, and hers' into his. Even though he didn't see a future for them, he wasn't about to risk not being able to reach her.

"How are you?" Sloan's voice was soft.

Axe knew what she was really asking, and he didn't know how to answer it. He was... a mess. The fire had brought up everything from the past. He had stayed focused the entire time he was on the ship, but as soon as they were out of the water, the memories assaulted him: Kyle burned so badly as they carried him out on a stretcher, Andy in the body bag. The nausea he'd dealt with right after the accident threatened to reappear right now.

Then, his CO had sent him to the hospital to deal with his own burns, but the pain of those didn't come close to the pain he'd felt at losing Andy and then Kyle. He'd tried to visit Kyle so many times, but his former buddy had refused to put Axe on the visitation list. He'd snuck in once, and Kyle had screamed at him. It was all Axe's fault he was still alive. He wanted to die, and it was on Axe that he was alive and suffering. Seeing the agony on his best friend's face was torture. Axe had left and never went back. He'd screwed up. He'd done what he thought was best, and it turned out to be the worst thing possible. A tremor went through his body.

Suddenly, Sloan was beside him, rubbing his back. He realized he hadn't answered her, but he had no words. He ran his hands over his face.

"Come on." Sloan gently tugged his arm. "You need a shower."

Axe slowly got to his feet and followed her to the bathroom. He had a room on the floor below, but that felt like it was miles away. He just needed to get clean and get some sleep. Sloan turned on the water and then started to help Axe get undressed.

He looked down at her, but she just went about pulling his dirty, ripped T-shirt over his head. He didn't want her to see his burn scars. He never liked her to see them but now with everything that happened, he didn't want to look at them nor did he want her to see them. They were a brutal reminder of how he'd failed in the past and how he'd almost gotten them all incinerated last night. He started to argue with her but she just ignored him. She helped him out of his jeans and pushed him toward the shower. He said nothing but groaned when he climbed under the hot spray.

Axe had no clue how long he'd been standing with the water running down his back before he felt a rush of cool air. Without looking, he knew that Sloan had stepped into the shower with him. This was a bad idea. He knew it and he knew she knew it, but he was absolutely powerless to stop it. Hell, he didn't want to. Getting lost in Sloan seemed like a damn fine idea at the moment. At any moment. She was an amazing woman, though, and he didn't want to hurt her any more than he already had. Nor did he want to risk his heart again.

"Sloan. Are you sure about this? It doesn't change anything."

She smiled up at him. "Yes, Axe. I am sure and I know it doesn't change anything. You and I might fight about everything else, but sex was never our problem. I think we could both use a distraction."

He glanced down over her generous proportions that had

turned pink in the warm water. "A distraction sounds fucking awesome right now."

He leaned down and captured her mouth. His body instantly reacted as it always did with Sloan. She slid into his arms, and they fit together like she was made to be there. He deepened the kiss and tightened his arms. She felt so damn good against him, he could almost forget everything.

Axe ran his hands down her back to cup her ass. She fisted his hair as their tongues rolled and twisted in a carnal dance. The water sluiced off their bodies, making them slick. Her skin slid against his. The need to touch her and taste her everywhere burned inside him.

"Axe," she whispered, arching into him as he kissed the hollow of her neck, "I've missed you."

He missed her, too. So fucking much. It was as if all the light had been sucked out of his life after their last fight. He'd driven her away on purpose to punish himself. To punish her for hurting him. Now he just wanted her. The need was so strong he was going to explode with it.

Sloan broke off the kiss and lowered her head to his nipple. She soothed her tongue over it as she ran her fingers down the length of his shaft. She reached back up and claimed his lips one more time as she continued to stroke him.

"You're gonna be the death of me," he groaned and then kissed her neck. He cupped her breast and sucked one nipple and then the other. Sloan moaned and said his name. Axe's gut tightened, and a wave of possessiveness washed over her. She was his. It was always this way when they were together. "Say it again," he demanded. He loved the sound of his name on her lips. She did, staring at him as she said it.

He grunted and then captured her lips again, deepening the kiss until they were both panting for air. When Axe pushed Sloan against the back wall of the shower, she let out a little yelp. "It's cold."

"I'll warm you up." He grinned and then alternated nipping and licking his way down her jawline to the hollow of her throat. She wound her fingers through his hair and lifted one of her legs over his hip. He shifted her, bringing her in direct contact with his cock. She moved against him, and he groaned.

He reached down between them and rubbed her hot center. She bit her lip and lifted her hips in response. He went back to sucking her nipples as he moved his hand over her. Her breathing was getting faster.

Axe removed Sloan's leg from his hip and went down on his knees. He moved so his mouth was over her core. She sunk her fingers into his hair. Axe," she moaned. She watched him as he lowered his head to taste her. She was wet and ready for him.

He licked her slowly with his tongue and then went in small circles. She fisted his hair and made small panting sounds. He gently slid one finger inside her and then another, moving in a slow rhythm as he glanced up at her. She had her head thrown back and was biting her lip. He loved how she looked during sex. She didn't hold back. He put another finger inside her and sped up the rhythm, her hips matching his pace. He captured her with his mouth, and she pulled his hair, holding him against her. Her hips were bucking wildly, and she called out his name as she came.

Sloan couldn't get enough of Axe's body. She loved the feel of it as she ran her hands over him. But when she touched his burns, he flinched.

"Axe, these don't matter. They are the reality of what

you've been through. Don't let these define you." She raised up one of his arms and pressed her lips to his skin. She planted little nips all the way from his wrist to his elbow.

His blue eyes turned dark, and he captured her mouth again in a scorching kiss. He pushed her against the shower wall again and used his body to hold her there. She loved it when he got aggressive with her. It turned her on more than anything. Axe was the only one she would ever allow to control her during sex. She trusted him implicitly.

Sloan ran her hands over the taut ridges of muscles of his stomach as he kissed and sucked on her neck and throat. "Axe," she moaned. She pushed him away and started working her way down his chest to his stomach and then lower, touching and tasting every inch of him. He swore in response when she moved farther south until her mouth was over his cock.

She softly touched the very tip with her tongue, and then she made small circles. First one way, then the other. Slowly, she drew more and more of him into her mouth, sucking and twisting her tongue. Axe growled her name, his rough voice sending tingles of pleasure through her. His hips started to move, and she matched the rhythm with her mouth.

Axe pulled away and brought her to her feet. She knew he wanted to be inside her. God, how she wanted that, too. He rubbed her nipples and kissed her hard. She moaned and arched into his hands. Axe bent and picked her up. She wrapped her legs around his hips and rubbed her center against his cock. She was wet and ready for him, so turned on she couldn't think anymore. The warm water washed over them both, making it easy to slide against him.

Axe pushed her back against the wall and then entered her slowly. She fisted his hair and kissed him hard, arching her hips to invite him in deeper, but he withdrew.

"Axe," she moaned, "now. I want you inside me now."

He obliged and she let out a yelp when he drove all the way inside her in one move.

Sloan was vibrating with desire. He started moving slowly, but she pumped her hips faster. She needed more. "Faster. Harder."

Axe complied, and within seconds, they were locked together in a dance as old as time. The rhythm was too much, and they careened over the edge.

"Sloan," Axe growled as he pumped into her one last time, "you're mine."

"Yes!" she yelled and then slid into oblivion.

Sloan moaned and slid down the wall as Axe slowly put her back down onto her feet. She smiled as he straightened. "Care for round two?"

Axe groaned. "You are going to be the death of me." He smiled and kissed her, but he couldn't hide the fatigue on his face. The man was exhausted both emotionally and physically, and even if he didn't realize it, she did. He needed sleep and some time to process.

She gave him a quick kiss and then grabbed a bar of soap. "Why don't we save round two for later? Let's finish the shower and grab some sleep. I'm exhausted."

"Me, too." Axe smiled at her and then stepped back into the full spray.

A few hours later, Axe woke with a start. He froze. Why had he woken up? There was a faint buzzing sound.

"Shit" he mumbled as he climbed quickly and quietly out of bed. He had no intention of waking Sloan.

The smell of smoke permeated the bathroom. Axe tried not to gag. He grabbed his jeans off the bathroom floor. His clothes were rank. He pulled out the new cell phone Nick had provided. A message appeared on the screen. A missed call from Nick Taggert.

Axe grimaced. He didn't want to call Tag back while in Sloan's room, but he was loath to put on the dirty clothing again and go down to his own. Last night he'd been so damn scared that he'd lost Sloan, he had a hard time letting her out of his sight. He'd gone up to her room with her to make sure she was okay even though he knew it was a mistake. Now he was glad he did. He needed her last night or this morning, whatever it was. And she'd needed him. But that was over and it was time to get back to work.

He glanced at the screen. It was going on seven a.m. Axe texted Nick that he needed a couple of minutes and then grabbed a towel off the rack in the bathroom. He tied it around his waist. He pulled his room key out of his jeans and then wrapped all his dirty clothes in a damp towel.

He walked out of the bathroom and glanced over at Sloan. She was still sound asleep. Her long chestnut curls had fanned out over the pillow, and a small smile was on her face. He wanted to remember her just like this because no matter what had happened earlier, they weren't getting back together. He might care about her—hell, he might even love her—but he couldn't trust her. Their lives were on two conflicting paths. She would always want him to share all the details, and he wouldn't betray his team like that. Not even for her. She would always put the story first. He would put his teammates first. Two divergent paths.

He turned and quietly left the room.

CHAPTER TWENTY-FOUR

"Tag, what's up? Is everyone okay?" It had occurred to Axe in the elevator ride down to his own room that maybe one of the guys was hurt worse than they'd thought. Did Elias or Finn have to go back to the hospital? Elias's leg had to be bothering him after swimming. What about Cain? His clothing had caught on fire after the first firebomb hit the deck and after firing at the raiders, he'd dived into the water. Had that saved him, or were his burns worse than they first thought?

"Everyone is fine. You need to get down here." He gave Axe his room number. "We have some new intel, and we need to make a plan."

"Okay. Um, I have a bit of an issue," Axe grumbled.

"What issue?"

Axe bit the inside of his jaw. "I have no clothes." There was a pause, and then the sound of laughter came down the phone line. "I can't wear the ones I had on yesterday. They're smoky and ripped. I don't have any others here. Wait, how do you have clothes?"

Nick was still laughing. "We had these rooms before the yacht was ready and left some stuff at the hotel."

"Well, I didn't get to do that, so I have no clothes."

"I didn't think about that. My bad." Nick chuckled and then asked, "Wait! How did you get to your room from Sloan's?"

"How did you know I was in Sloan's room?"

Nick snorted. "You wouldn't let her out of your sight last night. There was no way you weren't going to be with her and you would want her to be comfortable so, her room not yours. Elementary, dear Watson."

"Smart ass."

"So how did you get down to your room?" Nick asked again.

"I wore a towel." More laughter. "Okay, hilarious. I still need clothes."

"Elias is on the way up," Nick said and then started laughing again.

Axe ended the call with a bit more force than was necessary.

A couple seconds later, there was a knock on the door. Axe opened it to find a grinning Elias holding out a folded pair of jeans with underwear, a navy T-shirt, and socks on top. "Nice towel."

"Shut up." Axe took the proffered clothing and walked back into the room.

Elias followed him and shut the door. "Finn is bringing shoes."

Axe grunted in response. He moved toward the bathroom. "I'm grabbing a shower. I'll be out in five."

"No rush. You can take at least ten. Do you need a new towel?"

"Fuck off," Axe snarled as he slammed the bathroom door, trying to block out Elias's laughter.

He quickly turned on the hot water and dropped the towel. Stepping into the shower, he noticed that the cuts on his right hand from the jagged metal of the door they'd escaped through had started to bleed again. He'd lost the bandages in the shower with Sloan. He ran his hand under the water and then spent the rest of the shower trying to avoid getting any shampoo or soap in the cuts.

Ten minutes later, he opened the bathroom door. Axe glanced around the room. The whole gang was there. Nick was sitting at the small table across from Cain. Elias and Finn were lounging on the two double beds. Finn grinned at him and started to say something but broke off in a fit of coughing.

"Are you okay?" Axe stood just outside the bathroom door.

Finn nodded and managed to squeak out a "Yes" before coughing again. Elias handed him a water bottle from Axe's nightstand. Finn took a long drink and then smiled at Axe. "I hear you were strolling around the hotel in a towel. Bath size, or was a hand towel all you needed?"

"Funny." Axe gave Finn the once-over. He didn't look great, and his voice was still raspy. Axe started to comment and then caught his own reflection in the mirror over the dresser. He didn't look any better.

He'd been thinking during his shower about what happened last night. He took a deep breath. "Look, before we start the planning, I wanted to apologize to you guys." Axe put his hand on the bathroom door jam and swore. He examined the shallow cuts as he talked. "I should've realized Rohan Patel was behind this. I was sloppy, and it almost got everyone killed."

"Bullshit!" Finn barked out and started coughing again. "If it weren't for you, Elias and I would be goners. So would Saige and the FBI guys. *You* got us out of the engine room."

Axe shook his head. "You shouldn't have had to escape from the engine room. If I'd realized Patel was the shot caller on the *Sea Jewel*, then we never would have been that easy of a target for them. We would've gone after him, not the other way around."

Nick shook his head. "You couldn't have known, Axe. They had it set up from the beginning. They planned for interference from us. They were prepared. We weren't. Not your fault. You had no idea what you were walking into."

"Still, I should—"

"Cut the shit," Cain growled. "You did the best you could under the circumstances. You had no way of knowing about Patel. You got the boys off the yacht, and we're all okay. That's what matters." Elias and Finn nodded in agreement.

Nick tapped the table with his fingers. "Axe, you did what you were supposed to do. You stepped up and had your teammate's backs. No one can ask for more. No mistakes made. No need to feel guilty." He raised an eyebrow at Axe as if to ask m*essage received*?

Axe nodded. His gut loosened slightly. He hadn't realized how uptight he'd been until just now. These men were his friends, his brothers in arms, more importantly, his family. Thinking he'd let them down and put them in jeopardy was a hard pill to swallow. The fact they weren't blaming him was a relief. Now, he just had to stop blaming himself.

"So now that you're dressed, how about we figure out how we're gonna catch that fucker, Patel?" Elias asked.

Axe smiled. "Sounds good to me. So where do we start?"

"Germany," Nick said.

Axe raised his eyebrows. "Why Germany?"

"Do you remember when Mitch said there was a second cell phone on the *Sea Jewel* that was probably linked to MacGregor's men? We now figure it was Patel's, and the vast majority of calls on it were to Germany. The only other calls were to the other burner phones that were on board the *Sea Jewel* and then the *Green Leaf.*"

Axe leaned against the bathroom door frame. "So, you think whoever is behind this is in Germany?"

Nick nodded. "MacGregor and his pals are gone. Their cell phones went off grid just before the raid last night and haven't come back online, but the one we believe links to Patel came back online a short time ago."

"Let me guess," Axe snorted. "In Germany."

Nick pointed at him. "You got it in one."

"How did they get there so fast?" Elias asked as he massaged his leg. "I thought we had the airports blocked."

"Must have been a private jet," Cain said.

"Cain's right," Nick agreed. "There are too many private airports here to keep an eye on all of them without the Egyptian government's help. Someone flew them out. Probably had it on standby so MacGregor and his boys could light us up and be gone immediately. We need to check which airport they flew out of. There can't be that many that are close to here and had a private flight leave in the middle of the night."

"Agreed," Nick nodded.

"But how did they find out about us and where we were?" Elias asked.

"That's a fucking fantastic question," Finn growled. "Bertrand is going to have our asses for burning up the yacht. So much for low profile."

Axe's gut rolled again. He'd forgotten about Bertrand being pissed. "I think I can answer how they knew about us. Patel probably did actually have some of the rooms bugged on the *Sea Jewel* or he tapped Saige's phone. She'd discussed the plans on calls with me. Patel would have heard all of that.

As to how he and MacGregor found us, it couldn't have been that hard. I mean Sloan did it, didn't she? Not to discount her abilities in any way but she's not even trained for this sort of thing."

"That's true." Nick grimaced. "There aren't very many yachts waiting to go through the canal at the moment. It wouldn't have been hard to pick this one out if you had the list of who arrived in the last twenty-four hours. Besides if you're right, Axe, and he bugged Saige's room or her phone, he would have heard her say the name of the yacht."

Finn finished making another origami creature out of the laundry checklist that was left in the room. "Not to burst anyone's bubble, but do we know that MacGregor and his goons went to Germany? Just because Patel is there doesn't mean MacGregor is. Didn't Callahan say MacGregor and his people were Silverstone? They could be gone on another assignment or back in D.C. or wherever they're out of these days."

Axe grimaced. "Finn has a point. We don't know they're in Germany for sure. Maybe they didn't make it out. If Patel is the top guy, would he wait around for MacGregor and crew to firebomb us and then leave, or would he leave earlier? The faster he's out of the country the better for him."

Nick nodded. "You both make good points. We don't know for sure MacGregor got out, and if he did, we have no idea if he went to Germany. Unless the phones turn on again, we won't know for sure, and we may not catch up with them again. They might just get away with murder."

That statement sat heavy in the room. It was a tough nut for the guys to swallow, but especially for Axe. He hated injustice. It was one of the reasons he'd jumped at the chance to be part of the tactical law enforcement unit in the Coast Guard. He truly believed in bringing the guilty to justice.

Elias grunted. "But if we get the guy who paid for the shit to go down in the first place, it's at least something. I would love to bring down these assholes for firebombing us, but I'll take the guy who made the whole thing possible. It's not perfect but better than nothing."

Axe nodded. In the law enforcement game, they were always trying to go up the ladder. Get the bottom guy to turn on the next guy and all the way up. What no one ever talked about was sometimes it was just satisfying as hell to make the asshole who pulled the trigger pay. Fuck whoever paid him.

"It's better than nothing," Axe agreed.

"We have to catch him so don't get too excited." Nick's phone went off, and he looked down at the screen. "Bertrand," he announced and then answered the call. "Sir." There was a second or two of silence and then Nick put the phone down on the table and hit the speaker button. "You're on speaker, sir."

"What's your team's status? Is everyone okay?"

"We're all fine, sir. A few scrapes and bruises, the odd burn but nothing major."

"Glad to hear it. Now, what in the holy hell is going on over there?" Bertrand's voice boomed around the room. "I thought I made it perfectly clear this was to be a low-key operation. No one was supposed to know you were there! You weren't in Egypt for more than twenty-four hours before you were firebombed? The brass is all over my ass about it. You all are supposed to be good at keeping things quiet. What the hell happened?"

"Well, sir," Nick started, "we were unaware that there was a sleeper Silverstone guy still over on the *Sea Jewel.* When we—"

"Silverstone!" Bertrand swore. "Are they involved in this?"

"It looks like it, sir. We have it from a source that Hamish MacGregor, who appeared to be the lead man on the ground down here, works for Silverstone. We haven't had time to confirm it, but our source is impeccable."

"Hamish MacGregor?" Bertrand swore a blue streak. "He's involved?"

"You know MacGregor, sir? Sorry it's—"

"I know who you are, Cantor, and, yes, I know that son of a bitch. He was involved in a mess with the SAS that spilled over onto the Navy. We had a couple of guys doing training with them at the time. It was ugly. Hamish MacGregor. Well, that changes things. Damn hard to keep things quiet with him in the picture. He always likes to make a big splash."

"It was my fault, sir." Axe immediately cut in again. "I mean the firebombing. I failed to identify the shot caller on the *Sea Jewel*. I thought it was MacGregor, but there was someone else on board that was in charge, Rohan Patel. When I spoke with Saige Preston from the FBI about the raid, she either said something to Patel or he had her room bugged. Either way, he knew we were coming and decided to try and take care of us before we went after them."

"I see. Well, with what I know of MacGregor and Silverstone, I'm not surprised they had someone hidden in plain sight. They are crafty buggers. Not your fault, Cantor. I sent you into an impossible situation from what I hear. I also knew that I could count on you to assess the situation and let me know what's what. You did your job admirably." Bertrand mumbled the last words, as if unused to passing out compliments. "Now, what's the next step? Do you know anything else about who's behind this mess?"

Nick spoke up. "Not yet, sir, but we think they're in Germany. Patel has a burner phone that he only used to call MacGregor's men and a number in Germany. We're pretty sure he flew out last night from a private airport around here. If you could offer assistance as to which one, it might help us figure out if MacGregor and his guys were with Patel or not."

"I'll see what I can do. So, you're thinking your next step is you want me to authorize you all to go to Germany and track down Patel?"

"Yes, sir, that is correct," Nick said.

There was silence on the line. Axe's stomach churned. Either they'd be allowed to pursue this, or they wouldn't. It was way outside their jurisdiction, but on the other hand, they were boots on the ground, and Homeland Security would love to know who blocked the Suez Canal on purpose.

"It might be a bit of a hard sell. Panama was a bit different. You were doing your duties when the whole mess fell into your laps. This…" Bertrand paused.

"Axe was doing what he was assigned, sir. As a law enforcement officer, he was doing his duty and watching over a slain American citizen while waiting for the FBI to arrive when he discovered the canal was blocked on purpose."

"I am aware. I sent him on that assignment. Still, it's thin. A hard sell to the top brass."

Nick cleared his throat. "We think all this has to do with shipping, sir."

Axe's eyebrows went up. Elias and Finn both looked surprised, too. Cain looked, like, well Cain. Not much ever surprised him.

Nick continued. "Our working theory is that persons unnamed wanted to stop something from reaching the Mediterranean, so they blocked the canal. Since there are so many ships waiting to get through and some of the cargo on those ships is destined for the US, we are doing our jobs in that we are protecting US economic interests abroad. We are also defending our economic security, which is dependent on global trade. 'The US Coast Guard is, at any given time, deployed to and operating on all seven continents and in cyberspace to save lives, enforce laws, ensure safe and secure commerce, and protect the environment.'"

"Where did you get that from, Taggert? The handbook?" Bertrand barked on a harsh laugh.

Nick grinned. "Wikipedia, sir." The rest of the team chuckled. Nick continued, "But it does sum up our responsibilities, sir."

"Thin, Taggert, it's thin, but I'll give it a go. Pack your bags. I'm sure I can get you on a flight out in the next couple of hours. Once you're in Germany, we'll see what you're going to be allowed to do."

"Yes, sir. Thank you."

"Don't thank me yet Taggert. And stop getting firebombed!" Bertrand slammed down the phone.

Elias grinned. "Well, that went better than I thought. He was almost cheerful."

Finn snorted. "At least we get to go to Germany but, um, where in Germany are we headed?"

Axe nodded. "Good point. Do we know where Patel's cell surfaced?"

"Cologne," Nick stated as he stood up. "We need to get moving. Axe, go get your clothes from the *Fitz*. I'll make sure Bertrand gives your old CO the heads up. The rest of you, pack and be ready." Everyone started moving at once.

"Old commanding officer?" Axe asked. "Does that mean it's official, and we're back together permanently?"

The guys all came to a stop again and looked at Nick. He sighed. "I have no idea, but I hope so. We've never discussed it, but I personally would love this to be a permanent thing."

"Hell, yes," Elias chimed in. "This is the best gig I've ever had."

"Ditto," Finn agreed.

Axe straightened. "This feels like…home to me. Like we're family." He didn't mean to be so serious, but it just slipped out. He swallowed hard as the others stared at him.

Cain stood up and nodded. "What he said." Then he walked over, opened the door, and left the room.

CHAPTER TWENTY-FIVE

S loan opened one eye and reached out a hand. The bed
beside her was empty and the sheets were cold. *Damn.*
She'd been hoping for round two.

"He's gone."

Sloan's eyes popped open, and she clutched the blankets
to her chest as she sat up. "What the fuck?"

MacGregor sat across from her at the table. His gun,
lying on the surface, pointed in her direction. "He left about
a half hour ago. They're all on the next floor down."

Sloan's heart slammed against her ribs. Heat rose in her
cheeks. She clutched the blankets tighter around herself.
"What the fuck do you want?"

MacGregor smiled coldly. "You."

Sloan's lungs froze. She couldn't breathe or make a sound.

MacGregor's reddish blond hair was mussed and he'd
managed to fit his great bulk onto the small hotel chair but
he didn't remotely look comfortable. His icy blue eyes
snapped as he glared at her. "Oh, don't worry. You're not my
type. I need you to accompany me so I can get out of the
country. I seemed to have missed my flight and am having

difficulty getting another. You are going to fix that for me. Your friend is going to call off the dogs so I can get out of Egypt, or I'm going to kill you."

Sloan's mouth went dry. She tried to speak but nothing would come out. Finally, she managed to suck in a breath and get her lungs working again. "What? I mean why? I don't understand."

"There's nothing to understand. I need a way out, but your boyfriend and his pals have people watching the airports. I had a private ride, but it left without me and a few others. You are going to get him to ease up so we can leave."

"He won't do that." Sloan shook her head. "He won't change things for me. We have sex. We aren't in a relationship. He just isn't the type." She had to convince this man that Axe wouldn't help. She did not want to put him in danger or, worse, have him wreck his career over her.

MacGregor laughed. "You can try all you want to convince me of that, but I was there. I saw how he looked at you. He'll do it." His face went cold. "You'd better hope that he will, otherwise you'll be dead."

Sloan's stomach knotted. She had no doubt that MacGregor would kill her. She'd been afraid of him on the *Sea Jewel,* but that paled in comparison to how she felt now. Her lungs weren't working again, and her heart seemed to have stopped beating. *What could she do? Was there a way out of this?*

"Get up and get dressed. We have places to be." MacGregor glared at her, threatening her with a look.

Sloan refused to move. In truth, she wouldn't have been able to get her body to move even if she wanted to. She wasn't getting up. She was naked, and she was not going to be naked in front of MacGregor. "I—I—Y-you need to move so I can get dressed."

MacGregor picked up the gun off the table. "You are going to get up and get dressed or I will shoot you now."

"No, you won't," Sloan said with a bravado she didn't feel. "You need me. If you shoot me now, you won't get out."

MacGregor growled, "Don't push your luck."

"You need to let me get up and get dressed in the bathroom." Sloan wrapped the sheet around herself and pulled hard. It let go from under the bottom of the bed. She slid sideways across the bed. MacGregor's eyes followed her every move. She stood up and wrapped the sheet all the way around her body. Then she took a couple of steps toward her suitcase, which was lying open on the stand against the wall.

"What are you doing?" MacGregor shifted his gun to track her every move.

Sloan froze. She swallowed and tried not to stare at the gun. "I—I need to get some clothes." She pointed to the suitcase with her left hand while she held the sheet in place with her right.

"Okay, but don't try anything. If you attempt to get a weapon, you'll be dead before you can raise your hand."

Sloan nodded. She didn't have the capacity to speak. Her knees wobbled slightly, and she reached out to the bed to steady herself. *Calm. Just be calm. Don't panic. Panicking doesn't help.*

Who the fuck was she kidding? She wasn't calm. She wasn't ever going to be calm with a gun pointed at her. She stepped over to her suitcase.

Where the hell was Axe when she needed him? *That wasn't fair.* He'd told her it would be dangerous. He'd done his best to get her far away, but she'd been the stubborn one. She just *had* to go after the story.

Sloan stared down into her suitcase. She picked up a pair of jeans, a long sleeve light blue sweater, underwear, and socks. Her bra was still in the bathroom. She'd dropped it there when she'd gotten into the shower with Axe. Had it really been only a few hours ago that she'd been having fabulous sex with the most amazing guy?

"Get moving," MacGregor growled. "We don't have all day."

Sloan nodded again and headed for the bathroom. She went inside and started to close the door.

"No." MacGregor shook his head. "The door stays open."

"But you can see me."

MacGregor nodded.

"Obviously, I don't have any weapons. Let me get dressed and then we can go." She was not dropping the sheet in front of this man. It was too humiliating.

"You can get dressed right there. The door stays open."

Sloan opened her mouth to argue, but MacGregor raised his gun. She clamped her lips shut. She put her clothing on the counter. How was she going to do this? She took a steadying breath.

She first tied the sheet tighter around herself and tucked the end in under her armpits. She grabbed her underwear and slid it on under the sheet. She did the same with her jeans. Then she pulled the sweater down over her head. Once she had her arms through, she dropped the sheet.

She reached down and plucked her bra off the floor. She tucked one end into her jeans pocket. Then she pulled her arms in from the sleeves. She turned her back to the doorway and pulled the bra up and around her. Her back was bare as the sweater went up to her neck, but she got the bra on quickly and then put her arms back into the sleeves. She turned and adjusted her clothing in the mirror. She caught a glimpse of MacGregor's reflection. He was grinning. *Fucker.*

"Put on your socks and shoes. We're leaving." MacGregor stood up. Sloan did as she was told, and then reached for her cell phone on the bedside table.

"Leave it!" MacGregor snarled. "We need to be able to reach your boyfriend. He'll grab it when he comes looking for you." MacGregor gestured for her to go to the door. "Open it."

Sloan walked over and opened the door. She gasped. The tall blond guy from the *Sea Jewel*, Christo, was standing guard just outside. He clutched a deadly looking gun with a suppressor on the end which was pointed right at her belly. She swallowed hard and started to choke.

MacGregor came up behind her and pushed the barrel of his gun into her back. "If you try and fight me or scream or do anything to attract attention, you will be shot."

Sloan nodded and cleared her throat. "I understand," she squeaked. MacGregor pushed her with the gun, and she stepped out of the room. Christo moved back, and Sloan started walking down the hallway. They got into a waiting elevator and hit the button for the lobby. She prayed the doors would open on Axe's floor, but they went quickly to the lobby. When the doors did open, MacGregor pushed her out with the gun while Christo walked along right beside her with his gun tucked under his arm and pointed directly at her.

Sloan glanced around wildly, trying to figure out a way to signal someone, but her mind was blank. No one even looked at them. They were across the lobby and out on the sidewalk in seconds. Sloan tried to catch the eye of the valet, but he ignored her. Christo opened the door of a black SUV and cocked his head toward the interior, telling her without words to get in.

When she hesitated, MacGregor pushed the gun into her side again. "Don't do anything stupid. It won't go well for you."

Sloan gave one last frantic look around and then climbed into the SUV. MacGregor settled in right next to her, and

Christo got in on the other side, sandwiching her between them. The driver she recognized immediately as one of the men from the *Sea Jewel*. His name was Simon something. The other man slumped in the passenger seat was unfamiliar. He might have been on the ship, but she'd avoided MacGregor's men as a rule, so she might not have noticed him. He was sweating profusely, and he appeared to have his eyes closed, but it was hard for her to tell at her angle.

MacGregor touched the man in the passenger seat on the shoulder. "Styler, hang in there. We're heading to the airport now."

Styler grunted. He was alive, at least for now. But he wasn't looking so good. Sloan guessed he didn't have much time. "Is that why you missed your flight?" she asked as she pointed at Styler.

MacGregor glared at her. "Your boyfriend and his pals killed one of my men and injured Styler over here. It slowed us down a bit, but don't you worry. I'll make them pay for that right after you help us get out of town."

Sloan bit her lip, keeping silent when she wanted to rail at the thug. There wasn't a doubt in her mind MacGregor was going to kill her as soon as he didn't need her anymore. The question was, what was she going to do about it?

She knew Axe would freak out when he heard she'd been kidnapped, but she wasn't sure what the hell he would do. Would he try to rescue her? Would he even be allowed to try? They might not let him since he was personally involved with her.

MacGregor's cell went off. He answered the call. "Yeah." There were a few seconds of silence. Then, "The same one? What time?" He glanced at his watch. "We'll be ready." MacGregor clicked off the call.

"Good news. There's a jet coming for us. Same airport. It will land in two hours."

Sloan's belly churned as she processed the meaning of the call. *Did they need her anymore?*

MacGregor turned and looked at her. "Don't worry, lass, we're not done with ye yet."

Sloan's heart hammered against her ribs. She had no idea what that meant, but it didn't sound good.

CHAPTER TWENTY-SIX

A xe gathered his things, such as they were. He didn't
have much. Just the clothes on his back and the
damaged ones he'd worn during the fire. He picked those up
and then dropped them in the trash can in the room. There
was no point in taking those anywhere. He glanced at his
watch. Eight-thirty a.m. An ensign was bringing over his
other clothing shortly. They were supposed to meet in the
lobby. Sloan had to be up by now as well. She'd never been
one to laze in bed all day unless they were in bed together.

He glanced at the room phone. Should he call her? No.
That would be stupid. He just needed to get going. Seeing
her wasn't going to help him get over her. *Divergent paths.* He
threw some water on his face and then left the room. He
went to the lobby to wait for the rest of the team. He needed
more clothes, but it made more sense to shop in Germany
than it did in Port Taofik. There wasn't much choice here.

He took a seat in the lobby and people-watched. There
were quite a few reporters staying here. He could tell from
their camera bags and their chatter what they did for a living.
It was also one of the few good hotels in town or so the front

desk clerk said when he handed Axe his stuff. The ensign had dropped some clothes off for him early.

The reporters were congregating in the restaurant. His belly growled. He hadn't eaten breakfast yet, and he was starving. Axe stood up, grabbed his backpack and headed to the restaurant. He grabbed a table for two and sat down. The waitress brought hot coffee, and he had stood up to go to the buffet when a large man approached him. The man had white hair and a deep tan. He also had intelligent eyes. He was older and carried quite a few extra pounds.

"Are you Axel Cantor?"

Axe stared at the man. "Who are you?"

"My name is Charlie Philips. I am a good friend of Sloan Bishop's."

"Okay. Not sure what that has to do with me." Still standing, Axe shifted his weight. His instincts had gone on high alert. He wasn't getting a vibe from this guy, but something was off. He'd felt it all morning. He'd been chalking it up to everything that had happened in the last twenty-four hours. But now, worry started gnawing at his gut.

"Why don't we sit for a minute?" Charlie pointed to the table Axe had just left. "We don't want to draw any attention to ourselves."

Axe sat but stayed loose and at the ready. "What's going on?"

Charlie leaned forward in his chair. "I don't know if Sloan mentioned me, but I was good friends with her father. She is like a daughter to me. She texted me about what happened last night, and we were supposed to meet here for breakfast at eight. She didn't show."

Axe glanced at his watch again. It was only eight thirty-eight, but the worry ratcheted up another notch. Sloan didn't like to be late. Ever. "Maybe she just overslept."

"You don't believe that any more than I do. Sloan is never

late, and she has too much energy to sleep in." The waitress was approaching, and Charlie waved her off. "Listen, I spoke to the front desk already and they said she left just before eight with a group of men. I thought, initially, it was you and your team but when I asked for a description, the desk clerk said one of the men with her was a great barrel of a man. That's how she described MacGregor to me. I've been here ever since, trying to figure out how to reach you. The room isn't under your name so the clerk couldn't help. Short of banging on every door, I camped out in the lobby, hoping you would appear."

Axe's body went hot and cold at the same time. His heart raced double-timed. MacGregor was still here, and he had Sloan. Why? None of it made sense. Axe reached for his phone and immediately called Sloan. It just rang and rang. No voicemail kicked in because he'd kept her so busy last night she hadn't had a chance to set it up. He fired off a text to her new number. *Please, God. Let her answer back right away.*

Charlie shook his head. "I tried that as well. She didn't answer me either."

"She has a new phone. Hers was destroyed last night. Trying her new number. I have to cover all the bases." Axe stood up and looked around. He saw Tag and Cain in the lobby at the desk. Elias and Finn were walking over to join them. "Look, Charlie, I will do my best to find out what's going on with Sloan. Give me your number so I can reach you."

Charlie stood up. "You can't shut me out. I need to know Sloan is okay."

Axe caught Finn's eye and gestured to him. Finn nudged Elias, and they both tapped Nick and Cain. They all stepped away from the counter and started toward Axe.

Axe turned to Charlie. "Come on." He dropped a couple

of dollars on the table and went to meet his team. They came together in the middle of the lobby and moved over to where the couches were.

"What's up?" Nick asked.

"This is Charlie, a friend of Sloan's. He says MacGregor's got her." Axe gestured to Charlie. He didn't say anything else because he couldn't. Icy fingers clutched his heart and stole his ability to speak. His brain was going a million miles an hour and stuck in neutral at the same time. *MacGregor had Sloan.* Axe's gut churned and he was afraid he might puke. Charlie must have finished telling the guys what he knew because Axe could feel the weight of Nick's stare but he couldn't seem to get his eyes to focus on any one thing.

Nick turned to Elias. "Go talk to the clerk. Let's see what's on the security cameras. If they give you a hard time about it, tell them an American citizen has been reportedly kidnapped from here and we're American law enforcement. If he wants proof let me know. We'll get Axe to talk to him." Then he looked at Finn. "Go take a look at Sloan's room." Both men set out to do as instructed. Nick turned to Charlie. "Thanks for telling us. We'll take it from here."

Charlie frowned. "Look here, you can't shut me out like this. Sloan is like a daughter to me."

Axe heard everything but he couldn't seem to collect himself. He was struggling to remain upright.

Nick said. "You're also a reporter, correct? We can't have any details getting out."

Charlie looked at him. "Yes, I am a reporter but I wouldn't do anything to jeopardize Sloan's safety. I won't write a word about this."

"Now? Or at all?" Nick asked. "Because it's a problem for us either way."

Charlie nodded. "I see what you're saying. Just writing about the incident will cause you issues because you're probably not supposed to be here, and certainly you should tell the local authorities if Sloan has been kidnapped. Handling it yourselves is way outside of policy."

Charlie was smart and quick on the uptake. Axe would probably like him in any other circumstance but at the moment, he needed Charlie to stop talking and go away.

"I won't write about it unless you give me permission." Charlie raised his three fingers. "Scout's honor."

Nick glanced at Axe, but he could only shrug. "Okay, Charlie, we'll keep you in the loop for now. Just don't make us regret it." Nick gave the man a hard stare.

Cain, who was on Charlie's right, leaned forward slightly and said in a quiet voice. "We know where you live."

Axe had to bite the inside of his cheek to stop from laughing. It would have been hysterical laughter for sure because he felt like doing anything but laughing at that moment, but it was enough to snap him out of his trance. Cain's deadpan face was good cover for the smartass he could be. The shocked expression on Charlie's face said it all.

All the humor died, though, when Elias walked out from the security room behind the desk. Axe caught Elias's eye and cocked an eyebrow. Elias gave a slight nod. It was true. MacGregor had Sloan.

Blood roared in Axe's ears. His hands curled into fists. Adrenaline pumped into his veins. Sloan was in serious trouble. He needed to find her now. This minute. He also needed to kill MacGregor.

Nick put a hand on his shoulder. "Breathe, Axe. It will be okay. We'll get Sloan back."

Elias arrived at their circle. "MacGregor and another guy walked Sloan out of the lobby. They got into an old SUV with two other guys in it. The guy in the passenger seat looked like he was hurt somehow. He was slumped funny in the seat."

"I'm pretty sure I hit a couple of them last night just before all hell broke loose," Cain said. "Could be why they're still in town."

Finn arrived just in time to hear what Cain said. "You think they didn't make the flight because a couple of them were hurt?" He turned to Axe and held up Sloan's cell. "The room looks fine. No damage. Looks like she went peacefully, which is a good thing."

Axe took the cell and slipped it in his pocket. He was no closer to Sloan, but having her phone at least made it possible for MacGregor to reach them. Logically, he would assume they'd have Sloan's phone. He said a silent prayer of thanksgiving that he'd programmed his number into Sloan's phone. It might be the only way they'd find her. That fucker MacGregor better not harm so much as a single strand of her chestnut hair. Axe was going to enjoy putting that bastard in traction.

Nick nodded at Finn to indicate he'd heard him. "Your theory makes sense, Cain. The injured would slow things down a bit. If they were on a tight schedule, then the flight might have gone without them."

"But why take Sloan?" Axe demanded. "It doesn't make sense."

"It does if they don't have another lift out of town," Elias pointed out. "If they have to take a commercial flight, or at least go to one of the larger airports, then they'd need us to call off the Egyptians so they could get out. Sloan is their way of making that happen."

Axe could see it. "Then we need to check the larger airports around here. Port Said International and Cairo are probably the two closest larger ones. That's where they'd be heading."

Nick glanced at his phone. "Bertrand just came through with the name of a local airport where a jet took off from last night in the right timeframe. I think we should check there, too. At this point, we know they can't get through the larger airports until they call us and demand we call off the Egyptians. In the meantime, we can at least confirm who was on that flight."

Axe wanted to protest. He wanted to demand they go to the nearest large airport, but Nick was right. This was the next logical move, and it was a hell of a lot better than waiting around for a call that might not come. His lungs froze. He couldn't even contemplate that. Sloan had to be okay. He wouldn't survive it if something happened to her. He drew in a ragged breath.

Nick turned to Charlie. "We let you hear all that. You know what we know. You know where we're going. We are trusting you. Don't make us regret it."

Charlie nodded. "I won't. I know some people to call in airport security at Port Said. I'll reach out and ask them to keep an eye out for anything suspicious. I know they're on the lookout for MacGregor, but who knows what shenanigans he's capable of."

The man had a point. Axe was grateful for any help they could get.

Axe offered his hand, and Charlie shook it but held on an extra beat. "Keep me in the loop. I… Sloan means the world to me. I know you know what that's like."

Axe nodded and let go of Charlie's hand. He and the rest of the team headed out of the lobby to their waiting SUV. He knew what Charlie meant. Sloan missing with MacGregor was like someone was carving his heart out with a dull spoon. It was also what he was going to do to MacGregor when he found him if Sloan was hurt in any way.

CHAPTER TWENTY-SEVEN

Omar yawned again. He'd taken a redeye flight from Germany to Turkey. The woman at the bar had turned out to be less interesting than he'd hoped. Now he was home and wanted to celebrate his deal with his father. In truth, he wanted to rub his father's nose in it a bit.

"I told you, Father, that I would succeed. This is a fucking amazing deal for our company." Omar smiled. "And I did it all by myself. You should have more faith in me." He took a sip of champagne as he sat on the leather couch in his father's office. Soon to be his office if he had anything to do with it. The old man was slipping and hopelessly out of touch. He should have spotted this deal, but he didn't. Omar had made it happen.

Hakan looked at his son over the rim of his champagne glass. He was sitting behind his desk, across the room from Omar. "It is a very good deal. You did a good job bringing it to a close...although, you did end up giving the Germans more than necessary. Still. Congratulations. You were lucky." He raised his glass.

Omar ground his teeth. The old man couldn't just say

something nice without adding a criticism. Not once. It was jealousy, pure and simple. Omar had made the deal Hakan couldn't. "The Germans were worried. I offered them what I needed to in order for them to sign the deal. No more. No less. It worked, and now we are one of the largest, if not the largest, textiles company in the world. I made my own luck. You should say thank you to me father."

He *had* made his own luck. Blocking the canal had caused the Germans to be uncomfortable. And the Germans never panicked. Once it was pointed out to them that the textiles they relied on to arrive on time could be held up for weeks because of Australia being so far away, it was an easy sell. He had to throw in a few extras to sweeten the deal, yes, but they were necessary. The Germans had to feel like it was a win for them.

Hakan narrowed his eyes slightly but nodded his head. "As I said, it's a good deal. So"—Hakan put his champagne flute down on his desk—"what are you working on now? What is your next project?"

Omar almost spit out his mouthful of champagne. "Next project? The ink is barely dry on this one. I am taking some well-deserved time off. I want to catch up with some friends and spend some time relaxing. I'll be back in two weeks, three at the outside."

Hakan's lips turned into a thin line. "Omar, in order to stay successful, you must always have a goal. You must always have another deal in the works. This was a good deal, but it's yesterday's news." He pointed at the financial newspaper that was on his desk. "What are you going to do for tomorrow?"

Omar shot off the couch and walked over to stand in front of his father. "I just made one of the biggest deals this company has ever seen and you're lecturing me on how to be successful?" He slammed his champagne flute down on the desk, and it shattered. "I have pulled off an incredible deal, something you failed at twice I might add, and you are still lecturing me. Well, that stops now!" Omar slammed the surface with his hand.

Hakan stood up. "How dare you speak to me that way! I am your father and the head of this company."

"Not for much longer," Omar growled. "I have already spoken to the board. They are behind me as the new head of Balik Textiles. The vote will happen next week." He leaned across the desk and glared at his father. "Your days are numbered, old man," he spat and then he turned on his heel and stormed out of his father's office.

He walked across the reception room and slammed into his own office, causing the door to bounce off the wall. Then he whacked it closed. His father was dead to him. Dead! How could the man lecture *him*? Hakan was the past. Omar was the future. The board knew that. Or at least some members did.

A small frisson of doubt niggled at Omar's gut. He shouldn't have said anything about the board meeting. Now his father was warned, and he could fight back. Omar only had the slimmest of margins. He stood staring out at the Bosphorus. Maybe he should call his supporters on the board and warn them. They would be angry with him for letting the cat out of the bag. Still, he was the best choice to lead the company into the future. He would remind them of that. His father hadn't pulled off a large deal in some time. He was too busy studying the market, trying to figure out what the next big textile craze would be. It could be anything. Who knew?

It didn't matter.

No. He, Omar, was the man to lead, and the board would know it. This deal gave him a seat at the table. *He* was going to be the man in charge. He turned around and sat down at his desk. He might have to postpone his vacation again. He would need to be here for the vote. He'd go at the beginning of next month. The board would understand he needed a few weeks to recuperate.

His gaze hit the same financial newspaper his father had on his desk. There was an article inside that talked of his deal. It praised the deal, but it, too, said it was luck. If St. Claire's ships hadn't been stuck behind the *Sea Jewel,* the Germans would have gone into business with the Australian.

"Luck," he sneered. "I made my own luck." He'd beat Tristan St. Claire at his own game. *Ha*. Sending a bunch of ships with product for free to tempt the Germans had almost worked. Until they got stuck. Omar grinned. He really was a genius.

His office door opened, and his father strode in, newspaper in hand. He stopped on the other side of Omar's desk. "Tell me you had nothing to do with the Suez mess." His father's eyes blazed in anger.

Omar swallowed. His gut twisted. His father had always been able to tell when he was lying when he was a child. But he wasn't a child any longer. He stood up. "I told you I make my own luck. I capitalized on the situation. End of story." He glared at his father and Hakan glared back. Omar did his best to hold his father's gaze as sweat broke out across his back.

"Do you realize what you've done? If anyone finds out…"

His father seemed at a loss for words for the first time ever. Omar frowned. It wasn't that big of a deal. The ships are all moving again, and he'd made the deal of a lifetime.

"The Egyptians would sue us for everything we have. We would be sued by every shipping company in the world. We would be finished. Run out of the industry. It would be catastrophic." Hakan wobbled on his feet slightly. His face, which had been bright red when he'd entered Omar's office, was now white. Whiter than Omar had ever seen before.

"Well"—Omar cleared his throat—"it's a good thing I had nothing to do with it then, isn't it?" He met his father's gaze and then looked away. The man appeared unwell. "Perhaps you should take the rest of the day off, Father. You're pale and slightly unsteady on your feet. I can handle things here."

Hakan continued to stare at his son, and then he slowly nodded. He turned and wandered out of Omar's office. His gait was that of an old man, twenty years beyond Hakan's actual age. Was he right about what would happen if the world found out? Probably. Sweat broke out across Omar's whole body. He blinked. The money was lost. People would want restitution. Egypt would want to restore their reputation, and they would also want payment for blocking their canal. And the dead bodies. There were two people dead because of this whole mess. Maybe more. Omar had been afraid to ask after the last call. He really didn't want to know. He sat down heavily in his chair.

The phone on his desk rang. "Yes," he said into the receiver.

"The restaurant wants to confirm your dinner reservation for tomorrow evening. Shall I confirm for you?"

Omar had organized a little party for himself to celebrate with all his favorite people on Saturday night. Maybe he should cancel. Omar shook his head. Why should he cancel? He still had pulled off the best deal this company had seen in years. "Yes, confirm the reservation. And bring me more champagne." He clicked off the call. His father wasn't going to ruin his celebration or his success.

CHAPTER TWENTY-EIGHT

S loan stayed quiet in the SUV as they pulled up to the private airfield. Axe always told her to take in all the details of her environment. *Be situationally aware*. She looked around.

The airport was bigger than she imagined. There was a long, low building on the left with lots of windows, which seemed to be offices. There was also a long wall of windows that seemed to be part of a large room that looked like a typical airport lounge. There was a parking lot in front of the building as well as on the side closest to them, and a chain-link fence ran from the main building, across the side parking lot, to another building on their right. There was a gate that was attached to the building on the left with a guard booth to the right of it.

The building on the right was made of steel. It was big and sort of in the shape of a dome. The roof had to be sixty or seventy feet high and looked to be about one hundred and fifty feet wide. She'd noticed on the drive in that there were quite a few of them all in a row, leading away from the building on her left. They must be the airplane hangars. At least that was her guess. From the back side, they all looked the same, silver with a door in the back left corner.

Looking at the low building on the left, the most important thing she noticed were the people. Some in the offices and some in the lounge. People meant hope. Maybe she could signal someone for help. Charlie had to know she was missing by now. She'd missed their breakfast. Maybe he was already putting out feelers. If that were the case, the more people who saw her, the better.

MacGregor leaned in close to her ear. "Don't even think about causing trouble here."

She turned and stared at him but remained silent. He reached over and zip-tied her wrists together. "You are going to do everything I say, or I will kill you. I don't need you now. You're just an extra insurance policy, so don't push your luck."

Sloan nodded. She understood perfectly. MacGregor didn't trust that his people were sending the airplane back, so she was his backup in case it all went wrong again. The question was, would he kill her when the plane showed up, or wait until they were on board and push her out at twenty thousand feet?

She tried to quell the panic that was clawing at her throat. She wanted to scream and thrash and attack MacGregor, but she knew he'd shoot her. She wasn't that valuable anymore. Sloan drew in a ragged breath and then let it out again. She needed to keep her mind free of fear so she could concentrate.

What had Axe told her to do in these types of situations? *Look for an opening.* He'd said she would recognize one if it came along. He'd also stressed *don't panic.* A clear mind would help her get free. It was all well and good for him to lecture her on this shit when they were hanging out, but it was a whole different ball game when it was actually happening. How was she supposed to be calm? The man had just tied her hands together. At least he hadn't tied her feet.

When the SUV pulled up to the gate, Sloan realized the small structure to the right was there to stop people from having access to the tarmac. A man came out of a booth, and the driver put down his window. Sloan winced when MacGregor pushed the gun into her ribs. There was no way she could attract the guard's attention without getting shot. This was not her opening.

The guard spoke in Arabic and, to her surprise, Simon responded in the same language. She had no idea what was being said, but the guard gestured over to the right. Simon nodded, and the guard stepped into his booth and did something. The gate rolled open. Simon went through the gate and around the building to the right. He drove for another minute or so and pulled up to a hangar. It was wide open and mostly empty. There were some shipping crates on the left wall and some metal lockers toward the back left side. There appeared to be some shelves behind the lockers, as well. They stuck up about four feet above the lockers. Simon backed into the hangar into the far-right corner in front of the doorway that Sloan had noticed on their way in.

When they'd come to a stop, MacGregor reached for the door handle. "Drop the seats and get Styler into the back. He needs to lie down." He turned to her. "You. Don't give me any trouble, and you can live a bit longer." He slid out of the SUV and pulled her across the seat by her hands. She stumbled as her feet hit the floor.

MacGregor dragged her over to a table with some chairs at the very back of the hangar on the left side. She hadn't noticed them when they'd pulled up because of the lockers and shelves. There was a small bathroom to the left of the tables.

"Sit," MacGregor ordered as he pointed to a chair by the table. It was facing the shelving units so Sloan couldn't see the rest of the hangar, just the SUV parked in the opposite corner.

She sat where she was told and stared at her surroundings. There were various tools and wires on the shelves. There were also some mechanical pieces that she took to be airplane parts. A fire extinguisher hung on the wall next to the bathroom. Almost all the stuff on the shelves could be used as a weapon, which was good news. Now she just had to figure out a way to get over to the shelving, get her hands free, and grab something. *Piece of cake.*

Christo came over and stood next to MacGregor. "They should be here in another hour or so."

MacGregor nodded. "How's Styler?"

Christo shook his head. "Not good. He's not going to make it through the flight to Germany. Too much blood loss."

"You're sure?"

Christo nodded. "His blood pressure is dropping, and his heartbeat is getting weaker."

"Shoot him then. No point in dead weight. Too much to explain if we bring him back to Germany," MacGregor said and then took a seat on the opposite side of the table from Sloan. Christo walked back over to the SUV. He pulled out his handgun with the suppressor on it, and then Sloan heard two quick *thwap* sounds. She closed her eyes and shuddered. They'd just killed one of their own without hesitation. She had no hope that they wouldn't kill her. Her stomach rolled, and she gagged.

MacGregor smiled. "It won't be long now."

She swallowed hard. She didn't know if he meant until

their plane landed or until he killed her, but that was his whole point. This was his way of torturing her. He really was a son of a bitch. Sloan fervently hoped there was a hell because MacGregor was sure to be a resident when someone eventually managed to kill him. Cockroaches were so damn hard to kill.

CHAPTER TWENTY-NINE

Axe glanced at his watch. Nine-forty-five. Sloan had been taken about two hours ago. Two hours with MacGregor. He flexed his fingers. He wanted to strangle the man with his bare hands. It was his fault Sloan had been grabbed. He should have stayed with her.

"It's not your fault." Nick glanced over at him from the driver's seat. "You are working, and you had to meet with the team. Besides, it wouldn't have mattered if you skipped the meeting. You know as well as I do that if MacGregor really wanted to grab Sloan, he would have found a way, no matter what we did. None of this is your fault."

Axe grunted. "Maybe."

Logically, he knew Nick was right, but it was damn hard to let go of the guilt. Sloan always ran headlong into things. He should have known she wouldn't be fine on her own. He stared out the passenger window and watched the desert roll by.

"How long to the airport?" Cain asked from the back seat.

"About fifteen minutes," Nick replied. "We'll ask around

about the other jet and see if we can get the tail number to trace. Also, I want to know just how many of MacGregor's men made it onto the plane. From the footage we saw, it looks like there were four of them left behind, and one was in hard shape. That evens the odds a bit for us."

"Why do you think MacGregor is waiting to contact us? Doesn't he want to get out of town quickly? What's the hold up?" Axe ground his teeth.

"There could be variables we are unaware of, making it take longer. Maybe he took his man to a doctor. Maybe there's a specific plane they want to take. There are too many unknowns for us to guess. Don't read anything into it," Cain advised.

"Honestly, Axe, we're just guessing that they took her because they want to fly out. Maybe they took her as an insurance policy, but they plan to drive to Libya or Tunisia. MacGregor may not call unless he runs into problems."

Axe's gut churned. This conversation wasn't helping.

Nick glanced over at him again. "I know that's tough to hear, Axe, but you need to be logical about this. It could be a while before we hear from MacGregor. We had Charlie alert the Egyptian authorities. They'll keep an eye out for her, as well as MacGregor. He didn't take her to just kill her, Axe. He needed a hostage for some reason, and he wanted her to keep us at bay. She's still alive."

Axe said nothing. Alive didn't mean she wasn't harmed or sick. Nick specifically had said "alive," and Axe knew why. That was the worst part of this. He *knew* exactly what MacGregor would probably do to Sloan once he didn't need her anymore. He also knew what men like MacGregor were capable of. The rage churning in his gut went red hot. Axe realized this emotion wasn't helpful so he struggled to control his breathing, the way he had when the pain from his burns had been out of control.

Nick turned right into the small airport. All the signs were in Arabic except a small one right by the main door of the low building. *Suez Fixed-Base Operator.* Nick parked in a spot on the side of the building. He glanced at his phone. "Nothing from Finn and Elias yet. It's going to take them a while to sort through all of the information Mitch sent over. They're going to cross reference it with the stuff we pulled the other day. It's a long shot, but hopefully something will turn up."

The three men got out of the SUV and headed into the Fixed-Base Operations office where anyone flying private had to pass through. The main lounge was small but well appointed. There were leather seats and sofas for guests to relax in and various vending machines, as well as a snack counter for guests to grab a bite before their flight.

There was another counter with a tall, beautiful woman behind it. She was here in case anyone had questions about their flights and to organize ground transportation and the like. She smiled at the group of them. Her hair was covered by a blue hijab and her chocolate-brown eyes were warm. She wore a white blouse with a name tag that read *Raina.*

Axe observed all of this, but his mind was on Sloan. Where was she at this minute? Was she okay? Hurt? Dead? Having those thoughts run around his head was not helping. He needed to focus on something or he would drive himself crazy.

Nick and Axe approached the counter and the smiling woman behind it. Cain positioned himself in the back corner with a view of the entire room and the windows.

Nick smiled at Raina. "Hi, some friends of ours were supposed to meet up with us, but I think we got the time wrong. Can you tell me if a jet went out last night?"

The Egyptian woman immediately looked uncomfortable. Her warm brown eyes suddenly cooled. "I'm sorry sir. I cannot give you that information."

"Oh, of course. We understand. We don't want to put you in a difficult position." Nick smiled slightly, but Axe could tell he was trying to reformulate his approach.

Axe stepped up to the counter. "Sorry about my friend. We don't want you to get in trouble or anything, but we kind of need to know if our friends left already. We were out enjoying your country way too much last night and lost track of time. We thought we were supposed to meet here this morning, but unfortunately now we think they meant last night. If they've gone, then we have to find another way home and our bosses are not going to be pleased. We don't need names or anything. Just if a group of guys that look like us got on a jet to Germany." He offered her a wide smile.

She smiled back. "I wasn't working last night but…" She reached over and tapped away on the computer keyboard. "It looks like there *was* a jet to Germany, and there were supposed to be nine people on it. Only four actually made the flight. I guess that was the one you missed." She smiled and glanced around as if looking for the other two missing men.

Axe turned to Nick. "Looks like the other guys missed it as well. Maybe they'll come back for us." He turned back to Raina and smiled again. "Well, thanks—"

"You're right," she said with a bright smile.

Axe blinked. "I'm sorry?"

"I said you're right. It looks like the jet is coming back for you. It's going to land in about three minutes." She looked over her shoulder and pointed to a small dot in the sky. "There it is. It's going to park over at Hangar Four. They'll refuel and will leave shortly after that. So I guess you made your flight after all."

Axe's heartbeat ticked up. He smiled at Raina. "That's great news. Thank you! Can we go out to the hangar then?"

Raina nodded. "I will have Mohammed open the gate for you. You can leave your SUV by the hangar. I'm assuming it is a rental?" At Axe's nod, she smiled again. "Then just leave it with the keys inside, and we'll take care of returning it for you."

"Raina, you have made my day!" Axe offered her one last big smile and then turned on his heel and strode out of the FBO with Nick and Cain right behind him.

"They're here. We should call for backup," Nick said as he got into the driver's side of the SUV.

Cain slid in behind him. "We don't need backup." He pulled a handgun out from under his black T-shirt and checked it over. He immediately dropped it at his side when Nick drove over to the gate.

Axe nodded his agreement as Nick came to a stop and waved to the guard. The guard hit a button, and the gate rolled open. Nick drove through and turned to the right.

"I hear what you're saying, but we have no idea how many guys we're up against here." Nick drove slowly down the tarmac in front of a row of hangars.

"We also don't have the time to wait for them," Axe pointed out. "Once that jet is ready, they're gone, and Sloan…" he faltered. Even saying the words was just too much.

"Right," Nick said and pulled a sharp turn into a hangar on their left. It was two up from the one with the jet in front. He parked the SUV, and the three men checked their weapons one last time before hopping out of the truck. They met at the rear of the SUV.

"Axe…" Nick paused and looked directly at him with a serious expression on his face. "This is going to be tough. I need to know you can do your job here. You can't go off and do something stupid if Sloan's in danger. We have to work together as a team. These guys are…us. We probably have the same training and the same moves. They're good. Teamwork will keep us all in one piece."

Axe swallowed his rage. Tag shouldn't have to question his ability. He should know Axe would never do anything to jeopardize the lives of his team members. But could he really blame Tag for saying it? No. He knew what it was like. Nick's girlfriend had been involved in the mess in Panama, and it had scared the hell out of him. Axe realized Nick was speaking not just as his boss, but from a place of experience.

Cain slapped Axe on the arm. "He'll be fine. He'll do what's needed. We all will."

Nick glanced at Axe, but let it go. Axe nodded at Cain. Leave it to Cain to sum it up perfectly. They would do what was needed.

And he needed to kill MacGregor.

CHAPTER THIRTY

S loan shifted on the uncomfortable chair as she studied
the shelves ahead of her. At waist level was a pair of bolt
cutters. They would take care of the zip ties and then some,
but someone else would have to use them for her. She kept
scanning the shelves. There were pliers on the next shelf up
and a large file-looking thing on the shelf over to the left. She
could use that to break her bonds but there was no way she
could get it or hide what she was doing.

MacGregor and Christo had disappeared into the front
of the hangar. Simon was across from her, leaning on the
SUV. He had his gun down by his side. He glanced at her
every so often to make sure she was behaving herself.

Sloan studied the shelves some more. There were all kinds
of tools that someone else could use to cut her ties but
precious little that she herself could make work. She let out a
long breath. She was exhausted, and not thinking as clearly as
she would like.

She glanced around the hangar. The bathroom appeared
to be utilitarian. Clean but no frills. There was a sink, with a
mirror above it and a toilet. The fluorescent bulb on the

ceiling gave off a harsh white light. The mirror might be an option. Maybe she could ask to go to the bathroom and then break the mirror and use a jagged piece to cut the zip tie. Nah. They'd never let her close the door, and even if they did, they'd come in the moment they heard the breaking glass. She'd never have time to cut the ties before they were on top of her.

Sloan blinked back frustrated tears. She tried not to get discouraged. Axe and Charlie had to be out looking for her by now. Help was on the way. She just had to live long enough for it to find her.

She went back to studying the shelves. The far corner close to the bathroom door caught her eye. The shelf itself was bent. A jagged metal piece stuck out. From where she sat, the edge looked plenty sharp. If she had a bit of time, she could use it to cut the plastic cuffs. She knew it would work, but how was she going to distract MacGregor and his goons long enough to cut the ties and get away?

She glanced over at Simon again. How closely was he paying attention to her? She moved her arms suddenly, and he immediately looked in her direction. She just stared back at him, so then he went back to watching whatever was in the front of the hangar.

So, he was paying close attention. He'd never let her get up and wander over to the shelves on her own. She needed some sort of distraction to happen. Something that allowed her to get over to the broken shelf. She bit her lip. Her mind was blank. What could she do to create a distraction?

A sound hit her ears. It was quiet at first but got louder by the second. The jet had arrived. The engines were roaring. Simon straightened up. He turned toward the front of the warehouse and held his gun down behind his leg. Sloan noted the position of the gun. Simon was worried. Maybe the people on the plane were not so friendly?

She moved her arms again, but Simon didn't turn in her direction. Was now her moment? If she got up, would he notice? Moving slowly, she stood. Simon didn't notice. The sound was deafening now. The jet had to be just outside the hangar. She said a prayer that they didn't actually come in because then all the men would have to back up to be out of the way.

She moved a step and then another. Simon was focused on the scene outside of the hangar. The knuckles on his gun hand had turned white. He had shifted forward a couple of steps so now he would actually have to lean way back or step back to see her. This was her opening. She jogged over to the broken shelf and started rubbing the zip tie across the jagged edge. The plastic started to give.

Then the engines shut down on the airplane and the sounds started to die out. *Fuck!* Sloan wanted to scream with frustration. The plastic wasn't cut all the way through. Even if her hands were free, she didn't have time to get away. She made a split-second decision and went back to the chair. As soon as she sat down, Simon leaned back and looked at her. She just stared at him again.

She heard voices above the waning sounds of the engines. Whoever had arrived on the jet was now in the hangar and there was more than one of them. Sloan's heart rate skyrocketed. If she didn't get out of there soon, it would be too late, but there was nowhere for her to go. She couldn't get by Simon to the exit in the back, nor could she get by all of them to exit out the front of the hangar.

She looked over at the bathroom again. It didn't appear to have a window so it wasn't likely she could escape from there either. There had to be something. Anything. The sound of the voices was getting louder, and the jet engines had all but come to a stop.

"How's Styler?" a voice said. Rohan Patel. She'd know that voice anywhere.

"Didn't make it. Gut shot," MacGregor said. Sloan noticed immediately he didn't volunteer that he had Christo shoot the guy.

"So, it's just the three of you then?" Patel asked.

There was a pause. Then MacGregor cleared his throat. "We took a bit of insurance. We'll leave her here when we're ready to go."

"Insurance? What the fuck did you do?" Patel's British accent was thicker now.

"We weren't sure you were coming back. It's not like anyone contacted us, and they were ducking my calls, so we grabbed a woman that we know the Americans won't want to hurt. We were going to use her as leverage so we could get out of here."

"If you hadn't bollocksed the whole thing up then we wouldn't have had to come back for you." There was more swearing. "Where is she?"

"Around there," MacGregor answered. His voice was cold. He wasn't pleased. He didn't like Patel; that much was obvious. Sloan heard footsteps, and she braced herself.

"Well, I don't want to see her. What the fuck were you thinking? That just complicates things. Go get rid of her now."

There was silence. Sloan's blood pounded in her ears. Her breath froze in her lungs. Footsteps started coming closer until Christo appeared around the side of the shelving unit, the gun in his hand raised and pointing directly at her.

CHAPTER THIRTY-ONE

"How are we going to do this?" Axe asked as he glanced down the tarmac at the jet that was now parked in front of hangar four.

Nick hazarded a glance at the jet as well. "Good question. The engines have stopped, and the fuel truck is just pulling up. We don't have much time. I still think we should call the Egyptian authorities. They can stop the plane from taking off."

"It will take too long to explain things," Axe ground out. "We don't have that kind of time."

Cain leaned against the back of their SUV. "Call Saige. Have her tell her Egyptian contacts. It will have more authority coming from her."

Nick nodded. "Good point. Axe, you give her a call and fill her in. Cain and I will formulate a plan."

Axe stepped away and made the call. His voice was terse even to his own ears. He knew he was on edge. They needed to do something soon, or it would be too late. He wouldn't be able to live with himself if anything happened to Sloan.

"I'll do my best on this end. Good luck, Axe," Saige said, and then she was gone.

Axe walked back over to join Cain and Nick at the opening of the hangar. "Saige is on it. What's the plan?"

"In all likelihood, they haven't seen Cain and me up close, so we are going to approach from the front. I want you to go around and come in through the back door. We don't have comms so we're going to have to do this the old-fashioned way. Hand signals and timing."

Axe nodded. It made sense. They'd see Axe coming, but they might not recognize Nick and Cain. Coming in through the back meant that he was blind, though. He had to burst through the door and hope that no one was waiting on the other side to kill him. Tall order.

He glanced at his watch. He knew there was limited time, but he had to be thorough. He turned and ran to the back door of the hangar they were in. It was pretty flimsy. One good kick and it should come open. It wasn't really made to keep people out. Only to let them in when the big doors were closed.

He waved at Nick and Cain and then exited the building and rushed toward hangar four. When he got to the far edge of the building before it, he stopped and peeked around the corner. Nick's head popped up around the corner, and he gave Axe a fist in the air. Hold. *Fuck.*

Axe absently rubbed his chest over his heart. He was so close to Sloan. He needed to see her. To know she was okay. It took everything he had not to bust through that door right now. But he couldn't betray his team members like that. He might be putting them in danger. No matter how much he loved Sloan and needed her to be okay, he couldn't do anything that might hurt a teammate. He fucked up once and lost two best friends. It would kill him if he fucked up again and lost Nick or Cain. It would kill him if he lost Sloan. Knowing this meant he didn't care so much about living himself as long as everyone else would be okay.

A shot rang out.

CHAPTER THIRTY-TWO

The shot scared Sloan, and she let out a small scream. She stared in horror as Christo slowly slid to the floor.

"What the fuck did you do that for?" MacGregor demanded.

"Because you all are a liability. Too many dead bodies, Hamish. Silverstone can only cover up so much. You're a wanted man now. The FBI knows the reporter didn't just fall over the railing and neither did the Egyptian woman."

"But you killed those two." MacGregor pointed out.

"I was cleaning up your messes. And now I'm here to clean up another one. Silverstone doesn't want you and your men back, Hamish. Too much of an embarrassment."

There was the sound of a scuffle and then gunfire erupted. Simon now shooting at Patel and whoever was with him in the hangar as he moved behind the SUV. Sloan was on her feet and had started heading for the back door until a bullet hit the shelving unit beside her. She stopped and crouched down.

Simon took aim at her, so she turned and ran for the bathroom. There was another volley of gunfire behind her, and she heard a grunt. She flew into the bathroom and closed the door. It wasn't much, but it was something between her and the flying bullets.

Axe looked down the alley between the two hangars. Nick waved at him to go in. He hit the back door and sent it crashing to the wall and immediately started shooting. One of the guys from the boat was behind the SUV that was parked in front of the door. He whirled around and got a shot off that hit the doorframe right next to Axe's head before Axe put one in his chest. It wasn't the first time the guy had been shot. He was already bleeding.

Axe moved up to the SUV and glanced in the back. There was another dead guy lying there. It looked like he'd been shot a couple of times, too. Axe crept along the side of the SUV.

Nick and Cain were pinned down at the front of the hangar. They alternated popping out from behind the wall, taking shots at two men who were hiding behind some crates that had been pushed out from the side of the hangar. One of them was Rohan Patel. There was another dead man on the floor that Axe didn't recognize. He must have come on the jet.

A few feet away behind the shelves and next to a table, MacGregor lay in an ever-growing pool of blood. Axe squeezed off a couple of shots at Patel behind the crates. Patel returned fire. The jet engines started up. Axe looked around. *Where the hell was Sloan?*

He kept exchanging shots with Patel and his man behind the crates, taking turns with Cain and Nick to draw out their ammunition. He was going to be out shortly. The jet's engines started to emit a high-pitched whine.

Patel and the other man made a break for the open door of the jet with one firing constantly to cover their exit. Axe took aim and caught the guy in the shoulder just as he was going up the stairs. He fell into the jet, and it started rolling away.

Nick and Cain stopped shooting. There was no point. Hopefully, the Egyptian authorities would catch them. They walked into the hangar, guns still drawn, and looked around. Axe went out to meet them in the middle of the building. They checked the dead guy for identification, but he had none. There were sirens in the distance.

"Where the fuck is Sloan?" Axe demanded.

Nick and Cain shook their heads. "We didn't see her."

"Fuck!" Axe stormed around the lockers and shelving units where MacGregor had fallen. When he came around the corner, MacGregor was on his feet, and gunfire erupted. He had two handguns and was peppering the wall with both.

"MacGregor!" Axe yelled but the man didn't stop. *What the fuck?* Axe looked at the wall again. There was a door there. It was hard to see through all the bullet holes. MacGregor had shot off the doorknob. *Sloan.* Axe yelled one more time, but MacGregor kept unloading his guns. Axe shot him in the leg and the man dropped to one knee. He turned, and Axe saw blood gushing from a gaping stomach wound. He must have been shot twice, at least. MacGregor smiled and aimed at Axe. Axe shot him in the face, and he fell backwards to the floor.

Nick and Cain raced up next to Axe. "What the fuck was that all about?"

"Sloan." Axe could barely get his voice to work. He ran across the room, jumping over the now dead form of MacGregor as he yelled. "Sloan!" *Please, God, don't let her be dead.* The walls were riddled with bullet holes. MacGregor had unloaded both clips into the space. There was no way anyone could have survived the assault.

Axe pushed the door open, but what was left of it got stuck. He looked down. Sloan was lying on her belly with her hands over the back of her head. They were tied together with a half-broken zip tie.

"Sloan!" Axe dropped to his knees and tried to turn her over. There wasn't enough space in the bathroom, so he had to close the door to move her. He finally flipped her over. He cradled her head in his hands as he searched her body for holes. "Where is she hit?" Axe asked but Cain and Nick were on the other side of the door.

"What?" Sloan said.

Axe looked back at her face. Sloan was staring up at him.

"Where are you hurt, honey?"

"What? I can't hear a damn thing with all that shooting going on."

"Are you hurt?" Axe yelled. He looked her up and down again but could find no blood.

Sloan struggled to sit up. "I'm fine. Just dirty. I had to lie on the floor. Yuk." She made a face.

Axe gathered her into his arms and hugged her hard. She was okay. She was alive. *Sloan was alive.* He was having a hard time believing it, so he refused to let her go when she pushed against his chest.

"You're crushing my ribs," Sloan said, her voice muffled by her head being squished into Axe's shoulder.

"I can't believe you're okay." He swooped in and kissed her hard. She was okay. His Sloan was okay. Jesus, he'd been scared.

Sloan broke off the kiss. "Axe, I did what you told me. Kept low and tried to find cover. You never mentioned how loud guns are though."

Axe laughed as he scooped her up and took her out of the

bathroom. "Turn your head," he directed. He didn't want her to have to see MacGregor's lifeless body on the floor, but instead, Sloan stopped crying. She looked around the hangar.

"Put me down," Sloan said.

Axe hesitated.

"Now, Axe."

He set her on her feet. She turned and nodded to Nick and Cain. "Thank you for coming to get me." She looked back over her shoulder at Axe and smiled. "You, too." Then she turned back and looked at MacGregor. "I'm glad he's dead. He was an evil man. It was Patel by the way. He came on the jet with other men. He said MacGregor was a liability to Silverstone now. Does that make sense to you?"

Axe exchanged a look with Nick and Cain. "Yeah, that makes sense."

"Good," she nodded.

Axe wrapped his arm around her. "Let's get you out of here." He moved her around MacGregor's body and out from behind the shelving units. Then they came face to face with a dozen Egyptian policemen all with guns drawn.

"Shit," Axe mumbled.

CHAPTER THIRTY-THREE

S loan stared in the mirror. She didn't look too bad. A few bruises but nothing extreme. It was a good thing no one could see her insides, though. She was a mess. She always thought of herself as strong, but the whole thing with MacGregor had left her a hell of a lot more shaken than she imagined it would.

When all those bullets crashed around her and there was no letup, she'd honestly thought she was going to die. She would never see her mother or Charlie again. Never see Axe again. She swallowed the lump that was building in her throat. She was supposed to be grabbing a quick shower while they waited for room service and her debrief.

Sloan had told the cops everything she knew and answered all their questions. It had taken what seemed like hours. She was exhausted and strangely hungry. Axe and the others on the team would have questions as well. They'd been kept separate at the hangar, so she'd have to repeat her story for them. They were kind with her and patient. No one had asked her anything on the way back to the hotel nor had they said a word when she'd told them she really needed a shower.

Soon, though, she would have to speak to them. She just wasn't sure she could do it without sobbing. The last thing she wanted to do was ugly-cry in front of these guys. She needed their respect, but she also didn't want to embarrass Axe.

Axe. She had realized while she was sitting there in the hangar, trying to find a way to escape that she loved him. Like full-on, rest-of-her-life loved him. As in never love another the same way. What the fuck was she supposed to do about that? He cared about her, but she wasn't sure he had forgiven her or that he trusted her.

It was all too much. She reached in and turned on the shower. After peeling off her clothes, she stepped under the warm spray. She wet her hair. She reached for the shampoo and promptly burst into tears. She leaned against the wall and cried for the next ten minutes.

It wasn't just MacGregor and being kidnapped. It was Eddie and Zahra. It was Axe. It was her father and mother. It was what Charlie had said. All of it rained down on her like the water droplets from the showerhead. It was so much. So many years of trying to live up to her father and disappointing her mother. Years of doing things that she thought she needed to in order to be successful. The sadness of loss. And the realization that life did not have to be this way.

Tears spent, Sloan straightened and reached again for the shampoo. This time, she succeeded in washing her hair. Almost dying certainly provided some clarity. It was going to take a while for her to process everything, but a couple of things were resonating with her already.

One, she was done with trying to live up to her father's reputation. Charlie was right. She was better at the human-interest stories. She bonded with her subjects, and they responded to her. This was a way to move out from her father's shadow and still be a reporter. It was also less danger-ous, and after this whole mess, she was good with that.

Two, she was done with her mother. Or at least done with listening to her drunken rants about needing to be as good as her father and how fabulous he had been. Charlie was right there, too. Her father had been an asshole. That didn't mean she didn't love him, but she sure as hell didn't want to be like him, and her mother just needed to accept that.

Three, she did love Axe, and when the time was right, when things had calmed down, she was going to tell him and then she was going to convince him to trust her again. They were made to be together. She would just have to get him to believe that.

Sloan conditioned her hair and scrubbed her body. Lying on that bathroom floor in the hangar had been enough to skeeve her out. She was going to be scrubbing herself in the shower for months from the memory. Repressing a shudder, she rinsed off, and finally all clean and freshly scrubbed, she got out of the shower. Someone, Axe presumably, had left some clean clothes in the bathroom for her.

When they'd gotten back to the hotel after the police questioned them, she found out that Axe had arranged a new room for her. It was a suite with a separate bedroom and a kitchenette. She truly appreciated it. The bathroom was larger, too, and she would swear the towels were fluffier.

Sloan dressed in jeans and a white T-shirt. She towel-dried her hair and left it down over her shoulders. Giving herself one last look in the mirror, she noticed her eyes didn't look too bad. Axe would probably know she'd been crying, but none of the others would, and that would have to do. She pulled open the bathroom door to find the bedroom empty and the door to the living area closed.

Sloan walked over and opened the door. The guys were

all sitting on various furniture around the room. In front of her there was a sofa with a coffee table and a TV on the wall across the room from it. Axe and Elias were sitting on the sofa. Nick was in a club chair in front of the window and Finn was in the matching chair on the far side of the sofa. There was a coffee table in the middle of the room that had cans of soda on it.

Cain was leaning against the counter of the kitchenette off to the left. In front of him was a bunch of plates with silver domes over them. Whatever they ordered smelled good. Suddenly, she was starving. She glanced at her watch. It was going on four o'clock. She hadn't eaten since yesterday.

"Something smells divine," she said as she moved toward the kitchen.

"I think Axe ordered the whole menu, for which I am very grateful," Finn said with his hand on his heart.

Axe stood up. "Let's eat." There were plates and cutlery already laid out, so everyone got up and grabbed what they needed. Axe started removing the silver covers and Sloan helped herself to all kinds of goodies. She loved middle eastern food, but she also loved pasta and steak. A bit of almost everything made it onto her plate. Then she took everything over to the living area and set her plate on the coffee table. She sat on the floor in front of it with her back to the TV.

The others filtered over and found seats. The room was quiet as everyone ate. Sloan swallowed a bite of food and said, "I assume you want to hear what happened."

Axe, who was sitting across from her on the sofa, stopped chewing and quickly swallowed. "There's no rush. We can do it after dinner."

"I'd rather do it now." Sloan didn't want to have to look at the guys while she spoke. She was afraid the tears would start again. She took a deep breath and then launched into her story between bites of dinner. Axe and Nick asked a few questions. The others remained silent.

"When the shooting started, I tried to get to the back door, but I couldn't. So, the only alternative was the bathroom." She swallowed and looked up at Axe. "I remember you saying to get low and cover your head if I ever got into trouble. We'd been joking about it at the time, but it worked. I dropped to the floor and covered my head." She put her fork down on her now clean plate. "Anyway, you guys know the rest."

Axe had set his plate down a few minutes ago and was now just staring at her. He cleared his throat. "Thank God, it worked out."

"Yes," Nick agreed. "You were smart. You did all the right things, Sloan. Not many people would have had the wherewithal to do what you did. You should be very proud of yourself."

Sloan smiled. "I'm just grateful I survived." She got up off the floor and took her plate back to the kitchen. "Does anyone want more?"

Cain and Elias came over, and Sloan reloaded their plates. Then she started covering the leftovers. She yawned once, and then again. Axe came over and stood across the counter from her. She really wanted him to come around and give her a hug, but he'd been keeping his distance. She wasn't sure just what was going on, but now wasn't the moment to figure it out. A wave of fatigue hit her.

"Why don't you go crash?"

"It's not even dark out," Sloan protested.

"But you're exhausted, and you've been through a lot. Trust me. Your body needs the rest."

Sloan nodded. Axe was right. She was beyond exhausted, but if she went to bed, then the guys would leave and she'd be alone. A spike of adrenaline hit her system. She leaned on the counter. Her knees had gone weak.

Axe leaned across the counter and squeezed her arm. "Don't worry. The couch is a pullout. I'm going to sleep on that."

As the sense of relief flowed through her, tears sprang to her eyes. Axe knew her so well. They were truly destined to be together. She just had to make him see that.

Sloan tried to stifle her yawn, but it was no use. "I think I will go have a nap at least. I am done for." She smiled at Axe and came around the counter. "I'm really tired, guys. I'm going to crash for a bit. Thanks so much for coming to my rescue today." She swallowed the lump forming in her throat. "Just knowing you guys were out there was a comfort, but you all saved my life. For that, I will be eternally grateful." She tried to blink back her tears as she crossed the room and entered the bedroom, closing the door after herself. Five minutes later, she was in bed and drifting off to sleep.

CHAPTER THIRTY-FOUR

A xe let out a long breath and leaned against the counter after Sloan closed the door. It had damn near killed him not to hold her close, but it wouldn't help anything. He needed to get over her. He loved her, but their lives weren't compatible. He sighed, and Nick squeezed his shoulder as he walked by to refill his coffee cup. Axe turned to look, but Nick just gave him a small smile. He knew what Axe was going through, and Axe appreciated that to no end. It was one of the reasons that he had his fingers crossed Bertrand would let them stay together as a team.

"So," Nick said as he sat back down. "We got sidetracked. I got your text, Finn, that you and Elias think you've found something, but with everything that's happened, we haven't had a chance to catch up. Fill us in."

Cain walked over and took Axe's place on the couch next to Elias. Finn sat in the chair opposite Nick, and Axe stayed leaning on the counter. The guys all got comfortable.

"Anyone want coffee before we start?" Axe offered as he got a cup from the kitchenette and poured himself a mugful.

There was a chorus of "no and no thanks." Axe took up

his spot, leaning on the counter again, his coffee in front of him.

Finn glanced at Elias. "Why don't you start?"

Elias nodded. "We went back through the research that the Callahans sent us. There were a lot of fuckin' ships stuck, and they were from all over the world. I didn't realize how much traffic goes through the Suez Canal. Anyway, there were about twenty different companies that had a significant number of ships waiting."

"We decided that in order for a company to be included on our list, there had to be at least four or more of their ships waiting to go through the canal," Finn interjected. "Three or less, and they could have been taken care of other ways. It's an arbitrary number really, but it seemed to be a logical cutoff."

Elias continued. "We went through all twenty companies, and nothing jumped out at us at first. They were all just shipping companies moving their stuff. And then it occurred to us that it wasn't just the shipping companies we had to check. Who owned the cargo on ships was equally important. We needed some help getting that kind of information, so we called Charlie." He grinned. "I know he's a reporter, but he has some great sources and managed to get us the information quickly. Turns out he was already thinking along the same lines. Anyway, he got us the details and he helped us sort through it. We ended up adding another twenty-four companies to our list."

Finn took over. "We went through all of the new companies to see if any of them stood out, but nothing. Then, while we were taking a break, Elias sat up all of a sudden and started searching through the information again."

"That's right. A name rang some bells, but I couldn't place it, but then it clicked. Tristan St. Claire," Elias said.

"Okay, who is Tristan St. Claire?" Axe asked.

Elias smiled. "Tristan St. Claire is in the textile business in Australia. He's making waves because he is going all green, or as green as possible, with his textiles. People are taking notice. I read several articles about it when we were back on the ship. St. Claire was in talks with a conglomerate in Germany to ship them his organic green textiles. It was a big deal worth lots of money. There were seven ships that had his green textiles on them, waiting to go through the canal."

"So why do you think it was this St. Claire guy that someone wanted to stop coming through the canal? I assume that's what you're saying," Nick said.

Finn piped up. "Yes. We think it was these shipments of St. Claire's that someone wanted stopped. St. Claire hadn't made the deal with the Germans yet. They wanted to see the goods in person. St. Claire offered to send them the shipments on spec, and if the Germans liked them, then they could hammer out a deal."

"That's...unusual to say the least." Nick shifted in his chair. "Why would he do that?"

"Because," Elias said, "he was using it as a publicity stunt to get more notice of his green organic products. Everyone knew what he was doing. He made sure of it. The stunt got him a lot of press and a lot of interested buyers, not just the Germans."

"So, who didn't want him to get through?" Axe took a sip of coffee.

"That's the really interesting part," Elias replied. "On the surface, many different companies would like to see St. Claire fail, but we did a bit more research, and it turned out that one company had been working on a deal with the Germans before St. Claire approached them. They were in the final stretch when the Germans changed their minds and went with St. Claire. I guess the lure of being able to market their textiles as green was too great."

Finn smiled. "Green textiles would have given them a lot more tax breaks as well as good publicity. People are all about green-sourced materials these days."

"So," Nick summarized, "the Germans had a deal going with another textile company and then changed their minds and went with St. Claire for tax reasons. And then the canal was blocked."

"And once the canal was blocked," Elias agreed, "the Germans started to get cold feet. What if this happened on a regular basis? There was no real alternative route for the ships to take. The original textile supplier immediately capitalized on the German's fears, and a new deal was struck. According to several financial newspapers, the deal wouldn't have happened if the canal wasn't blocked."

"Who owns the other textile company?" Cain asked.

"Hakan Balik. He's from Turkey and has one of the largest textile companies in the world. His textiles do not have to go through the Suez Canal to reach Germany."

"You think this Balik guy is the one who blocked the canal?" Axe took another sip of coffee.

"No. His son, Omar," Finn responded. "Once we started doing some digging on Balik, we came across an article, one of those thirty power players under thirty type of lists. Omar Balik was on the list, but St. Claire was number one.

"A deeper dive into St. Claire revealed that he and Balik went to the same boarding school, and they were archrivals. They are rumored to hate one another. Or at least Balik hates St. Claire. He's bitter about always coming in second, I guess.

"Anyway, Omar Balik was days away from signing the deal with the Germans when St. Claire swooped in and stole the deal right out from under him." Finn leaned forward and rested his elbows on his knees. "Then suddenly the canal gets blocked, and the deal is back on. They signed it already, so it doesn't matter if St. Claire's shipment makes it through. The Germans are already committed to Balik."

Axe straightened. "How the hell did you find all this out? That's some serious research."

Finn looked at Elias and grinned. "Charlie helped. He's a decent guy, for a reporter."

"Just don't get used to chatting with reporters," Nick reminded them. "If he changes his mind and writes about this mess and about us, we're all sunk." He smiled. "Good job on the research. Looks like you guys found our man."

"It all fits," Finn said, "but there's absolutely no proof. I mean, there isn't another scenario that remotely fits the situation as well unless there's something out there that we missed entirely, but for now, it's all just supposition. There's even an article in one of the financial newspapers that outright says the deal wouldn't have happened if the canal wasn't blocked. The writer pointed out that it was just dumb luck Balik managed to make the deal, but we have no hard proof. Nothing."

Nick cocked his head. "We need to find Rohan Patel. He's the guy with the answers. MacGregor might have known something, but he's dead. Patel was the shot caller on the *Sea Jewel*. He was the guy who called Germany all those times. I am assuming Omar Balik was in Germany while the canal was blocked?"

"Yes," Finn responded. "He arrived the day before the *Sea Jewel* blocked the Suez."

"Well, that's something," Axe pointed out.

Nick shook his head. "Not enough. He could dismiss that any number of ways."

"So, what do you want to do?" Elias asked.

Nick hesitated. "Let me speak with Bertrand and see what he thinks. I'm not sure going to Germany will be helpful unless we know for sure Rohan Patel is there and we can track him down. It might make more sense to go to Turkey and speak to Omar Balik directly." Nick stood up. "Either way, it's been a long couple days for all of us. I propose we make an early night of it. I'll speak with Bertrand, and we will have a game plan for tomorrow."

The guys all stood up and made for the door. "Good work, Finn, Elias. You guys nailed it." Axe clapped each man on the back as they passed. Nick was the last one to leave. He turned. "You staying here?"

"Yeah, I promised her I would sleep on the couch. I think it will be a while before she's going to want to sleep by herself in a hotel room again."

Nick nodded. "Understandable. Just make sure you get some sleep. You're running on empty yourself."

Axe agreed. "Don't worry. I'll hit the hay early. I am tired." Nick left and Axe chained the door after him. He then spent the better part of a half hour cleaning everything up so the place wouldn't smell like old food in the morning. He opened the door again and placed all the trays in the hallway just outside the door. He came back in and called room service. They assured him they would be right up.

That done, he used the second bathroom to splash water on his face and get ready for bed. He pulled out the couch and lay down. His thoughts strayed to Sloan asleep in the next room. He longed to go in and lie down beside her, but he knew that would be selfish. The sooner she knew they were definitely over, the better for both of them. He rolled onto his side and grabbed the TV remote. It was going to be a long night.

CHAPTER THIRTY-FIVE

O mar stepped out of the restaurant and walked down the few stairs to the valet stand. He'd requested his car a couple of minutes ago, but it still wasn't here yet. No matter. He'd had a fabulous dinner with Ivan and the rest of his friends to celebrate his deal. They'd left to go clubbing, but Omar had begged off. Normally, he would love to continue the celebration, but he had to meet with some of the board members tomorrow to discuss his takeover of the company. He didn't want to be exhausted and hung over for that meeting. *See Father, I am taking things seriously.* He grinned to himself.

"Does it usually take a while to get your car here?" inquired the tall, lean gentleman who was standing at the bottom of the stairs.

"It's usually not too bad, but they must be shorthanded tonight." Omar was in a great mood. Life was good. He had put all of the canal business behind him. He even had an idea for his next deal. His father would be proud, if he was capable of such a thing.

"It's a nice night, so I guess waiting isn't too bad."

Omar took a closer look at the man. He seemed familiar somehow. His voice maybe sounded like someone Omar knew. The man was slightly older than Omar with a soft British accent. He appeared to be Indian, but Omar wasn't sure. The man's expensive suit seemed to be from one of Omar's favorite designers, and a Rolex that cost six figures adorned the man's left wrist. His shoes were designer as well. In short, Omar's type of people.

"I don't think I've seen you here before." Omar extended his hand. "Omar Balik."

"I'm new to Istanbul." He smiled as he took Omar's hand. "Rohan Patel."

Omar smiled back. "What do you do, Mr. Patel?"

"I am in crisis management. And you? What do you do?"

"I'm in textiles." Omar's Ferrari stopped at the bottom of the steps. He smiled at Patel. "Are you here to manage a crisis?" Omar smiled at his own joke.

"Yes. A new client. They just called yesterday. I'm here to stop a hostile takeover.

Omar nodded. "Well, it was nice to meet you. I eat here quite frequently. Maybe next time we can have a drink together."

Patel nodded. "Maybe, although I don't think I will be in town for very long. The crisis I was sent to manage is almost over. A father had a disagreement with his son over some actions, and he wanted some help straightening the boy out."

"You do that sort of thing? Personal crisis? Do you do business crisis as well?"

Patel nodded. "We handle any kind of crisis. We step in where necessary."

"Well, next time then." Omar nodded and went down the steps to his car. He tipped the valet and slid behind the wheel.

Patel watched him go. "Not bloody likely," he said and then smiled to himself.

CHAPTER THIRTY-SIX

"*Omar Balik was found dead this morning behind the wheel of his Ferrari. It appears Mr. Balik had too much to drink after dining at Maison Bosphorus, his favorite restaurant, and crashed his Ferrari on the way home. Police surmise he lost control of his vehicle and ended up smashing into a parked car at a high rate of speed, killing himself instantly. The investigation continues, but it's believed no other people were involved. Mr. Balik is survived by his father, Hakan Balik, a leader in the global textile industry.*"

Axe snorted in disgust as he closed the article on his phone and threw it onto the couch next to him. They were all in Sloan's hotel room again, since it had the most space. She'd left to join Charlie for breakfast.

Axe growled, "We find out this guy is responsible for the Suez mess, and he suddenly ends up dead. No fucking way that's a coincidence."

"Agreed," Nick said as he crashed down in one of the club chairs. "It does however wrap up the whole thing with one large bow. We can't prove Omar Balik paid the Silver-stone boys to block the canal. It's all supposition, so now there's nothing left for us to do. We can head back to the States."

"What about his father? He runs the company. Will the Egyptians go after him?" Axe asked.

"Unlikely." Nick shook his head. "They can't prove anything either. They'll hit up Pacific Overseas Express for some damages since it was their ship that blocked the canal, but they can't prove it was anything but an accident based on poor judgment and the weather. Pacific is unlikely to provide them with the data from the ship that shows exactly what happened because they'd be on the hook for more money. No one will pursue Hakan Balik. We don't even know if he knew about the whole thing. Omar put together the deal. He was the one with the rivalry with St. Claire."

Cain leaned on the counter and folded his arms across his chest. "A man like Hakan Balik didn't get to the top by pulling stupid stunts like blocking the Suez Canal. He knows the score. If it ever came out, he and his company would be finished. If I had to guess, I'd say he found out after the fact and took care of things."

Elias frowned and rubbed his leg while he sat in the club chair next to Nick. "You think he had his own son killed?"

Cain nodded. "Omar masterminded the blocking of the canal. That puts them on the hook for billions. They would be ruined. Hakan Balik is only in his mid-fifties. Plenty of time to have another kid. Not much time to build a new empire."

Finn, who was on the other end of the couch from Axe, whistled. "That's harsh."

Cain shrugged.

"Makes sense though," Nick agreed. "It's logical. No one else had motive to kill Omar. Silverstone got their money presumably. They wouldn't have done the work without it. So, they have no beef with Omar. The only one who takes a hit is Hakan Balik if Omar lives and the world finds out."

"Jesus. Killing your only kid over your company. That's some crazy shit." Finn shook his head.

Cain snorted. "No crazier than blocking the canal to make a deal. The apple didn't fall far from the tree."

"That's true," Elias agreed. "So, what does all this mean for us?"

"Good question, one I'm hoping we're going to get answers to—" Nick broke off to check the screen on his ringing phone— "now." He connected the call. "Admiral Bertrand," Nick said. "How are you, sir?" There was a moment of silence, and then Nick hit the speaker button on his phone and placed it on the coffee table in the middle of the room. "You're on speaker, sir."

"Gentleman, I assume you have heard of the death of Omar Balik. To say that complicates things in terms of pursuing those responsible is an understatement. He was the only one we could link to the blockage of the canal, and even that was tentative. We have nothing to link his father, and since all of the Silverstone men are either dead or they've disappeared, we have no way of creating that link." He paused and let out a long breath. "It's time to come home."

"Yes, sir," Nick replied. "Does that mean we should all head back to our previous assignments?"

Axe held his breath. He really didn't want to go back to the *Fitz*. He wanted to stay with Team RECON. They all wanted to stay together. It's where Axe felt the most at home.

"I have spoken with the top brass. They were not pleased about the inferno in the middle of the canal that incinerated one of their assets to the waterline, particularly since we were supposed to be low-key. The shootout at the hangar was just icing on that cake."

"But, sir—" Nick started.

"Hold your tongue, Taggert, and let me finish."

"Sir."

"As I was saying, all the commotion you gentleman caused did not go down so well. However, they do appreciate all of the work you put in and the fact that you discovered the true nature of the blockage before anyone else. You can bet the top brass at Homeland is crowing about it to the people over at the CIA, DOD, and anyone else who will listen. This is the second time you all have given them the edge in the intelligence war that exists not only worldwide, but in Washington.

"Because of that, they have agreed that you all should remain together as a team. It's unorthodox, but it seems to work. You're making the top brass look good, and they like to look good. So, you all will be permanently reassigned to a unit under my command. You will report directly to me as you have been doing."

"Yes, sir. That sounds excellent. We're all happy to hear it," Nick said, and every man in the room nodded.

Axe couldn't believe his luck. It was a dream come true. They were a great team, and he loved being part of it. Maybe something good had finally come of his burns. Without those, he wouldn't have been assigned to this group of men.

Nick leaned forward in his chair. "If I may ask, sir, where do we report? Are we relocating to Washington? To Coast Guard Headquarters?"

"No. The matter has been up for debate for some time. Assuming this assignment went well, Homeland wanted to be prepared. They decided that you needed to be located in a major city with easy access to Europe, South America, and Africa. They also wanted you to be on the water since you are, in fact, in the Coast Guard, something they need to be reminded of occasionally. The top brass said they have some space that fits the bill. It's in a bit of rough shape, but they feel confident you will be able to work with it."

"Where is it?" Axe finally burst out. The suspense was killing him. "Sir," he added belatedly.

"Miami. You gentleman will be stationed out of Miami. I'll send you all the pertinent details. You have a week to get your affairs in order before reporting in. As to accommodations, I'm sure you all can figure something out. More details to follow. See you in a week, gentleman." Bertrand clicked off.

"Miami. Fuckin' A." Finn grinned. "I love the heat."

Cain snorted. "You just like the lack of clothing."

"That, too," Finn agreed.

Axe grinned. "I like the good Cuban food and lack of snow."

"All good points," Nick agreed.

"What about you, Cain? You good with Miami?" Nick inquired.

Cain smiled. "Beats the shit out of Alaska."

"Elias, what do you think?" Axe asked.

"It's fine."

There was none of Elias's usual spirit in his answer. Axe had the distinct impression that he wasn't pleased with the idea of Miami, but Axe had no idea why. He shot a glance at Nick and cocked an eyebrow. Nick just gave a small shake of his head. It might be something they'd have to deal with later.

Axe let out a long breath. God knew, he was just glad to be with the team. Even if they had been out of Alaska, he wouldn't have complained, although he really wasn't a fan of the cold. "What about you, Nick? How does Miami work for you? I know Carolina is in Morocco."

Nick smiled. "I like Miami. It's a fun city with a lot going on and I happen to know Carolina loves it as well. I'm pretty sure I can convince her to come visit. A lot." He immediately turned to Elias. "Don't get any ideas. I'm not bailing your ass out of jail, or worse. No all-night card games or any kind of gambling."

Elias kept his face blank. "I wouldn't dream of it."

Another sign of trouble, making Axe believe Elias wasn't happy with the location. That wasn't good. Axe hoped that Elias would come around, but somehow he didn't think it would happen.

"Well, now that that's settled, I'm famished." Finn patted his belly. "Let's sort out food and then flights home. A week off sounds excellent."

"It's not a week off. You have to pack and get ready to move to Miami," Axe reminded him.

"Uh-huh. Two, three days' work, tops. Then relaxation. Doctor's orders."

Axe rolled his eyes. His belly rumbled. Finn had a point about food, but first he had to talk to Sloan. He glanced at his watch. She should be back soon. Just the thought of talking to Sloan made him suddenly lose his appetite. "I'll catch up with you guys," he said as they all started filing out of the room.

"Okay," Nick said, "I'll text you where we end up if we leave the hotel."

Axe nodded and closed the door after them.

He was glad they were moving to Miami. He'd spent a lot of time in his Virginia apartment with Sloan. It was better to be in a new place. No memories to haunt him.

Twenty minutes later, Sloan arrived back at her room. "Where is everyone?" she asked.

"They went to breakfast."

"You didn't go with them?"

Axe hesitated. "I wanted to speak with you first. We got our orders, and I'll be flying out later today. I also have to go back to the *William Fitzgerald* and get my stuff. There are a few people there I have to say good-bye to, and I need to check in with my former CO. This is sort of the only time that works."

"I see," Sloan said, moving to sit on the couch. "I want to talk to you, too, so I guess this is good."

Axe sat down in the club chair on Sloan's right. "How are you feeling today?"

"Better." She smiled slightly. "It will take me a while to process it all, but I think I'm making progress already. Charlie found the interpreter, and he is going to come with me to interview him and Zahra's family. He says he has to see some people, but I know he's going so he can keep an eye on me. He wants to make sure I'm really okay."

She gave him a genuine smile this time, and it made Axe's chest hurt just a bit. He rubbed it absently. Sloan never really felt loved by her parents, or at least so Axe thought. It was nice that Charlie was stepping into the role of father. She could do worse.

"Charlie says hello by the way, and thank you. He says he'll keep his part of the deal. I am assuming you all made him swear not to write about everything that happened, but what did he get out of it?"

"We kept him in the loop. He was very concerned about you. He really does love you like a daughter."

"I know, and I am coming to appreciate that more and more."

Axe leaned back in his chair. "Sloan, I am glad you're okay. When you were kidnapped by MacGregor, it was…" How could he describe it? Agony? Torture? "Difficult for me." The moment the words left his mouth, he realized how selfish he sounded. "I mean, I know it was obviously worse for you. It must have been terrifying. I—"

Sloan raised her hand. "I know you aren't being selfish, Axe. No need to apologize."

Axe nodded and then leaned forward and placed his elbows on his knees, linking his hands together in front of him. This was so much harder than he thought it would be. "What I should have said was, I know it must have been awful for you, but it sucked for me, too. Not just because I care about you." He looked up at her and captured her gaze. "I do care about you, Sloan. A great deal. Hell, I might even love you." He couldn't believe those words had left his lips, but they were true.

And they didn't matter one bit.

Then he looked down again. "But also…because having you in jeopardy put me in a difficult spot. I wanted to bust into the hangar and get you to safety. Knowing you were inside it was killing me, but I had to wait. As a member of a team, I have to put their well-being and safety first. I couldn't sacrifice them for you, nor would I have been able to live with myself if something had happened to you while I was waiting with the team outside."

"Axe, it's okay. It all worked out." Sloan moved down the couch so she was closer to him.

"But that's the point. It worked out *this* time. Sloan, all the articles you write put you in the thick of things. I know that's your job, but having you in constant danger makes my life difficult. I want to protect you all the time. Maybe I could live with it if our careers didn't make our paths cross. It seems, though, that every time I'm involved in something, you show up. The training exercise gone wrong off the coast of North Carolina. The thing down in Ecuador—"

"You asked me to come to South America," Sloan said, sounding slightly miffed.

"I asked you to write the story. I didn't say get on the next plane and come to the Amazon."

"You're splitting hairs."

"Am I? You were here to write about the female canal pilot, and you end up writing about Eddie's murder."

"That's not fair! You can't fault me for doing my job. Plus, I helped you guys. You wouldn't have known about Rohan Patel if it weren't for me."

Axe ground his teeth. "I'm not saying you aren't good at your job or that you should walk away from writing the articles you want to write. What I'm saying is we can't be together while you do it. My career and yours are too divergent. You will always want to know what my latest assignment is and when you can write about it. I can't be sure you won't show up in the middle of whatever mess is going on and cause me more issues." Axe stood up. "Sloan, I love you, but we just can't be together."

CHAPTER THIRTY-SEVEN

Sloan sat dumbfounded on the sofa. Axe had just admitted he loved her. Her heart raced. Her spirit soared. Not *maybe* loved her, but actually loved her. *Yes*! Now all she had to do was convince him he was wrong and they could be together.

Axe was walking toward the door. Sloan hopped up. "Axe, wait. Don't I get a say in this? You just get to say your piece and leave? That's not fair." She knew Axe would stop. If he was anything, he was fair. He would listen to what she had to say. She just had to be convincing enough to make him stay permanently.

Axe turned around. His lips were set in a line. "Fine. Have your say." He stood in the middle of the room and crossed his arms over his chest.

Shit. She definitely had an uphill battle ahead of her. "You're right. I have been involved in a lot of your assignments and maybe, just maybe, I didn't take the time to consider how my articles would affect your career. I admit it. I was being somewhat selfish, but the stories were accurate, and the public has a right to know."

Axe grunted but said nothing.

Shit. Shit. Shit. Old habits die hard. She'd just pissed him off more. "Anyway, I understand what you're saying. I get it. Having me involved in your work life puts you between a rock and a hard place. I do understand that because it does the same for me. And if I'm being totally honest, I didn't choose so wisely. You got hurt. Your career was damaged. The story wasn't worth all that."

She drew in a deep breath and then let it out. "The thing is, I don't think it's going to be a problem any longer. Charlie and I went to dinner before I was kidnapped, and he pointed a few things out to me, namely I was taking after my father and, in the end, that wasn't a good thing. My father wasn't necessarily the kindest person."

"I thought you wanted to be like your father." Axe leaned against the wall next to him.

"I thought I did, too, until Charlie pointed out my father was an asshole. Then suddenly it didn't seem so important anymore."

Axe's eyebrows went up.

"Yeah, it took Charlie to point that out to me. The fact that my dad missed just about every birthday and holiday celebration while I was growing up should have been my first clue. His job always came first. I didn't realize that wasn't a good thing. My mother praised him for it. She said it was what made him the best reporter out there, and she was right, it was, but it made him a shitty father and horrible husband. She just didn't mention that part, probably because then she would have to admit she made a mistake in marrying him and that she was unhappy. Anyway, it was an eye-opening conversation.

"Charlie also pointed out something I think I've always known but ignored because of my quest to be like my father." She clasped her hands together, knuckles going white. "He said I should write human-interest stories because I connect well with people. In this case, tell the world what happened to Zahra Nabil and why. People will read the facts in all the newspapers and online news outlets but no one else spoke with Zahra. No one else can do her story justice.

"And it's not just Zahra's story, Axe, I'm done with the hard-hitting news stories. I want to write about the human side of things. I want to bring people's stories to life and share them with the world because I think it's important for the world to know how major events impact humanity."

Axe stared at her and then slowly nodded his head. "I think you'll be really good at that, Sloan."

She smiled. "Me, too. Anyway, that clears the way for us."

Axe frowned. "I don't think that necessarily follows."

"Yes, it does. I'm not going after the big stories anymore. Our paths won't cross at work. Even if they do for some reason, I'll be writing the humanistic angle, not the news. It won't interfere with your job anymore."

Axe hesitated. "I see what you're saying, but Sloan, you've just been through a lot, and who knows how you'll feel about your career in a week or a month or next year. It could all change again."

"It could, but I love you Axe, and that won't change. Not now, not tomorrow…not ever. I knew that before all this, but with everything that happened, it just drove the point home." Sloan walked across the room to stand directly in front of Axe. "Axel Cantor, I love you. I am willing to do whatever it takes for you to see that we can be together. I promise you I will not report on any of your assignments"— she started to smile—"unless you ask me to, of course. Please say we can be together."

A smile tugged the corner of Axe's mouth. She was offering him the world, her world, so they could be together.

He had to accept it. He just had to. She wouldn't be able to pick herself up off the floor if he didn't. Her heart hammered against her ribs. She tried to swallow the lump building in her throat. He was taking too long to answer. He was going to say no. She searched his face for any glimmer of hope, but he remained stoic.

Then he straightened and opened his arms. Sloan flew into his embrace, and he claimed her mouth in a searing kiss. A few minutes later, he broke off the kiss. "You promise you won't write any more articles about my work, right?"

"Scout's honor," she said as she leaned up to kiss him again.

"Wait, you weren't a Scout," Axe complained.

Sloan grinned. "I always wanted to be, so close enough."

Axe frowned, but Sloan kissed him again, and soon all thoughts of anything but the man in her arms were gone from her head.

EPILOGUE

"I can't believe you have a place at the beach," Sloan declared as she leaned on the railing of Axe's balcony overlooking the Atlantic Ocean and all the holiday makers on the beach below.

"I know. I lucked out. My mom actually knows someone back home in New Hampshire who owns this place. The lady decided to winter in Arizona with her sister instead of coming here. She finds the humidity too much to take. She was going to sell but decided to hold on to it a while longer. Her winter tenant just left, so she let me rent it for the next year." Axe grinned as he handed Sloan a margarita.

"Cheers," he said, and they clinked glasses. He swooped in for a quick kiss and then drank deep from his glass. Life was good. He loved the heat and sunshine. He glanced down at his arms. It was nice to wear a short-sleeved T-shirt. Sloan had convinced him he needed to stop hiding his scars. Life was too short to feel guilty over something he'd had no control over. He missed Andy a lot, but having the RECON guys around made a huge difference.

"What are you smiling about," Sloan asked and then took a sip of her drink.

"I'm just happy. I like that you're here with me and we're having fun. I think Miami is going to work out well."

"I agree. I like the heat, and there are plenty of human-interest stories here. I'm working on one about some Cuban immigrants. It's fascinating."

"I'm glad you're happy." Axe leaned down and kissed her again. This one was longer. Finally, he broke it off. "What do you say we order in some Cuban food?"

Sloan shook her head. "No. I want to take you to this Cuban place I found. If we stay home, we'll just end up in bed."

"What's wrong with that?" Axe winked.

Sloan shook her head. "Nothing, but I would like to actually see some of Miami rather than just your bedroom."

"Fair enough. Go get ready, and we'll head out to dinner."

Sloan kissed him on the cheek and went inside. Axe leaned on the railing and took another sip of his drink. Life *was* good. His team was settling in nicely.

He frowned. That wasn't true. Elias wasn't happy. He wouldn't talk about it, at least not to Axe, but he definitely would rather be someplace else. Axe sighed. He was going to have to keep an eye on Elias. He knew Nick was doing the same. Maybe, between them, they could figure out what was going on.

Axe's cell rang, and he pulled it out of his pocket. He smiled as he hit the call button. "Kyle, how's it goin'? What did the doctors say? Are you gonna be sprung soon?" Axe was thrilled that his best friend had finally reached out to him just after he got to Miami. Kyle was going to therapy now and making good progress. He no longer blamed Axe for saving his life. He was actually happy to be alive.

Kyle was telling him of his latest progress as Axe watched the clouds blaze with the setting sun. Life was good, but how long would it last?

Would you like to know more about the Callahans?
Turn the page to read more of Mitch Callahan's brush
with Alexandra Buchannan, a professional criminal
*who has to lot to teach him about **romantic justice** in*
Break and Enter…

SNEAK PEEK: BREAK AND ENTER

Meet Alexandra Buchannan – the woman who uses her talents as a professional criminal to equalize the scales of what she likes to call, **romantic justice.**

She's the woman many of us wish we had on speed dial, at least at some point in our lives…

Your ex still has your favorite painting? He kept the bracelet he bought you for your 5th anniversary? They won't be his for long.

But Alex's latest job is her biggest challenge yet.

Her target just hired a new security company, and the team's leader is as smart as he is sexy.

Mitch Callahan pushed his brothers to expand the family business into private security, and their first major client is a complete pain in the ass.

It's no wonder the man has a target on his back, but **nothing could prepare Mitch for how seductive his adversary is.**

Mitch knows his ass is on the line, and he could drag Callahan Security down with him, but everything gets much more complicated as he begins to find Alex increasingly irresistible.

But their game of cat and mouse quickly explodes into a million pieces as another player enters the game -- with intentions that are far deadlier.

BREAK AND ENTER

Sweat trickled along Alexandra Buchanan's hairline under her wig. Her heart thudded in her chest. She was minutes from her goal, mere seconds from obtaining her objective. She had been planning for months. Her fingertips tingled as the seconds ticked by slowly. She itched under her red velvet Venetian mask. Its feathers tickled her face.

The humid air hung heavy in the grand ballroom. The smell of women's perfumes and men's colognes mixed with sweet scent of the dozens of flowers that were on tables stationed around the room. But none of it could mask the funk of body odor or the even stronger stench of money.

The room was filled with the elite of Venice, of Italy and beyond. Women wore eye-catching costumes. Sequins and jewels glittered in the light from the ornate chandeliers. Men wearing masks and capes flashed jewels of their own on their fingers and their wrists. The room was a swirl of color and sound. Everyone who was anyone was invited to the Santini's spring ball. And this year it was a masquerade. She smiled to herself. She couldn't have asked for a better cover. It was as if the stars had aligned perfectly just for her.

She glanced at her watch. Only another twenty seconds, and the song would be over. And then it was time. As always happened at this moment, her senses heightened. She could hear every voice distinctly, see every small movement. Time slowed down to a crawl.

Finally, the orchestra was playing the last few notes of the song. This was it, the moment she lived for, the moment when she either conquered her goal or she failed miserably. Adrenaline roared through her body. Excitement exploded in her chest.

Alex moved across the floor as dancers mingled, looking for their next partner. She had her target in sight. He was passing his partner from the previous song to another man. He turned and smiled at the woman standing next to him. He took his new partner's hand in his.

She increased her pace slightly so that she was directly beside her target as he swung his other hand around to clasp the woman. She didn't look at him as she jostled him slightly. It was expected in this crowded space. Her fingers deftly performed the task they had done many times before. Quickly, silently she had her prize. She made her way across the floor, smiling as she went. She slid her hand into a hidden pocket, depositing her bounty.

This was it—the worst and, yet, the best moment. Would he notice? Would he yell? Would he point her out?

She kept her head up and her steady pace as she broke free of the dancers and started up the stairs to the mezzanine. Sweat was a fine sheen across her body. She had a fixed smile on her face and nodded to several of the partygoers as she crested the top of the stairs. Walking across the floor, she made her way toward the restrooms but glanced around quickly. No one was close. No one was paying attention. She passed the restrooms and made for the hallway on her left.

She moved down the corridor and made it to the doors

that led to the terrace, but she kept walking. The security plan she'd gotten a hold of indicated they were tied to an alarm that would be on tonight. She went a few steps farther.

After making sure the hallway was clear, she did a little dance and slid her crinoline off. She wouldn't need it anymore, and it would just be in her way. She'd bought it from an online shop using a fake account and had it delivered to an office building. She hadn't touched it without her gloves so there were no prints, or at least not hers.

Glancing around she spotted a chair a little farther down the hallway. She put the crinoline on the far side of the chair, so it wouldn't be immediately seen by anyone walking down the hall.

Alex went back to a window at the far end of the balcony and unlocked it. Lifting it silently, she was once again amazed at how many people didn't alarm their windows above the ground floor. Tugging her costume up around the tops of her thighs so she could move her legs freely, she put one foot through the window, ducked under, and brought the rest of her body through onto the balcony. She lowered the window again from the outside.

"Where the hell did you come from?" a voice demanded from the darkness. She froze. No one should be on the balcony. She had planned this heist meticulously, and nowhere in the Santini security arrangements was there any indication that someone would be on the balcony.

A guest then? As she slowly turned in the direction the voice had come, a man dressed in a tuxedo emerged from the shadows. Damn. Security. They were wearing tuxes instead of costumes. But not Santini security. He didn't have the same type of ill-fitting tux as the Santini security guys. His fit him like a glove, like he was born to wear it. Someone else's security. A private bodyguard. Great. She'd been fifty-three seconds from freedom, and she runs into James Bond.

Her mind reeled as she tried to figure out a different escape route. The weight of the watch hidden in her skirt was a thousand pounds heavier. *Don't panic.* She smiled and moved forward a couple of steps, letting him take a long look at her.

The trick was to keep as much space between them as she could without seeming reluctant. She thanked her lucky stars once again that the party was a masquerade ball. For a thief, it was like hitting the jackpot. An *Asset Repossession Specialist Extraordinaire*, she mentally corrected herself.

Her duchess costume, which she'd had made especially for this job, not only showed off her assets but had a few hidden surprises. The security guy's gaze lingered for a moment on her "girls" as she called them. Not her norm to display them so blatantly, but she'd wanted to be sure anyone looking at her would be distracted, even the women. Better to show too much tit than too much of her face.

She took a deep breath. If she was careful, maybe she could still get away unscathed. After all, the mask she wore covered most of her face except for the lower part of her jaw, and the voluminous brown wig hid the rest of her head. Her heart rate started to come back down to earth. She could do this. The fine sheen of sweat had turned into a small river making its way down her back.

"What are you doing here? This area is off limits. No one is supposed to be up here." He walked closer to her, his stance showing easy confidence. They were about twelve feet apart, separated by an area bathed in shadow. The breeze ruffled the feathers of her mask, but it also brought his scent to her. He smelled of soap and citrus and something wholly male that had her taking notice.

"*You're* here," she said in her most sultry voice. She prayed he wouldn't come any closer. He was bigger than most men, much bigger than her diminutive 5'5". At least six feet, she figured, which wasn't necessarily a problem, but his shoulders were wide. Why couldn't he have been one of the doughy types she had seen earlier? The guys who'd gone to seed years ago. She could have handled one of those guys no problem. Years of kick boxing, Tae Kwon Do, Krav Maga, and general self-defense training meant she could have rendered one of them unconscious soundlessly.

But she had to get the keener who looked to be in fabulous shape. All narrow hips, broad shoulders, and solid muscle. One of the major lessons she had learned was how to assess her opponent, and this one would be tough. Her stomach roiled. A fight with this guy would be loud and painful. Fighting was off the table.

She smiled as she studied him. His hair was a light brown with blond highlights. He wasn't wearing a mask, but it was hard to determine his eye color. There was no mistaking his square jaw though, especially since it appeared to be clenched. He was also drop-dead gorgeous and sexy as hell.

His eyes narrowed and focused on her after casing the rest of the balcony. "Who are you?"

She ignored the question. So, throwing him over the balcony was not going to work. Physically impossible, and besides, she wanted to avoid a scene. The water in the canals would catch his fall, yes, but everyone would rush to see as soon as they heard the splash.

"Who are you?" he repeated as he stepped closer. The Venice breeze ruffled a lock of his hair so that it fell over his forehead.

She gave a girlish giggle while mentally rolling her eyes. Men loved that crap. "Well, doesn't that defeat the whole purpose of a masquerade ball? I can't tell you who I am. It would ruin the mystery."

"Then why don't you tell me how you got onto this balcony? Like I said, no one is supposed to be out here."

She pouted. "Well, *you're* here." Then she closed the gap between them with a sexy stroll. She smiled up at him while caressing the pleats of his tux shirt with her gloved fingers. She needed him to stop asking questions. "All by yourself, I might add." Yes, all muscle. She could feel it through his shirt. Warmth spread through her insides as she peered up into his startlingly gray eyes. She had never seen eyes that gray before. They were like polished steel.

If circumstances were different...she still wouldn't touch him with a ten-foot pole. She'd been down that road before. If she'd learned nothing else in life, it was that the best-looking men were the ones that couldn't be trusted. Not ever. Not even if they were family.

He grabbed her fingers and held them fast. It sent an electric charge skittering up her arm. Startled, she tried to pull her hand back, but he held on. Her plan wasn't working. *He* was the one who was supposed to be distracted, not her.

"You need to leave. Now." There was no sign that he was remotely affected by her presence, unlike her who was totally suffering from their closeness. Her pulse skyrocketed. She was surprised he couldn't see it with her chest on display. Maybe he could. Sweat was now running down her legs as well as her back. This man was sexy as hell, but he was like kryptonite. She needed a new plan and fast.

"Uh..."

"Go for Callahan," the man said as he pressed his earpiece. He dropped her hand. Then, turning around, he walked over to the railing and looked down.

Recognizing her chance, she quickly and silently moved the fifty feet to the other end of the balcony. She took off her shoes and stuffed them into the hidden pockets of her dress. Then she hoisted herself onto the railing. With a quick glance back, she saw the man was still on the other side of the balcony looking down. She quickly stepped onto the small decorative ledge running along the front of the building and, hugging the wall, slid her way carefully to the corner.

She reached up and grabbed the edge of the roof and swung herself around the corner. Regaining her balance, she took a second to breathe and rest her cheek against the building. She took one hand off the wall slowly and wiped it on her dress. Then did the same with the other. After she lifted her cheek, she carefully removed her mask and pushed it into the pocket next to her shoes. She put her hand back on the wall.

She loved Venice. The buildings were so close together here, and in her line of work, that was a big plus.

Want to read more?
Click here for the full book

READ THESE OTHER EXCITING BOOKS BY LORI MATTHEWS

Free with Newsletter Sign Up
Falling For The Witness
Risk Assessment
Visit my website to sign up for my newsletter

ABOUT LORI MATTHEWS

I grew up in a house filled with books and readers. Some of my fondest memories are of reading in the same room with my mother and sisters, arguing about whose turn it was to make tea. No one wanted to put their book down!

I was introduced to romance because of my mom's habit of leaving books all over the house. One day I picked one up. I still remember the cover. It was a Harlequin by Janet Daily. Little did I know at the time that it would set the stage for my future. I went on to discover mystery novels. Agatha Christie was my favorite. And then suspense with Wilber Smith and Ian Fleming.

I loved the thought of combining my favorite genres, and during high school, I attempted to write my first romantic suspense novel. I wrote the first four chapters and then exams happened and that was the end of that. I desperately hope that book died a quiet death somewhere in a computer recycling facility.

A few years later, (okay, quite a few) after two degrees, a husband and two kids, I attended a workshop in Tuscany that lit that spark for writing again. I have been pounding the keyboard ever since here in New Jersey, where I live with my children—who are thrilled with my writing as it means they get to eat more pizza—and my very supportive husband.

Please visit my webpage at https://lorimatthewsbooks.com to keep up on my news.

Printed in Great Britain
by Amazon